It had already been more than two months since Miranda had been killed by the American super-hero Golden Tiger.

Two months is a long time.

Angel City had fixed all the damage from that tremendous battle, painting over burn marks, replacing sheared-off telephone poles and broken glass, repaving a four-hundred-yard stretch of damaged pavement.

Standing on that exact spot, it would be as though nothing had ever happened there. No armored car knocked over on one side. No pool of Miranda Devereux's blood on the asphalt as she slowly bled to death at Golden Tiger's feet.

Supposedly, he had heroically striven to save her life.

Sure.

He had also hit her with the *ki-bolt* that ruptured her battlesuit and drove fragments of exotic metals into her lungs, causing her to drown in her own blood.

Kai Di remembered her friend. She remembered all the adventures they had from boarding school, as she stared out the darkened windows from the back seat of the luxury car. Outside, she approached the gates to the Devereux compound, in one of the nicer districts of Paris.

Paris always smelled so much more complicated than home.

White Crane
Modern Gods: I
Blaze Ward
Copyright © 2016 Blaze Ward
All rights reserved
Published by Knotted Road Press
www.KnottedRoadPress.com

ISBN: 978-1-943663-14-9

Cover art:
© Okalinichenko | Dreamstime.com - Girl Photo

Cover and interior design copyright © 2016 Knotted Road Press

Never miss a release!
If you'd like to be notified of new releases, sign up for my newsletter.

I only send out newsletters once a quarter, will never spam you, or use your email for nefarious purposes. You can also unsubscribe at any time.

http://www.blazeward.com/newsletter/

WHITE CRANE

BLAZE WARD

ALSO BY BLAZE WARD

The Jessica Keller Chronicles
Auberon
Queen of the Pirates
Last of the Immortals

Javier Aritza Stories
The Science Officer
The Mind Field
The Gilded Cage

Additional Alexandria Station Stories
The Story Road
Greater Than The Gods Intended
The Librarian
Siren
Demigod

Other Science Fiction Stories
Mymirdons
Moonshot
Earthquake Gun
Moscow Gold

The Collective Universe
Imposters
The Shipwrecked Mermaid

Collections
Beyond the Mirror: Volume 1 Fantastic Worlds
Beyond the Mirror: Volume 2 Fantastic Worlds
Beyond the Mirror: Volume 3 Alternate Worlds

WHITE CRANE

BLAZE WARD

Knotted Road Press
www.KnottedRoadPress.com

PART I:
KAI DI

鶴

OVERTURE: MODERN GODS

The world was not created on July 16, 1945 CE. It merely *Awakened*, a terrible flash of light illuminating the desert floor and announcing that things would be *different*.

As legends tell us, there was always power in the world, but only enough for a very few Gods at any one time. It took mankind to truly unlock the power of the atom, vaporizing all those exotic rare elements from the planet's core and blasting them up into the atmosphere where anyone could taste them, grasp them, possess them; to make power a truly democratic thing.

Now many people have become unto Gods.

And nobody really understands what the power is or how it picks and chooses. It's almost more like magic in this modern era, granting wishes to a few with the ability to unlock it and the dreams to transform it.

But while it is no longer as rare as it used to be, scientists tell us that only the exceptional person can truly use the power, embrace it, and shape it. And those few people are mostly concentrated in the nations that have seen atomic weapons tested and used.

Still, in a world with now seven billion souls, that means thousands, potentially millions of such beings, with the ability to alter reality to their desires, are walking among us.

Some choose to be heroes, others villains. Many remain hidden. But today, there are many Modern Gods…

Introduction from *Gods Walk Among Us* by Charlotte Yukiko Burnham-Lambert. Copyright 1974 Tamarin Press, 17th Edition 2014.

THE NEWS

It had already been more than two months since Miranda had been killed by the American super-hero Golden Tiger.

Two months is a long time.

Angel City had fixed all the damage from that tremendous battle, painting over burn marks, replacing sheared-off telephone poles and broken glass, repaving a four-hundred-yard stretch of damaged pavement.

Standing on that exact spot, it would be as though nothing had ever happened there. No armored car knocked over on one side. No pool of Miranda Devereux's blood on the asphalt as she slowly bled to death at Golden Tiger's feet.

Supposedly, he had heroically striven to save her life.

Sure.

He had also hit her with the *ki-bolt* that ruptured her battlesuit and drove fragments of exotic metals into her lungs, causing her to drown in her own blood.

Kai Di remembered her friend. She remembered all the adventures they had from boarding school, as she stared out the darkened windows from the back seat of the luxury car. Outside, she approached the gates to the Devereux compound, in one of the nicer districts of Paris.

Paris always smelled so much more complicated than home.

On the sidewalk, there were fewer protestors with angry signs than she had been expecting, but this was Paris. The police here were not as tolerant of that sort of thing as she would have encountered in Angel City, or Franklin, or back home in any of the Pacific Northwest Jewel Cities. And Jean-Michel Devereux was a popular and powerful industrialist in France, in all of Europe. That kind of money could shelter him from the revelation that his youngest daughter had gone to America, put on a cowl, and turned herself into the super-villain known as the *Scarlet Titan*.

Two months of government secrecy had passed before the Americans had finally decided to release her body for burial. Two months of sudden pain when certain songs came on the radio, or seeing trinkets Miranda had bought for her on one of their trips.

She would never again talk to her best friend in the world.

Kai Di brushed her long black bangs out of her eyes and forbid herself to cry.

At the same time, it had been two months for a deep rage to take hold of her soul, burning slowly, like a seam of buried coal.

If she couldn't cry, neither could she grind her teeth in anger watching the man who killed her friend be interviewed on the evening news.

She could only hold on, striving to live each day while she tried to come up with answers.

If there were any.

And then one sudden, early morning, a telephone call, only answered because it had come from Miranda's mother, Isabel.

How quickly could she make it to Paris?

A chartered, corporate jet waiting for her in a back corner of the smaller airport, well away from big jets shipping packages in and out of Emerald night and day.

Ten hours in the air, the only traveling guest for two young stewardesses; well, older than her, but not yet as jaded.

Ultra-class travel.

A long, black luxury car waiting for her in Paris when she touched down. Her own personal customs officer politely waiting at the bottom of the corporate jet's steps.

The long drive into the city, alone in the back seat.

On the street, outside the gates, the crowd was amazingly well behaved, but this wasn't one of the slums where the demonstrators might torch random automobiles as a sign of displeasure, or boredom.

Nobody even so much as threw an egg or a rotten tomato at the automobile as the black, iron gate opened and they sailed serenely through, into the safety of the Devereux compound.

"*Merci*, Étienne," Kai Di said as the chauffer parked the land yacht before the ancient, gray, granite mansion and hurriedly opened the back door for her.

Kai Di stepped out and hugged the older man. He had been with the Devereux family for two decades now, a fixture of her just-passed teen years when she frequently came to stay with her best friend from school during breaks, on their way shopping, or skiing, or causing trouble.

He had always been there, never commenting on the crazy things they did, or the times they nearly got arrested, and he had never told her parents of their adventures.

Truly, Étienne was yet another uncle across a tremendously large family, stretching from her distant paternal kin in Guangzhou, to her mother's family in Hong Kong, to now include all of Miranda's relatives across the United States and Europe.

There was a Chinese word for such an interlocked structure, largely unknown as a term to westerners, regardless of how much of the concept transcended all languages.

Guanxi. Connections. The great web of family connections.

Kai Di stepped back from his hug before they both started crying again. She turned and found Miranda's mother already standing in the opened front door, veiled and dressed in black. Like a proper, dutiful daughter, Kai Di presented herself before the woman she considered her second mother, even though they looked nothing alike.

Isabel Devereux had been a top fashion model once, decades ago, before she fell in love with Jean-Michel. The woman still had the lean, commanding height, the regal bones in her heart-shaped face, the elegant grace when walking across a room, the charisma to draw every man in the room into her orbit with barely a nod.

Kai Di was tall among her extended Chinese family, as much a result of good nutrition and world-class health care as simply growing up in America, when so many of her smaller kinfolk had lived through the upheavals of eastern Asia over the last three generations, and consequently were still tiny in comparison.

Still, she barely came up to Isabel's eyes.

Kai Di was five and a half feet tall, with the glossy straight black hair and almond eyes of pure Cantonese blood, never diluted in six generations of living in America. She was slender in all dimensions, too tall to be considered petite, but built like a short fashion model might be.

But Isabel was still her mother.

Today, the woman was a mess. Blood-shot eyes and nose red from a fresh round of crying. Her graying auburn hair pulled back with a simple strip of blood-red ribbon wrapped underneath and laced into a simple bow atop her head.

Only her perfume achieved perfection.

Kai Di wondered if the ribbon was an accident of timing, or a silent tribute to the costume her daughter, The Scarlet Titan, had worn.

Isabel did not speak. Instead, she took a step forward and wrapped her arms around Kai Di, pulling her into a fierce hug, like a western mother with a beloved child. Kai Di could not imagine her real mother, her first mother, the imperious and glamorous Yi Wen, showing such physical affection, certainly not in public.

And thus I am the Kai Di who is a proper daughter with her family, and Dr. Kate Peng, the youngest genius researcher in a laboratory full of them, when I am not at home. And beloved youngest-youngest daughter Catherine when I am in Paris.

Kai Di hugged her other mother.

"Come, child," Isabel finally said as she relaxed her tight grip a bit and leaned back. "Let us get you inside. I bought you a black dress that should be a close-enough fit, and the tailor is waiting inside to make final alterations. We will get you fed, and then the service is this afternoon."

Yes, that was mother Isabel, the whirlwind of organization and activity everywhere she went.

Kai Di let herself be led inside. Jean-Michel was there, waiting with another hug.

Truly, I am their fifth child, when they have just lost number four all over again.

It was so strange, so exotic, so much unlike her own parents. Yet it was her other home.

Now, she had to go bury her sister.

THE FUNERAL

The service was private.

Kai Di could not think of the right word to encompass the room she found herself in after lunch. Austere did not do it justice. It was not hollow, even though there were pitifully few people allowed in.

Simply empty, perhaps.

Dark, wooden walls. Polished granite floor. Beams overhead holding up a vaulted ceiling.

Isabel and Jean-Michel. Oldest sister Gabriella and her husband Anton. Middle sister Euphrasie seated with her ex-husband Kevin. Older brother Patrice and his lively wife Amber. A priest she did not recognize. An organist. Étienne. Arn, the stuffy, proper English butler and his tiny wife Carissa, the empress of the kitchen.

Nobody else.

No one was allowed.

In other circumstances, there might have been whole battalions of French politicians and ministers in attendance, filling a large auditorium or small stadium. Associates of Jean-Michel from all of European industry would have come. Cousins, teachers, neighbors, friends.

It would have been an event.

No one else was welcome. Not today.

Even Miranda's young nieces and nephews had been kept home.

How does one properly inter a super-villain? How does one mourn?

It wasn't like there were long-established customs for this sort of thing. Miranda was not a black-sheep child, buried in a potter's field in the dead-of-night and deepest secrecy, lest she soil the family's good name. Although, she already had done that to a certain degree, by dying as The Scarlet Titan.

Kai Di would not cry again.

She was afraid that if she did, one of these times the tide of tears would bear her away and drown her. Isabel squeezed her hand as the priest began to speak.

Kai Di let her mind unfocus, let the strange, sonorous, Latin words wash over her and numb the parts that hurt. Funerals were not for the dead, who were past caring.

They were, instead, for the living. A moment to remember all the good things. Whispered secrets in the middle of the night, secret crushes, the sorts of silly things teenage girls do when far from home and away from their families.

"It is acceptable to cry, child," Isabel whispered in her ear as Kai Di leaned over to rest her head on the older woman's shoulder. "No one could have imagined she would have turned out to be a super-villain."

But I knew.

Kai Di could not whisper those words out loud, even now. She had promised Miranda to keep her secret. Sworn a silly, little blood oath by pricking their fingers on a full moon night when Kai Di had been a fourteen-year-old university freshman, and Miranda was her sixteen-year-old senior roommate.

Gods above and below, had it been six years already?

Miranda Devereux. The sister she had never had. Older. More sophisticated. More exotic. Impossibly French. Rich, and lovely, and smart, and undoubtedly destined for a life of crime and adventure, however short it had been cut.

Kai Di had no doubt her sister-in-all-but-blood lived life right on the very edge.

Right up until the moment it killed her.

She would never see Miranda again. Never open the pounding door to Miranda's smiling face at six AM with bagels and coffee and wearing some unknown man's jacket. Never spend hours on the phone in the dead of night with her, giggling, and telling lies and secrets.

Her sister was gone.

Kai Di could cry now. That was okay.

But tomorrow, she was going to hunt down that bastard who had killed her sister, and make him pay.

HOME

A whole day had passed in a blur.

Kate/Kai Di was home again. Back to Emerald and her compact little apartment with the perfect view of the Sound and the Olympic Mountains beyond it. Back to her real life. Back to be being plain, ordinary Dr. Kate Peng again.

At least, tomorrow. She still had to face the rest of Sunday, to try to recover her poise.

If that could be done.

The tears that were threatening to blind her caused her to misjudge the books on the shelf as she reached up. Instead of just her current journal, she accidentally pulled her oldest diary down off the shelf as well, friction welded by the cloth covers on both volumes. It fell to the pseudo-hardwood floor of her tiny bedroom with a tremendous slap that caused her surprised tomcat to bolt under the bed in fright.

"I'm so sorry, Mr. Loh," Kate said between sniffles as she carefully bent down to retrieve the book, blowing her heavy, black bangs out of her eyes.

She moved slowly, awkward in rarely-worn high heels, hose, and that tremendously expensive, long black dress. She might have worn something more comfortable on the flight home, but she could not marshal the energy to change back into jeans and a sweatshirt before she left Paris.

Kate squatted down and leaned slightly against the heavy oak frame of her antique sleigh bed. She reached for her old journal, still holding the program for Miranda's funeral in her other hand.

The diary was not something petite. She still remembered very distinctly asking her father for a folio-sized book with rigid, blue-cloth covers when she was twelve and had very complicated information that needed to be carefully transcribed.

Twelve-year-olds girls were like that.

But he had bought it for her, the first of many like it where she kept her dreams.

Kate glanced down at the open page, marveling at the lines of tight Cantonese characters written down the page. They made her laugh in spite of herself, in spite of the pain in her chest and the loss of her best friend in the whole world. In spite of the anger underneath it all.

I have not yet confirmed it, her twelve-year-old self had confidently written. *But after the latest experiment, I am sure there is going to be glitter in the cat's poop.*

There had been. For weeks.

Mr. Loh meowed at her from under the bed, subtly rebuking her for being such a poor minion and so terribly frightening him.

Kate smiled at her sidekick and sat, carefully curling her legs under her. She patted her lap and smiled at her little gray tabby as he slowly emerged from under the bed to sniff the air. After a moment, he stepped carefully up onto her thighs.

Mr. Loh began to purr as she worked at his spine and under his chin with her nails. Kate knew she would be absolutely covered with his hair when she stood up, but right now she really didn't care.

She had never owned a black dress reserved exclusively for funerals before this. She had never needed to.

And she was never, ever, going to wear this dress again.

鶴

The day had slowly faded to evening. Kai Di checked the face of her cute little Swiss watch and decided it was time to head out. Her parents expected her for Sunday dinner at seven o'clock, regardless of her having just arrived back in Emerald from Paris less than four hours before.

She let the exhaustion wash briefly over her before she took a deep breath and pushed it away. This would be a night for dark, bitter coffee to keep her energy up. She only needed four or five hours of sleep most nights anyway. Caffeine-fueled insomnia tonight would not make that big a difference.

Kate checked herself quickly in the mirror. Bangs finally brushed into obedience. Long, straight, black hair French-braided to her shoulder blades. Dark blue silk blouse with a subtle floral print done in silver. Long, shiny black skirt. Low-heeled, lace-up, black boots with bangles on a stout gold chain around her right ankle.

Miranda had given her the little gold charm, a flying crane, for good luck on her eighteenth birthday. Kate would wear it tonight to honor her friend. It would be invisible under the skirt, but she would know.

Kate checked her smart phone. Her ride was five minutes away. She blew Mr. Loh a kiss and grabbed her nicer jacket off the hook and locked the door behind her.

Her parents awaited.

鶴

Kai Di flashed back to Paris as the car service deposited her on the curb outside her parent's home. The house was much smaller than the Devereux compound, and in the middle of a wealthy neighborhood on Capitol Hill rather than in the exurbs of town.

Kai Di could not imagine Wei De Peng and especially glamourous Yi Wen, living someplace out southeast like Hobart and possibly fitting in. Even Emerald's Nuevo-riche, mostly investors and software entrepreneurs across the Lake in their gated and secured little city on the Points, were too suburban, too remote.

Too modern.

Kai Di bowed ever so slightly to the two stone lions protecting the sidewalk and steps as she passed. On the porch, she checked that the *ba gua* mirror was protecting the front door from demons. Mother would be frantic if something happened to the *feng shui* of the ancient house, forcing her to either bring in a new geomancer, or worse, find a different house, somewhere else on the dragon's back that was Capitol Hill.

From the outside, there was little to distinguish the house. Wei De had subtly redone the corners of the roofline when he moved in, to tilt them up slightly, reminding her of a temple she had visited in Guangzhou when she was much younger, but he left the two great windows, overlooking the front yard, in their original, century-old, craftsman design. It was only inside that the space began to look properly Cantonese.

The backyard had been transformed, replanted with jasmine and tea trees, leaving only the semi-ancient mature roses from before. This late in the fall, there was almost no smell at all, save for the trace of salty air blowing in off the Sound.

Kai Di took a calming breath and rang the bell. She waited.

Father surprised her by answering the door himself, instead of Mu Ren, mother's maid and cook for forty years, a woman that had been a fixture of the Fong family from when mother had been younger than Kai Di was now. The family maid since long before her parents had moved here from Franklin.

Wei De was a gloriously middle-aged Chinese man from a very old family, rail-thin and seemingly made of bamboo. In her boots and low heels, Kai Di still looked up slightly at him. His straight, black hair was short and neat as always, and he seemed to be eternal, at least in her mind.

He surprised her even more when he reached out and hugged her quickly.

Wei De was not a hugging person.

"Jean-Michel called," he whispered in her ear before stepping back. "I'm sorry for Miranda. I know you loved her. Is there anything we can do?"

Kai Di nearly lost her remaining self-control as she processed her father's words. She had come here tonight mentally prepared for battle with Yi Wen. Mother had always been very insistent that Sunday dinner was to be a somber, family affair. The kind that required extraordinary expectations.

Her mother was the queen of extraordinary expectations.

Instead, Kai Di just shook her head, smiled at Father, and let him take her jacket, shocked and somewhat numb. She followed him deeper into the house, past the formal salon and little library/office, past the grand staircase, into the kitchen across squeaky hardwood floors.

The view there was even more shocking.

Mother sat on a barstool at the bar, silently supervising Mu Ren's cooking with a glass of red wine in her hand. Both women stopped talking when she entered.

Mu Ren reached her first, but only because tiny Yi Wen had to climb down off the barstool gracefully first. Everything Mother did was graceful.

Mu Ren was always good for a hug. Mother surprised her even more than Father had with one.

This was not a hugging family. They were Cantonese.

Kongzi, the great scholar and philosopher, had established very strict rules of behavior, hierarchies of relationships for honoring your emperor, your elders, your family.

He did not do *hugging*.

Kai Di somehow found it in herself, deep down, to giggle silently at the thought that her parents were becoming Americanized, even unconsciously, and however much against their will.

Still, she controlled her shock. Miranda had been as much another daughter in this house as Kai Di had been in Paris. Her parents obviously wanted to honor her as well.

Mu Ren poured Kai Di a glass of red wine and stuck it in her hand and then went back to her stove.

"Come," Mother said, leading her to the other barstool and seating her.

Kai Di started to speak, but Mu Ren turned and shooed them out of the kitchen, pointing imperiously at the grand dining room.

"Dinner will be served in five minutes," she announced gravely in Cantonese, an utter dismissal from her domain.

Kai Di smiled and allowed herself to be led by her mother into the dining room, already set with the finest porcelain and silver. She sipped at her wine after she was seated, something she could not do outside this house, with her much-older colleagues, since she would not turn twenty-one for another three months.

Mother smiled gravely at her.

"Was it a well-done funeral?" Mother probed.

Not *proper*, or *grand*. *Well-done*. Mother took the ceremonial aspects of things, of life and death, very seriously. She expected Catholics to be able to handle such a task with style and grace. Anything less would be unacceptable.

"It was," Kai Di replied with equal seriousness.

As much as you could do such a thing, they had managed.

"How are you doing?" Father surprised her by asking.

Again, nothing in the *Analects* prepared her for this manner of personal interaction with her parents. One was expected to show proper deference and respect, up a chain of relationships and connections. *Guanxi*. But her parents were obviously intent on trying.

Kai Di allowed herself to relax some. She felt her shoulders come down enough that she was no longer capable of holding a pencil between her shoulder blades as she sat.

"Tired, but well, Father," Kai Di replied quietly.

She could try, too.

It dawned on her that they might be a bit starved for conversation, for family now. They had reached the empty nest stage of their lives.

Kai Di was done with school, finished with her post-Doctoral work, and working as a Distinguished Researcher in a specialized laboratory down on the lake, with her own apartment. Both of her brothers were away at school. Ge Ke, commonly called Gregory by his American friends, was almost done with a Bachelor's of Science in Indiana. He would be eighteen this year. Han Rong, Harry, was in St. Clair, California, studying computer science with the best minds of his generation.

It was a family of scholars. Even Mother had taken a degree in literature. In China, that would have been enough.

In America, you needed money as well, to thrive.

The Peng clan had always been wealthy enough, but Father had taken it to an entire new plateau in the sleepy city of Emerald, once quaintly known only for making jet airliners. Wei De had seen the future, and moved up here to invest heavily in real estate, mere moments before personal computers transformed this entire region, the entire world.

He could have easily moved across the lake and lived among the technology billionaires.

If he cared.

The Peng clan did not do ostentation.

We have lived on the west coast of America for more than one hundred and fifty years, child, bound by links of family and favors to the mother city, to Guangzhou. We have lived quietly and watched other clans rise to prominence, and fall to arrogance and emperors.

We will survive. We will prosper, while history erases them.

Mu Ren interrupted any further commentary with the first bowls of soup.

She would allow no serious conversation that might ruin the digestion.

Father gave Kai Di a look that promised such seriousness later.

FATHER

Kai Di found herself in Father's study upstairs after dinner, alone with him. Mother had retired to bed, perhaps specifically so they two could be left to talk. Mu Ren would be down in her basement apartment, catching up on the latest seasons of her favorite television shows in one of her great weekly binges.

This room had always been where she and her father had come to have solemn conversations. Not that they excluded the rest of the family. She knew that Father had done similar things with both of her brothers once they had gotten old enough.

Retire to his study and have serious talks, ranging across politics, history, genealogy, money, culture, and languages. An education one could not receive in any school. The sorts of things that Mother's family in Hong Kong did not give serious enough consideration to, much of the time.

No, this was a shelter, for the Peng clan to consider what had made them, and how to retain it over the generations. A place to be safe.

Kai Di was home.

Father sat in his great, ancient chair, red leather and overstuffed and oh-so-very-English. He held a snifter of expensive brandy in one hand and watched her across his big wooden desk, perched on the comfy love seat to one side, holding a glass of her own.

The walls were sheathed in a dark, red oak, stained almost to black, and then enameled to shine. Carpet had been laid over the original hardwood floor; a deep, lush shag in pale jade that swallowed every footstep. On the walls, two bright watercolors hung, presumably of the English countryside. They had that faint whiff of faded imperialism and unquenchable perseverance.

Kai Di always expected the room to smell of sweet tobacco smoke. If an Englishman lived here, this would be his smoking room. Father had decorated it as such, the only room in the house not traditionally Cantonese in nature. But Wei De was not a traditional son. Dutiful, but not traditional.

Like father, like daughter.

Instead, jasmine leaves and sweet oils in a side-table vase made it smell more like the traditional apothecary she occasionally visited down in the International District, no longer just Chinatown as the Vietnamese, the Thai, and various other immigrants came in and pushed the Chinese families up the hill and into the middle class.

Father eyed her speculatively. Kai Di awaited his wisdom like a dutiful daughter.

"I have given much thought to your friend Miranda," he began solemnly. "Who she was, what she was like, how she died."

Kai Di nodded. She had taken a few days off work when the news first broke, to sit at home and cry. She might do it again, now that the funeral was done.

And yet…

She was familiar with the western concept of the stages of grief, but had managed to get them in the wrong order. Anger had decided to come last, after acceptance.

She could accept now that Miranda was gone, but she couldn't get over her rage at the how or the why. It had been a slow burning, deep inside. Embers almost hidden, but never going away.

Instead, Kai Di had spent the last month learning to control the edge that would suddenly appear in her voice, lest she take it out on people with no greater crime than they happened to be closest when she bubbled over.

She might spend a lifetime recovering.

"Perhaps a year after you went away to college," Father continued carefully, "one of your professors contacted me directly."

Kai Di blinked in surprise at the sudden direction of the conversation. This was news to her.

"He mentioned the Japanese scholar, Burnham," he continued. "And asked if you had ever exhibited extraordinary characteristics."

Burnham? That wasn't a Japanese name. Oh. Yukiko Yamanaka, known by her adopted name, Charlotte Burnham. Storyteller and distinguished scholar of the special humans she had called Modern Gods.

Kai Di was aghast.

Her? One of them?

But then she realized.

Miranda.

Her sister *had* been one of them. The sister that had helped her, gotten along with her, understood her better than any of the other students, even those in the exceptional program for accelerated education. The so-called super nerds, none of whom had started college after they turned fifteen.

Her sister, who had turned out to be one of the ones called *Modern Gods*.

Automatically, Kai Di checked the door, but it was closed. No one else could listen in.

"I assured him that you had not," Father stated flatly.

Father smiled at her, more warmly than he had all evening.

"After all," Father concluded. "Extraordinary is a very flexible word in English. And he was not family. Our secrets are not for outsiders."

Kai Di opened her mouth, but could not speak. She couldn't summon demons, or fly, or throw lightning bolts, like the costumed heroes and villains on the evening news.

"I am not a witch, Father," Kai Di said automatically.

"And I am not a warlock," he replied serenely. "That does not make either of us entirely human, beloved daughter."

Kai Di's jaw hit the floor. She felt like her eyes were probably that bugged-out size that characters got in Japanese anime. In her mind, a precipice suddenly appeared at her feet.

Father? One of them as well? What did that make me?

Kai Di temporized by taking a sip of her brandy. Father had brought out the very finest tonight. It behooved her to appreciate it correctly. Especially when she couldn't trust her words.

They stared at each other in raw silence for several seconds, Father Buddha-like in his great chair, Kai Di aghast on the love seat, trying to find words, in Cantonese, Chinese, or English.

There were none.

"But Miranda was your sister," Father continued. "In soul if not birth. And we are Peng. I know what I would do, if I stood in your place. I would know your thoughts."

Kai Di looked inside herself, still shocked by the turn of conversation tonight. The grief and loneliness persisted. But anger still shaded her soul red.

She sipped the brandy and smelled the jasmine. Anything to ground her in home, when *adrift* threatened her.

"What does it mean to be what Burnham calls a *Modern God*, Father?" she asked finally, quietly. "What can the power do?"

Wei De leaned back in his chair and swirled his glass. She watched his eyes focus on a distant, invisible horizon.

Moments passed. Or eternities. It was hard to keep time straight in her head right now.

"Power is power, daughter," he said after a time. "According to Burnham, the only limits appear to be imagination and discipline, to use her words. If you can dream it, and will it, you can bring it into being."

"I always wanted to fly," she murmured, partly to herself, partly to the universe.

"Yes," Father agreed with a sharp edge to his voice. "But you did not *demand* it."

What?

Kai Di brought her attention back to the present, to see the serious look on Wei De's face. There were lines around his eyes and down his cheeks, not obvious at any other time. Save for lacking a flowing, white beard, he had the look of one of the Christian Patriarchs from their great book, aloof and angry and *Intent*.

She could not find words.

"You demanded science," he continued flatly, speaking to her from the mountaintop.

Science?

"You looked at a problem," he said. The words seemed to thunder at her, for all their quiet inflection. "An equation, a formula, something. You solved it in your head intuitively, faster than anyone else could. I have seen you do it."

Yes. Was that a super-power? Could it be one?

There were hundreds of heroes and villains in costumes, doing flashy things with their power. Could she?

Kai Di suddenly felt that ability unfold. Clarity from confusion.

She saw to the root of her Father's reasoning. Perhaps there was power there.

"Will I use my power to avenge Miranda?" Kai Di observed evenly.

"Indeed," Father agreed, still aloof, but warming slightly. "There is an old American saying. If you would seek revenge, you should begin by digging two graves."

Two? Oh. Yes. One for Golden Tiger, and one for me.

She tasted the possibilities of revenge. Of actually transforming her private, little vengeance fantasies into something more concrete, more real.

It was sweet, and bitter. Exhilarating. Imposing.

Ominous.

"I have never considered that I had that power in me, Father," she replied finally.

"I know, beloved daughter," he said. "But you would have, at some point. Better we have this discussion now."

"Why?" she asked honestly.

Nothing in the Analects had prepared her for this moment. She had envisioned a life of science and intellectual exploration. Of friends and family and vacations to exotic locations. Or, at least, even more exotic than her adventures with Miranda.

"I fear you are at a crossroads, my daughter," Father continued. "There are many paths that lie open before you at this moment. A proper father would impress upon his most-dutiful daughter the correct choice to make, venerating the ancient teacher while honoring her clan and her parents by following those wishes. Even at cost to her own."

He paused to take his own sip, gauging her. The Patriarch was gone. In his place, perhaps a slightly angry Buddha. If one could envision such a thing.

Kai Di could retreat behind a carefully Cantonese façade as well.

Dutiful daughter.

But she was utterly at sea. She could never remember him being like this. But then, they had never been *here* before.

"Instead, Kai Di, I would tell you that not all answers are to be found in the Analects. We live in an age of gods and heroes. I believe I have raised you well. Whatever choice you make, I will be proud of you."

He swirled his glass and drank.

Kai Di did the same, unable to put coherent words in order, even in her head. She had been raised to be the proper, dutiful daughter, to sublimate herself to the wishes of her parents, of her clan. Of her emperor, had there been one. She had been expecting him to expressly forbid such things.

She might have even honored those wishes.

To be free to choose was a modern thing, an American thing. It was at once intoxicating, and terrifying.

She sought within to find the words, but could not grasp them.

And then she saw a picture on the shelf behind Father's desk. It had not been there the last time she sat in this place.

It was a picture of her and Miranda, arm-in-arm at the reception that followed Kai Di being awarded her Doctorate in Chemistry. And it occupied the place of honor in the section where one would look for kinfolk.

Miranda was family, as far as Father and Mother were concerned.

It would be Kai Di's duty as next daughter to avenge her sister.

Thus, she could best honor her sister, and her family.

She felt a cold smile grow on her face.

Kai Di turned to her father and saw the same smile there, so unlike any she had ever seen before.

It was feral, hungry, angry.

Yes, this man has lost a child. And he will have blood for it as well.

Kai Di raised her glass mutely. Father did the same.

They toasted silently to vengeance.

THE LAB

Kate woke at her customary time, well before the alarm on her phone that she kept as a backup. Outside, it was still dark. This late in October, the sun would not rise for hours. Even if it were summer, she would still see the dawn arrive.

She took a deep breath and stretched, opening her curtains to watch the moon slowly set over the Olympics before making her way to the kitchen to make coffee. She put water on to boil and filled up the hand-grinder as she prepared to reduce the beans to magic.

It took a moment for Kate to locate the mug she really wanted this morning, tucked back in a corner of the cupboard. She pulled it out and studied the outside with care and a secret smile. The United States Patent Office let you order a coffee mug with your patent information on it. This was hers.

Correction, my first patent. There will be others. Perhaps one day I will have an entire dinner service for parties.

Kate sat the mug carefully on the counter and got to work. Her Cantonese parents took their tea very seriously, but this was Emerald, the City of The Mermaid, and people here matched that level of devotion in their coffee. Perhaps surpassed it on some days.

Press and funnel set atop the mug. Beans ground and transferred into the press. Hot water poured over the grounds, stirred to just the right amount of foam, pressed through until the grounds were merely damp. Extra water poured into the mug to cut the thickness down from something almost Turkish to something merely adequate for her morning.

Kate added just enough cream to soften the blackness, just enough honey to blunt the bitterness. Today was going to be a hard one, it needed to be approached with a ceremonial level of seriousness, even as she began her normal routine.

She turned on the television and sipped her coffee while she sat on the floor in front of it and slowly stretched, letting the east coast financial information wash over her like a warm summer tide. Kate could not see the future, like some of the Modern Gods, nor cast fireballs with her hands, nor tame demons.

She could, however, absorb staggering amounts of information, remember it, and process it.

Maybe that was enough. She had no basis against which to compare, except for Miranda, who had been one of *them*.

Other people she had known were able to memorize pages of texts, and recite it years later. But they could not analyze it in three dimensions in their head and locate fascinating new connections, hidden underneath, the kind that intuitively worked. Those people could not rotate a molecule of some organic chemical in their mind, seeing all the possibilities. They did not instinctively understand some entirely new way to bond it with a completely different chemical and transform it into something amazing and powerful.

Kate could do that. Had done that. At twenty years old, Dr. Kate Peng already had more money than she knew what to do with. More than the entire rest of the Peng clan combined. And more came every quarter in the form of licensing payments and stock dividends.

Chinese women probably *were* willing to sell their souls for a weekly pill that would make their skin young, pale, and utterly blemish-free. Jean-Michel Devereux had certainly made the two of them both fantastically rich by understanding and exploiting that. By telling her what invention might be useful to a young woman with a head for exotic organic chemistry.

It would never win her a Nobel Prize, but at this rate, she might be able to buy Sweden one of these days as a consolation prize.

Kate finished properly stretching on the floor and emptied the last of her coffee. She rose and centered herself in the middle of the living room.

Her apartment was all space, in spite of how small the footprint was. Here in the living room, a television was mounted flat to the far wall. A comfy green cloth couch across from it. Two bookshelves, one for science and one for literature. Mr. Loh's little carpet-covered palace by the window for climbing and observing. For being the lord of all he surveyed, like the God-Emperor Woodchuck she and Miranda had seen once on a hike in the North Cascades.

The middle of the room was empty. She preferred space, not clutter.

Kate took a deep breath and began the first movements of *Tai Chi Chuan*.

The ancient forms helped focus her. As her teacher had once described them, *Meditation In Motion*. Hands just so. Feet perfectly placed. Breathing evenly paced. Movement. Calm. Center. She needed that, especially today.

Kate traveled inward and considered her day ahead.

Father was right. Many paths had opened.

鶴

The Lab had an off-putting feel this morning. Something Kate could not place.

Nothing had changed that she could see.

It still had that smell of fresh-cut flowers resting fitfully atop the ammonia and other powerful cleaning agents regularly blasted everywhere to keep strange chemical concoctions at bay. There was a new security guard in the lobby, but he smiled politely as he stared at the badge she wore on her hip as she walked by.

Perhaps he was staring at her bottom as well. There wasn't much there as a result of too much running and not enough walking, but Miranda had told her it was a nice bottom.

Kate blushed ever so slightly and sped up a little. She quickly badged her way through the reinforced, bullet-proof glass doors and disappeared into the facility. She was not yet ready for *people* today.

Inside, things were still off.

Maybe *she* was off, and everything else had continued to sail along perfectly well in her absence.

Certainly, it had been a rare entire weekend with no emergency messages on her phone. And there were no deadlines looming for her team. Hopefully, everyone else had relaxed, possibly even enjoyed themselves.

Kate stopped first in her office to drop off her purse and hang up her rain shell, before she went down to the kitchen for more coffee.

A bouquet of flowers on her desk stopped her cold. Roses. White, red, pink, and yellow. A dozen of them, patiently waiting in a glass vase filled with water.

A note attached to the front caused her heart to race for reasons she could not name. Her hands trembled as she fumbled it open, nearly dropping it twice.

Inside, a single linen-paper card.

Much love, it said in French. *Papa.*

Jean-Michel.

Kate realized that everything *was* the same around her. Her sheep-skins hanging on the wall, part of what her assistant, Abigail, had called her Brag Wall. A generic motivational poster her boss Emmett had gotten her that said *Fail Originally*. A plain desk and sideboard. Even the standard-issue white lab coat that everyone wore because it was tradition.

She was the one who had changed.

Somewhere, during the time Kate had finished her morning workout routine, showered, dressed in jeans and her favorite sweater from New Zealand, caught the bus across town to the Eastlake Biochemistry neighborhood, and walked into this room; she had changed.

Become someone else. A *someone* who did not belong here.

And yet…

Was this growing up? Kate was only twenty years old. Twenty-one in January.

She still thought of herself as wet behind the ears, even if the ink on her PhD was finally dry. She had never had a real job. This lab certainly didn't count, since she got to play with chemicals and models all day. And didn't need the money.

What had happened? Who was she? *What* was she?

A sound interrupted her wool-gathering.

Kate blinked and came back to the present. She turned and found Em standing in the door to her little office, sipping from a mug that said *BOSS* in great big letters, with *Touch my coffee and I'll cut you* in fine print below that.

Dr. Emmett Tanaka. Chief Research Officer, Devereux Pharmaceuticals America. He was a great bear of a man, wearing jeans and an ancient tie-dyed t-shirt under his lab coat this morning. Apparently, it wasn't a day to video conference with Paris, what he referred to as *calling the mothership*. On those days, Emmett wore shorts with a dress shirt, tie, and jacket. At least until the call was done.

Emmett was too young to have been a hippy, but was doing a good job of making up for it these days.

He smiled down at her.

"Jean-Michel called," he said. "Told me about your weekend. I know I told you already, Kate, but I'm sorry for your loss. If there's anything you need, lemme know."

Jean-Michel called.

Kate knew *Papa*, Jean-Michel, meant well. He was trying to insulate her from the shocks that had been accumulating. Perhaps he was unconsciously trying to divert her from the path she had found her feet on this morning.

He was acting like a businessman, trying to keep the golden goose happy. But at the same time, he was a worried father, probably concerned that she would go off and seek revenge for Miranda.

That he might lose another daughter.

He was French. They worried over such things.

First Father, Wei De, had understood her mad need. Had already told her that this path was honorable. Had opened the way. Now she just had to figure out how.

"Thank you, Em," Kate said carefully, striving to keep as much emotion as possible out of her voice. "Right now, I want to bury myself in work for a while."

"Sounds good," he replied, stepping back out of her doorway, out of her light and space. "If you have time this afternoon, I'd like to go over some of the testosterone experiments we have ramped up this quarter. Something's not quite right and I'm hoping your genius spots the holes in my theory."

Kate blushed at the compliment. The other lead researchers in the lab were all brilliant folks. Jean-Michel liked to joke that he was planning to remodel his den for a dozen Nobel Prizes on the mantle, from his staff. It was not that far-fetched a dream.

"I should have time after lunch," Kate replied.

Em smiled and departed, leaving her alone in the strange, crowded space.

Emmett Tanaka, while brilliant, was not in Kate's league. Nor was Abigail, her assistant, who was fantastically smart herself.

Kate considered her colleagues. Yesterday, she had considered herself slightly smarter than them, a result of the genetic lottery and a lot of hard work, balanced against their impressive smarts and greater experience.

Could it be that they were merely human? That she really was another one like Miranda, or apparently like Wei De?

One of the *Modern Gods?*

A new path had opened this morning as she traveled the more mundane one to work.

Could she actually take possession of the power that was out there and make herself over into a god?

DISCOVERY

Kate sat in the main conference room on the third floor, the one with the extra-comfy green leather chairs with nine different knobs and levers to make them do all sorts of strange things when you wanted to be relaxed while calling the mothership.

The whole far wall was lit up, twelve huge monitors hung together in such a way as to create the illusion of a single wall of light, a screen twelve feet across and nine feet high.

It was just her, Emmett, and Abigail today.

Dr. Abigail DuBois. Thirty-five, twice divorced; currently, to use the analogy she preferred, *a free agent*. Extremely French. Perhaps half an inch taller than Kate in bare feet, if you ever caught her out of six inch heels. Addicted to men.

Kate wondered if Abigail was a nymphomaniac. Clinically so. Certainly, she went through men fast enough, they generally being unable to keep up with the *breadth and scope* of her sexual demands, as she phrased it.

At least it was illegal indoors these days to smoke those nasty, little, home-rolled cigarettes with the imported French tobacco that Abigail preferred. It gave Kate an excuse to send Abigail out into the rain, outside the secured perimeter of the building and well away from the air intake systems. And gave Kate space to think.

Kate had considered turning her work towards something she could mist all over Abigail when the woman came indoors again, to eliminate that rank smell of smoke. She suspected she could make a fortune if she could make it easy.

Another fortune.

She made a note to ask Jean-Michel sometime.

The giant glowing wall displayed a molecule, slowly rotating on the horizontal axis.

Testosterone. The primary hormone that made males what they were. Important in the growth of muscle and bone mass, one of the triggering keys of male sexual characteristics.

Two decades ago, a random side effect of a drug for hypertension turned into a cure for male erectile dysfunction. And a license to print money on a scale not repeated until Kate discovered how to make Asian women look young and beautiful again.

Vanity was a very powerful way to make money, legally or otherwise.

Jean-Michel Devereux wanted to make more. Lots more. Slobberingly lots more. And she would have her slice, through stocks and licensing agreements that her first father had carefully negotiated with her second one. She would never lack for money.

Was that why she found it so hard to focus this afternoon?

Kate's heart just wasn't in it. She knew that inside.

Emmett had made his presentation, gone over the designs, the testing regimen, everything to find a drug that would make middle-aged men virile again, without killing them from cancer or some other side-effect. Build up muscle again. Tighten the stomach. Do for the skin of the male of the species something loosely akin to what she had done for Asian women.

Make them young and sexy.

Another license to print money.

Em sat in the chair across from Kate and watched her, waiting. Abigail practically vibrated with energy, but whether that was a need to smoke or something else was open to interpretation. She reminded Kate of a six-year-old who needed to pee and was too shy to ask.

Kate sighed. She really owed it to Emmett to pay closer attention. There were millions of dollars riding on these experiments. Anything she found this afternoon would probably save Jean-Michel enough money to actually register on the quarterly statements. Especially if they were on the verge of another wonder drug.

She studied the rotating display one more time.

And felt her heart skip a beat.

Something must have shown on her face. Emmett leaned forward suddenly, feet slamming into the floor from his regularly reclined spot.

"You've got something," he pounced, brown eyes boring into hers from across the table.

Kate blinked, looked again.

Yes, she saw something. But not what Emmett wanted her to see.

She saw herself standing over the corpse of a costumed hero in Angel City, a man known to the world as Golden Tiger. Saw the key to that man's death on the screen in front of her.

One of the keys. There were many. Signposts between here and that ugly demise.

Something that Wei De had always taught her.

Assume success. Plan for victory.

Kate turned to Emmett and felt her skin flush as she quickly prevaricated.

"Maybe," she lied as convincingly as she could.

The dutiful daughter could tell many lies. To outsiders.

Emmett and Abigail had just become outsiders, threats to her vengeance. Humans.

"What?" he asked breathlessly.

"Possibly a negative androgenic side-effect you haven't controlled for," Kate said. "I can't be sure."

Emmett scowled.

She flushed again.

"I need to look something up to be sure," she continued.

Emmett fixed her with that perfect raised eyebrow thing he did.

"You?" he asked sarcastically. "I thought you had everything you had ever read carefully filed in The Vault against need."

Kate speared him with a look so hard that it actually made him lean back and blanch in embarrassment.

"It was published forty years ago," she enunciated carefully, grinding the words between her teeth like coffee beans as she spit them out. "In East Germany. I've only ever read parts of it that were translated as reference material in another study."

"You don't speak German?" Abigail inquired suddenly, as if that made her a barbarian from the distant steppes. With Abigail, it might. "Really?"

"No," Kate replied coldly. "That language is too *mean.*"

Every possible variant of Chinese, both spoken and written, from the Classical period to the present? Yes. French, English, Italian, and a little Spanish? *Absolument.* But not German.

It made a useful lie now.

"When will you know?" Emmett asked carefully, obviously afraid he might get fingers bitten off.

Kate watched the path in front of her turn into a super-highway.

"Tomorrow," she decided aloud. "I'll head home now and spend the rest of the night digging it up and translating the bits I need, to see if it says what I remember."

Or, locating an interesting article that would make a wonderful red herring for the others.

What she saw, floating on the wall in front of her, might have won her a Nobel Prize after all. But in the process, it would have cost her the vengeance demanded by her soul.

EAST GERMANY

Kate stretched out on her sofa with her laptop open. Her personal laptop. Not the company-issued version with software that could track what she did, where she went, who she talked to, what she learned.

That was a useful tool in a world of stolen secrets and corporate espionage, but Emmett and Jean-Michel were not allowed to know what she was up to.

Not anymore. Possibly never again.

Kate's personal filing system in her head, what she and others referred to as *The Vault*, had not led her astray. She found the article she had remembered, part of a secret East German study of Olympic athletes, and dutifully translated the bits she needed.

What she would tell Emmett tomorrow wouldn't be a lie. It just wouldn't be the whole truth.

Sin by omission.

After all, that study did have some bearing on Emmett's work. They could either choose to replicate one part as a control, or assume it from the earlier study and spend the time and effort elsewhere. Money saved. A lot of money.

There.

Kate set the machine to one side and looked over at Mr. Loh, stretched out on his palace and watching his kingdom. She patted her lap invitingly, but he just blinked at her with an ear twitch and a kinked tail.

I am being a very bad, very lazy minion.

Kate rose and grabbed the metal cat brush, the one that looked like a saw blade in a circle, attached to a handle. Mr. Loh immediately rolled onto his side and began to purr, so Kate began to extract handfuls of gray hair from the little master of the house.

She wondered absently how smart Mr. Loh really was. And if he might actually live forever.

Some of her experiments on her cat, when they were both younger, might have killed Mr. Loh. Accidentally. Playing with fire, really. But for a twenty-year-old kittie, he still moved like a two-year-old. And seemed to be much smarter than any breed of dog she had ever met. Still fundamentally aloof in that way that only cats have mastered, but much more cognizant.

Considering how much money people in this country spend on their pets every year, I wonder how much money I could make with a treatment that would multiply a cat's lifespan?

It wouldn't work on humans. It had never been intended to. Humans didn't have the right gene sequences anyway. Well, not unless they decided to go all in on the were-kitty thing, half cat and half person. At the speed science was pushing the envelope, that might be an option in her lifetime, especially if there were Modern Gods doing research.

Kate's breath caught in surprise.

How many of the great geniuses of the last few centuries were really advanced beings who used their power for brains instead of brawn? Like Miranda? Or me?

How many more were out there right now, inventing the future? What might we humans be like in another few generations of mad scientists and heroic inventors?

Once again, Kate considered the two pathways open before her.

On the one hand, vengeance for Miranda, with all the attendant risks: violent death, arrest, dishonor. Would she really do this thing, even with Wei De's approval?

Wealth was no longer a driving factor in her life. She would never be poor again. Her clan might never be poor again, although she remembered the ancient Cantonese wisdom of sudden wealth over four generations: *coolie, tycoon, playboy, coolie.* Something to strive against. Something that required discipline.

To be arrested risked all that. Everything she owned might be confiscated by an angry government.

Would that truly be the best way to honor Miranda's memory?

Kate knew she could return to work tomorrow and invent something fantastic and exotic, like a potion that would turn a person into a were-tiger. She could let go of the mad dreams of vengeance that had plagued her for weeks, and instead make the world a better, safer place.

Her eyes fell on a picture on the bookshelf. Her and Miranda. The Tower of London. Summer before last.

Her best friend.

Dead.

A touch on her hand brought her back to the present. Mr. Loh's paw. He made a mournful chirp, rather than the disappointed yip she would normally get if she stopped brushing too soon.

Again, she wondered just how smart her kittie really was. Certainly perceptive. Almost empathic. She went back to brushing him.

There really was only one road.

The world could go to hell. She was going to have Golden Tiger's heart on a plate.

POLAR BEAR DREAMS

Kate woke from a dream of polar bears. The clock read two in the morning. It was far too early to actually get up. But she was completely awake.

And rumbling.

She found herself on her side, facing the curtained window, stretched out. Mr. Loh was not in his usual spot, curled up in a furry ball against her stomach with Kate wrapped around him for warmth. Instead, he was stretched out flat against her spine atop the covers, deep asleep in some important kittie dream, alternately purring madly and squeaking as he slumbered.

Rumbling. Polar bear.

Carefully, she slid away, letting him sleep while she let the mad adrenaline fade. Dreams of polar bears, flying through the skies with pegasus wings, stalking her. Herself as a great bird, flying as well. In Angel City. In the middle of summer. She wasn't sure what it meant, but she was too awake to fall back asleep quickly.

Instead, she climbed out of bed and added sweatpants to the t-shirt she normally slept in. Quietly, she moved to the living room and sat on the couch to consider her options.

She had finished translating the German paper into English so that she could forward it on to Emmett and Jean-Michel in the morning. They would take it from there. She would be free to explore the other topic, the thing she had seen, had lied to them about.

Kate wondered again if it would have come to her in any other mental state. If she hadn't been emotionally exhausted, frustrated, and pushing herself so hard. If her need for revenge hadn't been so great, would it have been there to see?

Testosterone. The male hormone. The thing that gave men size, and bulk, and muscle. Made them mend quicker, recover faster.

Women could take it, but they would bulk up, grow hair in all the wrong places, possibly begin to develop secondary male sexual characteristics. She had seen pictures of female weight lifters who were indistinguishable from their male counterparts, except usually with the addition of ugly, fake boobs.

But what if she could edit the chemical instead? Keep most of the anabolic effects, and none of the androgenic? She could be stronger, faster, tougher. Heal faster. Become the physical peer to the strongest men, possibly some of the Modern Gods. And keep the side-effects to an absolute minimum. Remain a woman.

Be girlie, if she ever figured out how to do that.

Kate considered the moon out her window, visible after a fast squall line had passed and wet everything just enough to make it Emerald in winter.

She could take this discovery to work tomorrow, and all but guarantee herself a Nobel Prize one of these days, and Jean-Michel another fortune. She could make the world a better place, treating the sick, the weak, and the elderly and make them whole.

All she had to do was walk away from her revenge.

Nothing, right?

After all, the Scarlet Titan had been a super-villain. She had been in the process of attempting to rob an armored car of a fortune. Committing a crime. Breaking the law.

Kate wasn't clear what Miranda might need with that kind of money. What did super-villains require? What did they do with it? Or were secret lairs and armies of minions? Did Miranda have a hideout, a lair somewhere?

Before tonight, the Modern Gods, both heroes and villains, had been characters in books and movies. A presence on the evening news when they fought. Toys and licensing deals on television and in the stores for the holidays.

Kate considered her revenge from a technical standpoint.

Going after a super-hero meant that she would be seen as a super-villain, at least in the popular press.

What did it mean to be a villain?

Did they get up each morning and consider their villainy? Cackle madly at some evil scheme, like in the movies?

Everybody probably saw themselves as the hero in their own story.

Knowing Miranda, being Scarlet Titan hadn't been about wealth or power, but the rush of adventure. That mad burst of excitement, riding right on the edge. Like skiing too fast, trying to outrun an avalanche. Or BASE jumping.

Yes, Miranda had always been a rush-junkie. And it had gotten her killed. And that bastard had killed her.

He had to die.

Maybe Kate was going to have to be a villain in this scenario. She was okay with that. But she was going to be smart about it.

After all, dancing with death is a dangerous-enough task. Best do it right.

Kate spied her boots by the door as she day-dreamed. She had left the little gold chain with the bangles and charms on it from Sunday dinner.

The golden crane spoke to her. Whispered lovingly. Called her name.

Kate suppressed a shudder and considered another of Miranda's secrets.

Inspiration. There was a way to do this.

Kate knew where to start, how to become a super-villain.

Would she?

She rose from the couch and made her way to the hall closet.

Carefully, she opened the door, as if to a terrible basement dungeon in a bad slasher movie.

There. On the floor, all the way in back. Behind a box marked Christmas ornaments, in one labeled Medical Research Text Books. Another present from Miranda. Hidden. Secret.

Kate considered just how many secrets she and Miranda had accumulated over the last few years.

The box was heavy as she trundled it over to the sofa and sat down. She danced quickly into the kitchen for a knife to attack all the strapping tape wrapped around it. Careful not to cut herself or cardboard, Kate got the box open.

Inside, under several old books, was an anvil case. That was what Miranda had called it. About two old-fashioned-briefcases-thick, by their regular dimensions long and wide. Fashioned out of some incredibly light but durable bronze-colored metal Miranda had been working with, apparently in her super-villain identity.

Miranda hadn't gone into science and business after school, but had become an inventor. Kate had filled the role of dutiful daughter, taking up the family business for the Devereuxs.

Or had, until a few hours ago. Now, she wasn't sure. Perhaps being the dutiful daughter to the Peng clan took precedence. Vengeance over money.

Kate moved the anvil case into the middle of the floor and laid it on its side. The locking mechanism, Miranda had assured her, would defeat anyone but the two of them. Kate put both of her thumbs on optical scanners and waited while the machine decided she was her.

It unlatched with a solid thump. The case moved a fraction as bolts retracted.

She took a breath, willed herself not to cry, and opened the lid.

Last summer, Miranda had taken her flying.

That was what they had told people.

It hadn't been much of a lie.

How they had done it, however, was a terrible secret.

Another one.

Kate's specialty was organic chemistry. Being able to see how to transform one chemical into another one that did what she wanted. It was profitable. It could be very useful.

Miranda, on the other hand, was a genius at mechanical engineering. She could look at a machine and see instantly how to take it apart, and how to put it back together better. Faster. Smoother. Stronger. Something-er.

Or, in this case, she could look at a bird flying and realize how to make a machine that made it possible for a human to do the same thing. Or rather, a harness that would unfold, wrap itself around her, power up special little generators that would lift, and let her fly. Possibly another Nobel Prize for the wanting. Had she wanted.

Miranda had assured her that nobody else would be able to make the machine fly besides Kate.

At the time, Kate hadn't been able to process what Miranda meant. Had she somehow tuned it specifically for Kate?

Now, Kate understood.

Miranda had seen in Kate another person capable of reaching out and grasping the energy around them, to use the phrase Burnham has first written down. She could pull it in, and harness it.

They could use *Power*.

For Kate, *The Vault* inside her head. For Miranda, inventing wonderful toys.

And this one had been tuned to Kate. Or rather, only someone like the two of them, one of the Modern Gods, would be able to use the device, to power it with nothing but force of will.

To fly.

Kate kneeled and pulled the device from the opened case and held it in her hands. She placed one hand on the palm-print plate and felt the machine grow warm.

Because she was paying attention this time, because she was expecting it, Kate felt the machine draw power out of her own body, out of her soul, and begin to transform itself.

Instinctively, Kate reached out her consciousness and studied the air around her.

There.

Floating like a thin fog on a cold winter morning. Almost transparent, even to the new, heightened senses she was using. Kate wanted to reach out a hand and grasp it. Instead, she envisioned herself as a vacuum, like Miranda had taught her.

The world resisted.

The power was content, just floating by. It did not want to give itself up to her, regardless of how great Kate thought her own need might be.

It did not fight her. The power was not like that.

Instead, it passively pushed back, like a layer of rime frost wrapped around a container just pulled from the deep freeze. Kate had no source of heat.

She did, however, have her will.

Kate wanted to fly again. She wanted to power this machine, using the almost-magical frost ice she saw all around her.

Kate pulled harder.

It felt like trying to pull an oak tree out of the ground.

Kate envisioned herself as a terrible giant, standing over a tiny forest. She growled, although if it was in her mind or her throat was hard to tell. Godzilla would have been pleased with the sound.

She reached down in her mind, suddenly thousands of feet tall, and grasped the oak tree that was now a tiny sprout sitting on the forest floor. It became a strawberry in her hand as she tugged it free.

Kate put the berry in her mouth and crushed it, letting the sweet juice run. She swallowed in triumph.

The machine surged into action.

Kate opened her eyes to a moment of panic. She smelled ozone floating thickly in the air around her, where there had been only a thin taste moments earlier.

The fog was coming towards her now, like a stream flowing towards a waterfall with a terrible roaring in her ears.

This was the power Burnham had talked about. The energy of the cosmos, cracked by the efforts of Mankind when they learned to break the higher atomic elements under fission and fusion, blasted skywards and only slowly settling.

The machine telescoped.

It extended bands that carefully, almost lovingly, wrapped themselves around her waist and then crawled up her back and over her shoulders, tickling her like a feather's kiss on her skin. The bands came around front, crossing between her breasts like a racing harness she had seen in a Formula One car once, before encasing her chest.

Other lines ran down the outside of her legs to her ankles, wrapping with bands to anchor the joints tenderly and swelling out to become boots.

The bands opened slats that expanded, like thin sheets of bronze-colored scale armor, to cover her legs and protect them from the thrusters on her waist that she knew would open up when she willed them hard enough.

From just below her shoulder blades, the greatest part opened now.

Kate could feel the lines extend from her sides, wrapping themselves around her shoulders and upper arms like a titanic edifice. She looked at her right arm, watched a plate, perhaps two inches wide and one thick, grow down the back of her arm to her elbow, to her wrist, wrapping the arm joints just as it had the legs.

It continued onward, though.

The two lines went more than a foot past her fingertips, coming down to a dull-edged tip, like a saber-blade.

Feathers unfolded from the back of the bar down her arms.

These were bronze, like before.

Kate smiled, remembering flying with Miranda, up in the North Cascades, where there was nobody around. Fulfilling her dream to walk the clouds.

Being a great hawk, terrorizing the smaller birds. Laughing.

Flying.

She considered herself, standing in the middle of her living room, a giant, bronze hawk.

Kate decided things needed to be a different color, especially if she was going to be a super-villain.

She needed an identity, a cowl.

A masque.

Another secret.

Kate envisioned the bronze surface turning white. After all, if the power was as close to magic as modern science could admit, then the only limits were those she was willing to acknowledge.

It said so in all the fairy tales.

Kate was not willing to submit.

She pushed.

The metal pushed back, content in the form Miranda had chosen for it. *Change is entropy. Entropy is bad.*

Kate would not be denied.

She looked up, found an especially strong bit of ephemeral spider web in the aether above her. She grasped it, pulled it into her soul, wove it into something new.

She envisioned the new burst of energy flowing out through her spine into her new legs, her new arms, like an extension of her being.

The bronze still resisted. It had achieved perfection of form. Why did it need to change?

Kate pushed harder. She growled again, louder this time.

She showed the mindless lump of metal the new form she demanded of it. The beauty. The elegance. The august majesty.

The bronze relented. It would allow this change.

She felt the metal relax itself under her patient strength.

Kate reached into its soul and remade it from one of Miranda's little toys into her own sword of vengeance.

The metal understood. The power understood. They agreed.

Everything *shifted*.

Kate closed her eyes and delved into the atomic structure of the metal itself.

Color was just a pattern of reflection of the light bouncing off. It was bronze because the top layer absorbed most light and only bounced back a specific fraction on a certain wavelength. There was no bronze in the metal, just something exotic Miranda had invented.

In itself, it was an elegant beauty fit for one of the great eagles. Miranda was French. Such an image would be appropriate.

Kate was Cantonese. She demanded a different bird take shape around her. Less a predator, but much greater within her own culture.

The machine finally came to understand that an eagle was a lesser bird. It must become something greater.

Kate ran mental hands over the surface, polishing them with her power. When it faltered, she looked up and took a deeper breath, drawing more into her.

Finally, the machine *became*.

Kate opened her eyes and held out both arms straight forward to study them.

Where things had once been a rich, dark bronze, now her legs and boots were black. Where the body of the machine wrapped around her hips and chest, everything was the purest white. Even the arms were snow white with only a row of black feathers from the shoulder to the elbow, before turning white again down the rest of her arms.

It was almost perfect. Almost enough.

When they had been flying, she had needed no more. This would take her to the sky, let her dance with Miranda's ghost, Miranda's memory, among the other birds.

But she was to be a super-villain now. More secrets. More things hidden.

Kate took a deep breath and envisioned the rest of the bird from her dreams. The crane whose symbol she wore on her boot.

The machine was mindless, but Kate called out to the goddess of birds for her help. This would be something Miranda never envisioned.

But it was *necessary*.

Kate felt her lungs expand like a bullfrog getting ready to croak. Power flowed into her body like electricity and pain mixing. For a moment, her will quailed under the assault.

Kate called out to all the Chinese gods and goddesses she knew, seeking their help to bring her vengeance to being.

Something answered her. Perhaps.

The machine turned pliable again.

Acquiesced to her might, her hunger.

Her rage.

Became.

Kate felt the metal on her back flow upward, wrapping loosely around her neck, and then coming up her jaw, her temples, her skull.

The task was done.

The machine felt like a second skin around her.

Kate let go of herself enough to breathe again, and started to stumble. She caught herself and staggered slightly as she made her way into the bathroom.

The wings should have made things awkward. With all the extra mass, she weighed almost half again her normal amount. The machine compensated.

Or rather, she could pull power from the air and let it flow into keeping the machine powered.

Miranda must have done this for her, when she had taught Kate to fly.

Kate had to learn now.

She turned on the light and stared at the apparition in the mirror.

She had neck and head armor now, black-throated as it should be. The black faded into a soft gold around the opening for her mouth, but continued up her cheeks and around her eye holes. She could see and breathe, but the rest of her head was covered, protected.

She turned enough to the side to make sure, but she already knew what she would see. The back of her new helmet was white, with a crest of bright red metallic feathers, like a mohawk or a horse's mane, running from the top of her forehead to her neck.

She had succeeded. This was no longer the costume of a flying eagle.

Kate had transformed herself into a Red-Crested Crane. In China, a symbol of nobility and immortality. Of power. Of purpose.

Of vengeance.

Mr. Loh surprised her with a chirp.

She looked down and smiled at him as he rumbled loudly and began to rub himself against her leg. She could feel his fur through the armor, as if it was a super-soft skin itself.

But she had taken it, owned it. It was hers now, transformed into an extension of her body, of her will, of her revenge.

She could do this and not lose her soul, no matter how Faustian she had been prepared to go.

Would she really have offered her soul up for that ability?

Yes. It was for Miranda. For losing her. For that bastard who killed her.

A flash of insight nearly caused her to collapse.

Had Miranda been grooming her to become a sidekick one of these days? Would she have taken the opportunity?

Grooming.

Kate felt the blush start around her belly-button and quickly work its magic all the way to the tips of her ears. She was happy the armor hid it.

Perhaps Miranda had been preparing her for other things as well?

Kate flashed back to a night in her dorm room, after Miranda had graduated, but come to visit. Miranda teasing her about boys. Kate complaining about the truth in the old line *sweet sixteen and never been kissed.* She had always been too busy with books, laboratories, and legal contracts, to take any time for boys. And none of the boys around her had been interesting enough to pursue.

So Miranda had kissed her.

It hadn't been a simple peck, platonic. It hadn't been two French women saying hello, cheek to cheek. It had been a stirring kiss, heavy with fire. It had been arms wrapped around each other, tongues dancing, breath growing hot and wild, before Kate broke it.

She had liked it. Wanted to taste it again. But that would mark her different, especially in a Cantonese culture that did not accept such things.

Did Kate like girls instead of boys? She had never considered it before that moment, simply assuming that she was a woman and would find the right man someday.

Miranda never had differentiated all that much, seeking pleasure and excitement, however she might find it.

It was one of the few places where the two women were magnetic poles apart.

Since then, Kate had still never kissed another person, beyond a simple French greeting. Never once been with a boy, or a man. Had never found one capable of turning her head.

They had all seemed so boring. So transparent. She knew she was attractive enough, but her mental abilities quickly frightened them off.

She was too smart. Too driven. Not emotional enough.

And she didn't need anyone else.

Kate had always been self-contained, emotionally independent in ways she could not explain.

Perhaps being the dutiful daughter was enough to explain? She just never felt the need to share herself with another person. And Miranda had been there when she needed a friend.

Beyond Mr. Loh, she had never needed anyone else.

And now she had lost Miranda.

Kate looked at herself in the mirror again. She saw another being stare back.

At home, she was Kai Di, the dutiful daughter. At work, Dr. Kate Peng, resident genius in a group of them.

And now?

Kate had turned herself into The White Crane. Now, she was Vengeance. One of the Greek Furies made steel-bound flesh.

In the morning, she would need to prepare. The road to killing a man would be long and dangerous. Particularly a man who was also a Modern God. But she had taken the first, hard steps.

And nothing would deflect her from her chosen path.

BECOMING

Kate had given up on sleep, eventually.

Reluctantly, she had powered down the flying crane armor, packed it back up, and changed into running tights and a rain shell with reflective tape everywhere. And a very, very warm knit cap.

She didn't run every morning, but many of them. Today would be one. Hopefully, it would clear her mind.

Upper Queen Anne Hill was quiet this early. Nobody was out this late on a Monday night, very few people were up this early on a Tuesday morning. Most of the people she saw were either early bird runners like herself, or people headed in to jobs servicing the morning food and coffee rush. Mostly coffee. Emerald was like that.

It smelled wet and wintry this morning. Just enough damp from overnight squalls, just enough breeze off the Sound to bring in a taste of salt.

Kate had too much mad energy pent up this morning to run just a couple of big squares atop the hill. Instead, she set her sights on the big mountain, way southeast of town, and headed downhill. There was a fantastic 24-hour dive called *The Fifth Point*, on the other side of City Center, where she could stoke up on chicken fried steak and eggs, with a slice of the blackest, bitterest coffee in town on the side.

She would need the energy today. It wasn't every day she had to lie to her father, Jean-Michel, and make him believe it. Wei De would understand. Jean-Michel would need convincing. She would have to spin tales of angst and heartbreak.

She would need time to properly mourn Miranda and find herself. That sort of thing.

Hokum.

She really needed to do things in a research lab without him watching over her shoulder. She had to transform herself, physically and emotionally, without him asking questions. She had to get serious about Tai Chi Chuan again, and find someone to help her remaster the animal forms of southern Kung Fu, techniques she hadn't concentrated closely on since she was twelve. All things considered, she would need to know the Crane form better than just what she remembered from the old lessons.

And then she needed to learn ways to fight against the person expecting her to continue to fight like a bird.

She needed a biker, or something. Maybe a bouncer. An expert in no-holds-barred, blood-on-the-peanut-shells, close combat. And he had to be someone who wouldn't tell any of her family, either family, what she was up to.

Tall order.

Kate pounded the pavement silently as her brain processed options at a million miles an hour.

Being a super-villain was going to be a pain in the ass.

And she would need a cat-sitter for those times when she traveled to Angel City to study her target and plot his demise.

Maybe she needed to move there when she was ready. Just put everything up here in storage and go live down in Paradise for a while. It was fashionable. People might believe she needed to be a beach bum, to surf, to *find herself*, or whatever she could get people to believe these days.

Planning and work. But first, a very non-Cantonese, non-Emerald breakfast.

Kate smiled as she ran. What would she do without rain?

The Laboratory was already a strange place.

Alien. Weird.

After breakfast and a run, Kate had taken a nice, long shower and put on her smallest pair of jeans and a tight, green t-shirt. It was nothing like the slacks and blouse she normally wore to work.

Kate smiled back at the security guard today, instead of rushing past him while trying not to be embarrassed.

Four cups of coffee and a bucket of food was what it had taken for her to finally feel full this morning. She wondered if that was an after-effect of tapping the power as she had. Perhaps she would need more calories on a daily basis, like a professional athlete. She remembered reading that the average male consumed about 2,500 calories in a day, while top athletes might need 5,000 to stay at their peak.

Hopefully, she wouldn't need that. It would be exceedingly difficult explaining to people how she could do that and not turn into a blimp, let alone why.

Of course, if she was serious about disappearing off the local radar and re-inventing herself, very few people would have any baseline against which to compare, if she timed her disappearance right.

So many things to plan.

Maybe she should just chuck the idea of ever returning to being Kate Peng, and become The White Crane full-time. It would simplify things.

White was the color of death, or mourning. It was appropriate.

She could build a secret lair. Recruit a small army of henchmen. Do crime for a job and a hobby.

Of course, cash flow would quickly become a problem if she had to feed a mob. She might be reduced to robbing armored cars, which was the sort of thing that got Miranda into trouble in the first place.

She would need to be quieter about it.

And she had one thing that Miranda did not.

Guanxi.

English had no truly equivalent word. She had heard it translated as networks of connections or relationships, but that didn't cover the word.

Kate considered what the best translation might be as she passed through the secured, bullet-proof doors, and entered the facility.

She paused, looked back, and blew the guard a kiss. It was something Miranda did constantly, but shy, quiet Kai Di Peng would never have done.

She barely even blushed as she did.

She still wasn't sure who she would be tomorrow, or where, but it most certainly wouldn't be here.

Kate just needed some help.

Guanxi.

A web of favors owed and expected. Almost a Marxist tenet: From each according to his ability, to each according to his need, with stratifications of class and power thrown in. Perhaps Marx meets Kongzi, lacing in the Five Basic Relationships, so that you provided favors up the pyramid, and were afforded protection down from above. The Italians had long ago figured out how to make it work.

She would need to use the power of connections across the entire Peng clan, on several continents, to get certain things, quietly. Things she did not, could not, tell the Devereux kin.

And there would be things from the Devereux side as well.

She was another daughter to Jean-Michel and Isabel. Best to use that. Exploit it as much as she could, within the bounds of family.

Kate already had an annotated list of needs in her head, growing by the minute as she explored new avenues.

Revenge was a complicated business.

Being a super-villain would just make it harder.

In her office, Kate quickly hung up her rain shell and grabbed her coffee mug. It was still too early for anyone to be here. Most of the lab ambled in after nine, and it was barely seven, but she had already put in four hours of work this morning, and was just hitting her stride.

Kate felt free.

Was this what it meant to be truly alive?

The coffee machine asked no questions and offered no sage advice, beyond the need to consume more caffeine. She asked. It served. They both achieved bliss.

Kate had already gone through all her usual news and entertainment blogs and web sites once this morning. She had emailed Jean-Michel and Emmett the study she remembered, the cover story for so many of the lies that were coming.

She returned to her office and powered on the desktop to check her mail for late-breaking surprises.

All that was left to do this morning was to prepare herself to lie convincingly to her boss and her second father.

And then she would be free.

The conference room had not changed in the last twenty hours. Not that Kate had expected it to.

Expensive, comfy chairs. The wall of monitors. Marble-topped conference table with enough layers to seal it against most damage. An organic chemistry lab was never entirely safe from something accidentally sticking to the bottom of a coffee mug, even when everyone took care to wash them regularly.

Kate activated the secured channel and sent a ping to Jean-Michel. Paris was nine hours ahead of Emerald. It would be late in his afternoon, but he routinely kept hours more like the East Coast of the US. Up early to study the markets, have a proper breakfast, into the office in the late morning Paris time, work a while, talk to Americans on the West Coast, dinner, workout, bed.

Jean-Michel was as regular as a clock, six days a week. Even when he vacationed with Isabel, he was never far out of reach, although he was not working unless something happened. One of the reasons his lovely wife had put up with his hours for so many years.

The line clicked as he answered. There was a short pause while he activated the secured links at his end. One could never take communications security too seriously in this business. There were always competitors, often with powerful government assistance, trying to listen in.

Sometimes she thought that Devereux Industrial was just a very powerful telecommunications and information security company that also happened to do pharmaceuticals on the side.

"Good morning, beautiful," Jean-Michel smiled at her as the image came live.

He looked like a benevolent ghost, staring out at her from the wall with a head three feet tall. She had a flashback to George Orwell's villain, but this was just her father.

Kate could see the tired lines etched into his face. The leonine mane was finally starting to transform from sandy blond to gray, just around the edges. At sixty, he looked forty, and could still out-marathon men half his age.

But he was worn. And this was not going to help.

That couldn't be helped.

"*Bonjour, Papa,*" she replied diffidently.

Kate worked very hard to keep the right amount of bright in her voice and her face, while shadowing it with her own layers of care and wear. He did not need to know how much she was looking forward to this. It would send entirely the wrong signal.

This was not forever. She told herself again that it would only take her a year, possibly two, and then she would be back in this lab, happily puttering away as she turned twenty-three.

The villainess known as *The White Crane* would be gone, retired, and she could get on with her life, happily avenged for all of them.

She even believed it.

"What's wrong, *chérie*?" he asked, noting something about her face that disturbed him.

Kate took a deep breath and glanced down at the table-top. She drew strength from its solidity. She looked up, and realized there was another source of strength, of comfort, that she could tap.

Kate opened her senses to the power, floating in the air even here, and reached out. It felt like a sip of her other father's mulled wine, settling in her stomach and warming everything.

"I have been thinking," she began slowly. "About Miranda. About me. About life."

"Oh, ho," he half-smiled. "Has my little bird grown up?"

Kate felt a catch in her chest at his words.

What did he know? Had he guessed what she was up to? Was she predictable? Would he help or hinder her?

Jean-Michel Devereux had far more to lose than she did. Would that make him a foe, or an obstacle?

She blew out her breath slowly, loudly, trying to relax her suddenly-tense muscles.

"I do not know," she replied simply. "I know Miranda was enjoying herself, enjoying life. I know it killed her, but I cannot imagine she would have chosen any differently, except to duck faster."

"I would agree with you, Catherine," he said. "She was alive. And now you feel that you are missing something, no?"

"How did you know?" Kate let a little of her surprise show.

Jean-Michel leaned back in his chair. She could tell by the way that the camera adjusted itself.

"Ah, youngest daughter," he smiled sadly. "It comes to every parent, eventually. You protect your children as much as you can, preparing for the day when they must fly the nest."

Kate silently bit her tongue as she envisioned just how she would fly this nest. The White Crane. Vengeance. Probably not what he expected, whatever it was he expected.

"I think so, Papa," she replied diffidently. "I was up all night last night thinking."

Kate let the words trail off. Everything was still God's honest truth.

So far.

"I think I need to take some time off," she continued, strength edging into her voice. "I have never really taken the time to enjoy myself, even when I was with Miranda. We were always busy doing something, going somewhere. I want to see the world while I'm young."

"I see, little flower," Jean-Michel consoled her. "It can be hard, facing death so suddenly. As a businessman, I do not wish to see you go, even for a day, but as a father, you have my blessing. I know your team has no pressing issues at present that Abigail cannot handle, assuming we can find you somewhere in the world with a satellite phone. Should I tell Emmett?"

Kate felt the energy surge out of her stomach, all adrenaline, and bile, and power, as she controlled the muscles in her face and hands, kept everything calm, and relaxed, and a little sad.

"No, *Papa*," she said meekly. "I will tell him. I do not know how long I will need to be gone, so I should say proper goodbyes."

"Very well," Jean-Michel said sadly. "Will you at least be here for Christmas? Isabel would be very sad not to see you."

"It is still on my calendar," she let her smile grow ever so slightly warmer, as if the memories of past Christmases might ease the burden of her mourning. Certainly, her Cantonese parents did not celebrate Christmas, except to go out to dinner with their Jewish friends. She could still be back in Emerald for the New Year and a proper family event.

"Very good, *chérie*," he said. "Hopefully I will talk to you several times before then. And I will make sure Carissa prepares her kitchen for a truly wonderful celebration."

"Thank you, *Papa*," Kate signed off with a heartfelt smile.

She could not imagine trying to keep someone as sharp and intelligent as Jean-Michel Devereux as far in the dark as she had planned. She couldn't tell him anything at all.

A moment of inspiration flashed across her senses, like someone walloping her in the head with a four-days-dead flying fish down at the Market with all the tourists.

Guanxi.

She did know someone with the right sorts of connections to do the things she would need. And she could trust him with silence, and secrets.

After all, Étienne had already kept so many.

鶴

Kate let the doors to the Laboratory close behind her like a bank vault sealing. Or a nautilus shell closing off a room.

She was free.

It had been hard, getting out of the building without losing her patience, accidentally dropping the façade of a mourning friend needing time to heal. Kate had never realized just how many teary hugs she could generate, just by telling everyone she needed time off.

Emmett had been even worse than Abigail.

But now she had everyone's promises to connect via social media, even as she told them she was going dark for a while.

Kate didn't need witnesses or friends to go drinking with.

She needed time and space to plan.

And, if it worked, she could always come back in a few years and win a Nobel Prize or three.

Kate let her feet carry her to the parking lot, past the cute security guard who looked like he might ask for her phone number if she smiled at him.

Did she want a relationship? Physicality with a male?

A female?

No. Her fire could only be quenched by one man. *Golden Tiger.*

Now she just had to find him. Stalk him.

Kill him.

And this parking lot was absolutely not the place to have the phone conversation she had in mind.

Kate crossed the little side street and got onto the walking path next to the lesser lake. As long as she paid attention to the idiots on expensive bicycles pretending like they owned the entire damned planet, she would be fine. At least the sun was finally up and they wouldn't have any excuse for almost running into her.

Besides being assholes.

Still, better safe than having to beat someone to death this morning. Kate moved to the water side of the path and began to walk quickly. Worst come to worst, home was only a few miles away, around the base of the lake and up the hill. Or maybe she would find a coffee shop without a mermaid on the door and relax.

The whole world awaited her.

She checked her watch. Late morning in Emerald. Just after dinner in Paris.

She pulled out her smart phone and typed a text.

Call me as soon as possible. Please do not tell J-M or I.

Sent.

She started walking, wondering how long it would take.

Moments. Her phone rang.

Kate checked the name. Étienne. Good.

"*Bonjour*, uncle," she answered as she walked.

"*Bonjour*, niece," the man rumbled back. "What kind of trouble are you causing now?"

Kate nearly tripped as her mind blanked for a moment.

What does he know?

"What, what makes you say that?" she stammered back at him.

"How many times did you and Miranda ask me to do something without telling your parents, little bird? Just like this."

Oh. Right. Uncle Étienne.

Kate blushed in spite of herself.

Maybe he was why we never got arrested.

Still, she smiled. Some amount of immense weight slid off her back and fell by the side of the path as she walked.

"This will be even worse, uncle," she said finally. "I must swear you to utter secrecy."

Something in her voice carried across the thousands of miles. Étienne grew serious.

"*Bon*, Catherine," he said.

It barely even sounded like him, voice suddenly down half an octave and lacking any of the bright cheeriness there just moments ago.

Kate took a breath and stepped out into air.

"I remember you telling me once, uncle," she said carefully, enforcing the bounds of *guanxi* to a man who would not recognize the word, but who would know the meaning. "You have a nephew of some ill repute. One who grew up to be the blackest sheep in a very dark family."

There was a moment of silence on the other end. She heard him breathing, but he did not speak.

"You mean the jewel thief," Étienne replied finally, heavily. "Thibault?"

"Yes," Kate said, letting herself relax. She felt the bands tie him closer to her. There were very few people she implicitly trusted to lie to both sets of her parents if necessary, to protect her.

She cherished Étienne like a priceless relic.

"And why would you need such a person?" Étienne continued carefully.

"Because you have said he is a man who keeps his word, uncle," Kate said simply. "And he has certain contacts that I need, to acquire certain goods that I cannot simply order from the world's largest online retailer, even as I walk by their headquarters in Emerald."

Kate looked around. Her feet were moving her faster than she had expected. She was already at the south end of the lake, passing between the monstrous new construction towers transforming the city and the old Coast Guard station that was now a museum. There were very few tourists about this morning. Probably the threat of drizzle.

Again, silence from the other end of the phone. Kate heard the wheels turning in Étienne's head. She found herself holding her breath as she waited.

Why *does* one need a jewel thief? To steal things, obviously. But what things did she need stolen that she could not buy or borrow? She was rich, educated, American.

Finally, he spoke, having made peace with himself. And probably mentally setting an alarm to get up and go to Confession sometime this week, for sins he had not yet determined.

"Let me make a few calls, little bird," he said slowly. "I will let you know what I find out."

"Thank you, uncle," she replied, equally serious.

The phone line went dead.

Kate tucked the device back into her pocket and took a deep breath.

This was barely past step one, but she was on her way to an encounter with a hero in Angel City.

And his death.

THIBAULT

Kate had expected to be waiting for days, possibly longer, before she heard anything from Uncle Étienne. Instead, it had been barely three hours. Lunch was just beginning to happily digest itself as she sipped the last of her iced tea and watched birds squabble angrily over old tortilla chips in the parking lot, next to one of the best Taco trucks in the city.

Her phone chirped.

+33-. International telephone number. *France*. A number currently unprogrammed into her contacts list.

"*Bonjour*," she said neutrally as she answered.

"H'Allo," a man replied in English with a heavy French accent. "I am looking for Catherine Peng. My name is Thibault."

"How did you get this number?" Kate asked in a tight voice.

"I was told to say that Uncle Étienne needed a favor from his favorite black sheep for his favorite niece."

His voice had a wry smile. She could envision him sitting in a sidewalk café with bitter black coffee and a loaf of bread. There would probably be a beret and a neck scarf. Étienne had said Thibault was a tall, wiry man in his late forties, close enough in age to Étienne that they had been fast friends as children.

Oh, what a strange world and the paths we take.

"*Bon*," Kate said. "We need to talk privately, face to face."

The phone grew silent. She heard noise in the background at his end, so he was thinking, instead of having just hung up on her.

"I would not be welcomed by US Customs," Thibault said quietly.

Considering some of Étienne's stories, she could see that. This man had been arrested a score of times, but only twice had French or Swiss authorities been able to make anything stick, and even then, it was barely enough to keep him in prison for more than a year or two.

And he had never given up his cohorts or his employers.

That made him useful.

"Then I will come to you," Kate decided. "Where?"

It was one of the many benefits of the money she had squirreled away against a rainy day. Occasionally, like today, it rained.

"Just like that?" Thibault was surprised, almost taken aback.

But then, a good jewel thief probably never did anything on the spur of the moment, as a matter of good survival instincts. A man like Thibault probably had a plan for escaping the restaurant where he would eat dinner tomorrow night. It would be a good plan, too.

"Yes," Kate replied. "Just like that. Where should I fly to? And when will we meet?"

The way he turned silent reminded Kate of Étienne. Neither man stammered or stuttered when he was deep in thought. Instead, Étienne turned inward, silent and still. She imagined his nephew the same way, poised, like a fox, waiting.

"It is Tuesday," the man said finally. "Can you be in Milan by Friday?"

"I can."

"Good," he said. "Text your flight information to this number and someone will meet you."

The line went dead.

Gruff. Bordering on rude, but he was a Frenchman, talking to someone he thought was an American woman. She would insult him more personally, more directly, when she saw him. Then, perhaps, he would be more sociable.

Or not.

He was a means to an end, as well as part of the extended family.

Guanxi.

One more step on her path.

ITALY

Kate always thought that Milan existed for tourists.

Get them in, quickly shuttle them up to the mountains, transport the next batch coming down and home. Show them a fabulously wonderful time.

Keep all their money.

But then, she had always had money when she traveled.

For this flight, she had decided not to do the private, corporate jet route again, as lovely as that might be. One of these days, someone might be looking at her history, and those sorts of things would likely raise red flags. Here, she could pretend to be a tourist.

So instead, she had flown first class through London. The British knew how to make travelers feel loved and appreciated, both inbound and outbound.

The airport in Milan somehow managed to look like every other airport in the world, both inside and out. Kate wondered if there was a school of architecture dedicated to making sure all airports felt exactly the same, no matter where in the world you landed.

Only the travelers and conversations around her gave any clue as to where she was, if she had somehow gotten lost and ended up on the wrong flight and landed somewhere else.

Since she did not know what Thibault's plan was, Kate had packed a little of everything. She and Miranda had once woken up in southern Germany in a heavy rain in June, driven to Innsbruck through a snow-storm, continued, and eaten lunch at a lovely sidewalk café in northern Italy in the sun. It was not that far away from Milan, even on Italian roads.

Now, she had a small suitcase, really a large overnight bag, so she could travel light and close to the ground, slung over one shoulder as she passed out of the secured area and looked around.

Kate's eyes fell on a tiny blond woman, not much older than she was. The woman was perhaps in her mid-twenties, thin and wiry, dressed in a quiet black suit, suitable for a private car driver like the taller and older men around her.

She was holding a sign in Mandarin, where all the others were in English or German. It said Dr. Kai Di Peng.

Kate felt like a giant as she got close. This woman might have been five feet tall, and weighed perhaps one hundred pounds, but there was nothing soft about her.

Kate stopped in front of the other woman and addressed her in Mandarin.

"Can you understand me?" Kate asked politely, nodding at the sign.

"Yes, ma'am," the driver replied in reasonably-passable Mandarin. "Are you Dr. Catherine?"

Kate blinked. She had been expecting a tall, skinny, French, male, jewel thief.

"I am," Kate replied. "And you are?"

It felt odd having a conversation with an Anglo stranger, in Mandarin, in an airport in northern Italy. But nothing about the situation was normal.

"My name is Itala, ma'am," the driver replied. "I am Thibault's niece, Étienne's grand-niece. I'll be your driver. The crew is waiting."

Weird, but acceptable.

Kate suddenly realized that she might be interrupting Thibault's regular work, whatever it was that a career criminal might be doing, since he didn't have a real job. She had asked Étienne for a favor, and expected him to make it happen. With no thought for others.

Guanxi.

She had forgotten that others had lives. It was one thing to demand someone's attention. She needed to be aware that they had responsibilities.

At least she was prepared to pay well for the things she needed. Hopefully, that would help.

"Very good. Shall we?" Kate smiled at the woman, pushing her bag back around to rest more comfortably on her butt as she walked.

Itala nodded and folded the sign, stuck it into an inside pocket of her black jacket, and turned to her right.

Something about the way Itala walked caught Kate's eye. The woman moved very deliberately, walking in a single line where one foot was almost exactly behind the other, like a gymnast on a balance beam. It made her hips float back and forth in a way Kate decided she needed to practice, mesmerizing in its metronomic pattern. That would be very distracting to most men. And many women.

Outside, they walked a great distance to where the private cars were parked, almost at the far end of the lot. Itala chirped the alarm on a newer model, gray, Type S Mini Cooper and opened the back for Kate to set her bag.

Kate realized only then that other woman had not spoken a single word, all the way out of the airport and to the car.

Itala closed the back and moved around to the driver's door, opening it and quickly hopping in.

Kate climbed into the passenger side.

As Itala dropped the clutch in and started the motor, Kate studied her profile.

Very, very serious. Quiet. A woman of few words and fewer defining mannerisms. Almost a cypher.

Itala was not a classically beautiful woman. Her dark eyebrows were a little too heavy. She wore no makeup at all, at least today. Her lips were thin and pale. She did not move like Kate expected, but more like a professional gymnast.

Not very girlie. But who am I to judge?

Kate smiled to herself.

"So where are we going?" she asked Itala as the engine settled down.

Itala grinned at her briefly as she slipped the car into reverse.

"Bressanone," she said simply. "Thibault and the crew are staging there."

Staging?

Yes, she had blundered into their china shop. Hopefully, she wouldn't break anything while she was here.

Bressanone was just as beautiful as Kate remembered, from her lunch here with Miranda sixteen months ago. It had taken Itala a little more than three hours of climbing valleys to get to this picturesque little village, just a half hour south of the Austrian border. The town was a tiny place, almost a tourist trap, but it was close enough to the border that someone could drive here from Germany for lunch, as they had.

Itala dropped off the highway and circled around the tourist walking areas in the old town, heading uphill east of town to a small chalet with a fabulous view overlooking the valley and the town.

A remote control opened an electric gate, closing it as they passed through and entered into a circular drive with a large, gray panel truck parked in front. Kate could see the Germanic influences in the architecture. The house was three stories, bright canary yellow in the places that were not polished wooden beams, and looked like a miniature version of a Swiss skiing lodge she had stayed at once.

Itala parked the Mini and hopped out with a quick "We're here, ma'am," in French.

Kate got out, grabbed her bag from the back, and followed the tiny woman up the walk to the front door. The sidewalk had been shoveled since the last snowstorm, and possibly salted. The air was very crisp, but not the sort of brutal cold it could be.

If they were going to be out for any length of time, she would need to pull out a heavier jacket, and maybe a sweater from her bag. For now, she could suck it up and get inside quickly.

Thibault was standing just inside the door when Itala entered, Kate trailing just behind her.

He looked like a younger version of Étienne, in much better shape. Étienne was not in bad shape. Perhaps average for a man in his early fifties. Thibault showed what Étienne could be, with some serious exercise and a little better diet.

The jewel thief was wiry, like his niece, but very tall, several inches over six feet. There was not an ounce of spare flesh on the man, except perhaps in his face, which was just starting to wrinkle with age. His brown hair was kept short and neat, and was in the first stages of turning gray along the edges.

He was too old for Kate, but she still felt his magnetism.

She was reassured that she found men attractive.

He stepped forward with a hand out and a smile.

"Dr. Catherine," he said quietly in French as he took her hand. "We have not met, but I have looked you up. And Étienne has very proudly told me about you and Miranda over the years. My condolences on your loss."

Kate shook his hand as an icy jolt of adrenaline poked her in the stomach. Grief was a complicated bitch. She hoped she never got used to it.

"How should I address you?" Kate replied. "You were always Nephew Thibault, or *The Black Sheep*, when Uncle Étienne talked about you."

The man screwed his face up into a sideways smile. He had a firm handshake, steady and rather dry.

"If you call him Uncle Étienne," the man said finally, "then that would make us cousins, of a sort. Call me Thibault. You have met my niece, Itala. I sent everyone else down into town for dinner so we can talk."

Yes, definitely interrupting their plans. Apparently someone, somewhere, would be losing some expensive trinkets soon.

Hopefully, she didn't ruin everything just by being here.

Thibault released her hand and turned a serious look on Itala.

"Coffee's fresh," he said to his niece. "Any problems?"

"None, uncle," Itala replied.

"*Bon.*"

Kate followed the two deeper into the house, to a kitchen at the back.

The house had the feel of a rental that one would take for a week, or a month, while using it as a base camp for skiing holidays.

Or preparing for a heist, as one might do when one was a jewel thief.

The kitchen was blandly industrial, with none of the personal touches that one accumulated in their own home. There was a cheap coffee maker with a fresh pot of ink-black heat waiting. Bags of chips, cookies, and dried jerky lay strewn across the counter, some open, most closed. A large cooler like one would take to a tail-gating party.

Itala grabbed a mug from the mismatched group on a drying towel by the sink and poured herself the first batch.

"Would you like some, Dr. Catherine?" she asked as she held out the pot.

On the one hand, it had been a long day getting here, and a long drive. On the other hand, too much now and she wouldn't sleep. Not that she needed much, as wound up as she was.

"Please."

Itala grabbed another cup.

"Cream in the ice box," she said as she poured. "Honey bear on the counter behind the chips."

Thibault walked around to the kitchen table and sat. After they finished fixing up their coffees, both girls followed him, ending up seated across from each other.

Thibault's hands twitched the same way Abigail's did when it was time to go outside and smoke, but the man said nothing. Instead, he watched Kate like a hawk.

"So, Dr. Catherine," he said simply. "Let me be blunt. Étienne told me to help you as if you were family. So here you are. Why are you here?"

Kate watched his eyes glance briefly at Itala, but he maintained his focus on her as she sipped.

She didn't need to order her thoughts. She had spent two days doing that, and the whole flight over. And the drive up here.

But how to approach this man? How to convince these people she was worth helping?

She set her mug down and placed her hands on the table top, fixing him with her own stare.

"I need to acquire certain materials," she said, equally bluntly. "Most of them are perfectly legal, but only if you have all the right corporate certifications. I want them for myself."

He stared at her hard, eyes squinted as if he could see her soul through her skin.

"You have a list?" he asked finally.

Inside, Kate relaxed. She nodded and reached for her overnight bag, resting on the floor beside her. From an outside pocket, she pulled an envelope, crinkled slightly from all the travel and being warped by her clothes.

She handed it to him silently and waited.

He pulled out the three pages of printout from the envelope, listing all the chemicals, exotic and mundane, that she had felt she would need for this experiment.

Thibault handed the pages to Itala and waited.

The only sound was steam coming off the coffee as Itala read them in turn.

A nod passed between the two of them.

"Étienne tells me that you work for Devereux," Thibault said heavily. "You cannot simply get them there?"

It was not an easy question. She felt the edge of menace under his words.

Kate let the anger bubble up from where she had been keeping it carefully hidden.

"I took a leave of absence from Devereux on Tuesday," she said with a hard tone. "I had access to everything on that list, right up until that moment."

"And now?" he asked, skillfully fencing with her over the table.

"Jean-Michel Devereux is not allowed to know what I am going to do next, Thibault," Kate said simply, almost harshly. "Ever. I turned to the one person I could absolutely trust for help. Étienne must not know either, but he trusts you. I flew to Milan with no questions asked."

Kate let the moment linger as she looked at each of them in turn.

"I have money. I am happy to pay you for time, expenses, and risk, and then I will be gone from your lives. Simple?"

"What is the purpose of these chemicals?" Itala asked suddenly. "You cannot manufacture narcotics with this crap. And certainly not in these tiny amounts. There is simply not enough."

Kate let the rage loose. It was already too close to the surface to hide. She let the energy bleed out into her eyes, her smile, her hands.

"Most of that is for me," she rasped, hearing an entirely different voice come out of her mouth from the dutiful daughter she normally was. The edge of menace had transformed into an angry raptor, screaming with rage in her soul as she considered Miranda and the man known as Golden Tiger.

"You?" Itala asked, leaning back slightly.

"Me," Kate agreed, grinding her teeth. "I'm going to find the man who killed Miranda Devereux, and I'm going to kill him."

"Miranda was a villain," Thibault said quietly, almost diffidently. "She was killed by an American super-hero, a man named Golden Tiger."

"Yes, Thibault," Kate replied. "If I was hunting a rabbit, I would only need a small weapon, something simple. For this, I need something much bigger. He will not die easily."

"All this for revenge, then?" the man asked with an edge of sarcasm.

"Miranda was my sister, Thibault. Surely you understand the value of family?"

He jerked back just as if she had physically slapped him. For a moment, his own anger came to the surface, and then transformed into a wry smile.

He pursed his lips and reconsidered her.

"Most of my family have disowned me, Dr. Catherine," he rumbled. He nodded at Itala. "A few have chosen to remain in the family business, but most have become boring and safe. They have turned their backs on us. And they have certainly forgotten their lust for life."

Something passed between the two thieves as she watched. Kate wasn't sure, but she could see the messages flowing back and forth as Thibault and Itala looked at each other.

"We will do what we can to help, Dr. Catherine," Thibault said finally. "How soon will you need all of this?"

Kate felt her heart finally start to slow down.

"Stalking a tiger is a slow and dangerous business," Kate said quietly. "I plan to complete each step with great care before moving on. Even with those chemicals and materials, and a lab to work with, I will be several months preparing."

"*Bon*," he replied.

Kate watched the man's entire body language shift as he turned to his niece. All the subtle tension was gone, replaced by a professional, an expert at the top of his game, a general calmly marshalling troops for battle.

"I have made a reservation for her in town," he said to Itala, pulling a piece of paper from a pocket and handing it to the woman. "Get her settled and join her for dinner. The rest of the schedule is still as expected."

Itala nodded and slid her chair back silently to move around the table.

"Dr. Catherine?" she said, smiling impishly down from her little height.

Kate stood to join her.

"We will be departing no later than Monday morning," Thibault continued, standing as well and holding out a hand to Kate. "There will be a week with no news, hopefully, and then you will hear from Itala. How long are you here?"

"I bought a one-way ticket to Milan," Kate said. "I could return home in a few days, or remain in Europe for a while. Perhaps I will spend the weekend in Venice and return to America after that."

Kate saw a spike of jealousy in Itala's otherwise-guarded eyes, gone after a single, fleeting glimpse. What must it be like to be a criminal living in the shadows, always preparing for the next job, never able to just *go to Venice for the weekend*? Perhaps she could find out more about this woman over dinner.

"Very good, Dr. Catherine," Thibault said, nodding to Itala and sending them on their way.

Kate had a moment to realize just how much her wealth insulated her from such things. This quest was already educating her in ways she had never imagined.

And all this, just to kill a man.

BRESSANONE

Kate found herself seated across from Itala in a tiny bistro in town, a few blocks down from her equally tiny inn, eating a specialty of the Franco-Swiss chef who should have had his own Michelin star from the quality of the chicken alone, to say nothing of the mousse she had eaten for dessert. The entire establishment was barely six tables and a bar with three stools.

Thibault had apparently made them reservations, or they never would gotten a table. Even then, he must have called in a favor. The place was wall to wall with people. Cozy, but not crowded. And the food was simply amazing.

Kate held up a glass of white wine and gestured with it as she spoke. The conversation had been wide and exotic as the two women probed each other, Itala asking about Kate's background in ways that indicated deep poverty, Kate finding out more about the various black sheep of the family.

"Why Mandarin?" Kate asked finally.

Itala smiled ruefully and sipped her own glass of chewy red.

"A French tourist in Shanghai is looked down upon by the locals," she said. "Largely invisible except as a source of Euros. It is the same in Beijing."

Itala shrugged as she edited what she was going to say next.

"We occasionally get hired to do jobs in Asia," she continued. "And I am generally the wheelman right now."

"Wheelman?" Kate was lost by the term.

"A driver who specializes in, uhm, fast and possibly dangerous maneuvers on crowded streets," the French woman continued with a grin. "Getaways. Boston does not bother me."

Kate felt her eyebrows go up. Just from her experience riding in a vehicle on the East Coast, those people were insane.

"I see," Kate said diplomatically.

"Thibault is still the aerialist," Itala continued carefully. "In a few more years, he will probably finally retire to planning and let me handle those things."

The woman shrugged Gallically. "We shall see."

Kate felt the energy bleed out of her suddenly. She had been in motion for a whole day at this point, flying halfway around the country, then driving, and finally dinner.

"I need some air," Kate said quietly. "And then bed, I think."

Itala nodded. They both finished off their wine and stood. Kate paid for both of them and kissed the chef on both cheeks before leaving.

Outside, the weather was cool and headed for cold quickly. Kate had pulled on a sweater, and that plus her rain shell kept her warm enough. Itala walked beside her in companionable silence as the two women moved. There were few people out tonight.

As Kate and Itala walked down an alley, two shadows detached themselves from a wall ahead of them.

Men. Big men.

Kate glanced back and saw two more enter the alley behind them.

She was tired from the trip. She was relaxed from the wine. She was already skating lightly atop all the anger she had been holding in all week.

"Give us your money," one of the shadows ordered her gruffly in Italian. "Nobody has to get hurt."

Kate saw red.

"Fuck you," she snarled distinctly in English. She did not expect them to understand her words, but there was no misunderstanding her tone. She continued to walk forward, aiming to pass around the one on her side of the alley.

He grabbed her shoulder with one hand as she got close, trying to stop her.

Enough.

After enough years, Tai Chi Chuan becomes automatic.

Kate pivoted, moving her hands up to grab the man by the wrist and elbow of the arm holding her.

Because she could, she opened her senses as she did so and found a thread of power flowing above her. She snagged it, sucked it into her lungs, and twisted on her hips.

The first mugger's face made a satisfying crunch as he slammed hard into the alley wall. He started to slide down bonelessly.

The other one grabbed her from behind in a bear hug, trying to lift her off the ground.

Kate relaxed and let the growl emerge from the depths of her soul.

One elbow hammered backwards, and then the other.

Ribs crunched under the impact. The man lost his hold.

Becoming The White Crane in her mind had awakened the training and the reflexes of her youth. Kate spun inside the loose grip of the man's slackening arms and drove the back of her wrist into the side of his head, fingers pinched together in the southern Kung Fu form known as Crane.

She was The White Crane in her head now.

The sound was the crack of the bat on a line shot up the middle for a single.

The man's eyes rolled backwards as he went down.

Kate turned to find the other two men before they got too close.

Itala had already stepped away from her, towards the two muggers, coming to rescue their friends from being thrashed in an alley by two, tiny, tourist girls.

As Kate watched, Itala ran three steps, as though trying to get by the one on her left. At least, that was what the man probably thought as he pivoted to grab her.

Kate watched as Itala leapt a few feet in the air, planted her right foot on the wall, and twisted her whole body to the right as she got into the air. Because Kate had managed to empower herself, even for a few seconds, she saw the entire thing, as if in slow motion. Or perhaps she saw it at speed, and could slow it down in her memory, like an instant replay.

Itala turned in the air like a cat, bouncing off the wall and kicking across her body with her left foot. Her boot connected with the third man's head as she went by.

She continued in the air like a gymnast coming off a vault, grabbing hold of the fourth man as she flew over him and using his weight to anchor her. Itala collapsed as she landed, dragging the man over her and letting inertia and surprise slam his shoulder and skull into the wall.

Kate gasped and let the power flow out of her body.

Time returned to normal.

She started to say something as the smaller woman stood up, but Itala grabbed her hand and dragged her quickly out of the alley.

Once in the light, Itala continued to jog, pulling Kate along towards her inn.

At the hotel door, Itala silently gestured for her to quickly enter, then followed. She did not seem inclined to talk until they got upstairs and into Kate's room.

Finally, Kate sat on the edge of the bed and watched Itala questioningly.

"If someone heard or saw anything," Itala said. "They would have called the authorities. Best if neither of us was there, since we do not want to have to file a police report, or be involved in a police investigation tomorrow."

"I see," Kate said.

It made sense. Police would ask unanswerable questions, and start pulling on threads to see where they led. That could not be allowed.

"Tomorrow morning," Itala continued. "Eat a good breakfast early, and then walk to the train station. You might have to wait a while, but it is Saturday, and the tourists will be everywhere, so you will be safe. Then you catch a train to Venice and relax. In a week, when all is quiet here, Thibault or I will call you and we will go from there."

Kate reached out and grabbed the other woman's hand as she started to move away, tugging Itala to sit close on the bed as Kate began to jitter from the adrenaline.

"What was that you did?" Kate asked. "When you jumped off the wall, kicked him, and then tackled the other with a judo toss?"

Itala grinned proudly as she sat.

"I was a gymnast in school," she began, gripping Kate's hand excitedly. "I also study Savate, and Parkour. That was what happens when you combine the three."

Kate made a note to look those terms up later. They meant nothing now, but obviously were useful, powerful even, if they could show a woman how to fly, and how to beat up bigger men.

"Could you teach me?" Kate asked sideways.

Itala stared at her closely.

"It would take years," the Frenchwoman said. "Even for someone who has studied martial arts, like yourself."

Kate nodded to herself. It probably would. But it would be necessary.

"What do you do between, uhm, jobs?" Kate inquired diplomatically.

"I study," Itala said. "I train, I—"

She looked closely at Kate.

"Why?"

Kate looked deep into her own soul and leapt off a cliff.

"I need to learn to fight better," Kate said. "And other things. And I can afford to hire you, when you are between jobs."

Kate fell silent.

Itala did as well.

The tiny Frenchwoman stood abruptly, turning to look as much down on Kate as she could.

"I will consider it," she said, before turning, grabbing the door open, and disappearing.

Kate let go of her breath.

She wondered if she had just hired her first henchman.

ITALA

Venice had been wonderful, even as late as the season was. The rain and cool weather had spoken to Kate's soul as she walked among all the end-of-season tourists.

She would miss the parts of the old city that were still sinking and might disappear in her lifetime, but change was the nature of things, and Kate had spent her week thinking about change.

About transformation.

About *becoming*. Not just an adult, but a particular kind of adult. The kind that would willingly give up her quiet, happy life in order to hunt down a total stranger and commit lethal violence against him.

In some ways, it felt like planning to murder a police officer, or a government official, but in the end, Golden Tiger was just a private vigilante, meting out his own brand of violent justice. Granted, largely with the support of the authorities and the people of Angel City, but still a vigilante.

And he had killed Miranda.

Every time she stopped and thought about whether this was a smart idea, whether she could just let it go, it always came back to that fundamental point.

This wasn't about justice. Miranda had been a criminal engaged in a criminal act. A policeman might have shot her. Might have used lethal force. Might have been completely within his duties to do so.

Golden Tiger was a private citizen. And he had killed her sister.

For that, Kate was going to kill him.

She was back in Emerald now. It was late fall. The rain was a relentless drizzle that did just enough damage to force drivers to turn on their wipers, and to expose the California drivers for the amateurs they were on the freeways.

Ten days had passed since she had seen Thibault and Itala.

Kate wondered if they had succeeded in their task. Had some businessman been relieved of something valuable? Gems? Art? An exotic car?

Kate wondered what a jewel thief would be after. At least there had been no news of a crew of brazen thieves having been arrested, nor news of a major heist stumping the police. She had been carefully wandering through a number of news boards and web sites for just such a thing.

Silence was, hopefully, good news.

Mr. Loh had finally decided to forgive her. While he liked the professional cat sitter that occasionally came to feed and entertain him, five days with no Kate had caused his pique to climb off the charts.

He was curled up against her left thigh right now as they sat on the sofa. Kate had her laptop open, reading the latest issues of several research magazines as she tried to decide what to do next.

The phone ringing caused Kate to flinch and nearly drop her laptop. Mr. Loh jumped down and scampered into the bedroom with an angry chirp.

+33- international telephone number. *France.* Another number currently un-programmed into her contacts list.

Hopefully, good news.

"*Bonjour,*" she said neutrally as she answered.

"Dr. Catherine?" Itala asked in French.

"Yes," Kate replied, letting go of a breath she had not realized she was holding.

"I have your delivery ready," Itala said matter-of-factly. "The total came to thirteen thousand, two hundred and forty-three dollars US and ninety-seven cents. I will be arriving to Emerald late tomorrow."

"Do you get to fly first class for that total?" Kate asked politely.

Either they had stolen large chunks of the chemicals she had requested, or ended up paying not much more than Devereux Pharmaceuticals would have paid their supplier wholesale. She had been expecting Thibault to quote her closer to twenty thousand when they called, at least as an opening bid, from which everyone would negotiate.

Perhaps she was getting the friends-and-family rate.

"No, ma'am," the petite French courier replied professionally. "Strictly coach."

Kate could hear the smile in the other woman's voice.

"Well, upgrade yourself and add it to the bill, then," Kate said. "Shall I meet you at the airport, or somewhere else?"

"I've never been to Emerald before."

"Then we will have to do the tourist thing," Kate said.

"Very good," Itala replied. "I will text you the flight information and let you organize things."

"It will be fun," Kate said.

They both hung up. Kate programmed the number for tomorrow and considered how to best play tourist in Emerald.

Kate owned a sporty little hatchback, but rarely drove it, Emerald having a blessing of good mass transit downtown and a horrid dearth of parking places everywhere. It was usually easier to take a bus or black car service anywhere she wanted to go in the city. Plus, she could run down to the airport on the light rail.

That would be a good introduction. Ride the train to downtown. Watch the men throw fish back and forth at the market. Get reservations at a nice restaurant.

It would be important if she was going to convince Itala to turn her into a combat machine. Or a super-villain.

And maybe, just maybe, she needed her own sidekick, one of these days.

Nothing about Itala suggested the capacity for super-powers, but she was certainly extremely well-trained, and very well connected if they had already managed to get Kate all the chemicals she needed. And not every hero and villain out there could throw fireballs or fly. That didn't stop them from putting on the spandex.

Kate considered her plan. She hadn't even seriously started looking for a space as a lab for herself in which to work.

One step at a time had been her mantra.

Still, Kate felt a tide beginning to run behind her. Or an avalanche. It would be interesting to see which.

She was truly living in interesting times.

THE DEAL

Just because, Kate had dressed in black today.

Not a formal suit like a driver waiting for a passenger, but she had dug out her black boots, the ones with the little gold crane charm still on the chain. Black jeans tight enough to pass for leggings if you didn't look too close. Her softest sweater, darkest charcoal gray and made from the best New Zealand Merino, over a black mock-turtleneck shirt. Today, the longer rain jacket, just to keep her thighs dry when they were out walking in the mist.

With her black hair pulled back into a simple pony tail, Kate had all the hallmarks of a modern goth, except for a fundamental lack of visible piercings, tattoos, or makeup as she checked herself one last time in a bathroom mirror at the airport.

Tough shit. This is me. Deal with it.

She surprised herself with the thought. And the language. But it was her. The *new* her. This strange new being who had taken up residence in her soul, beside the dutiful daughter and the mad scientist.

If Father, Wei De, not Jean-Michel, had asked, she would have told him a story about a little girl who went off to Europe and never came back. Perhaps one of the northern European fairies or trolls had stolen her and replaced her with a look-alike.

Stranger things had happened.

Kate checked her phone. Itala's flight should have just landed. She would still need to wait while the plane taxied to the gate, fight all the idiot tourists who didn't know how to exit a plane, as well as all the idiot businessmen who didn't know how to do it politely, and then finally deboard. Then Customs, and the long walk up the concourse to get to the security gates, and Itala would be free again.

Kate looked around, feeling a touch of paranoia. Technically, owning these chemicals was not illegal, even if importing them this way probably was. It was possible that Thibault and Itala had set her up, but it wasn't like they were transporting narcotics.

Still, she didn't see anybody that looked like a narc waiting to pounce on her.

Of course, having sixteen thousand dollars in cash, in two thick bundles, wrapped against her stomach underneath all the layers, didn't help.

Wei De had taught her well. Kate kept a hollow book on her shelf, a trashy biography hardcover, where she had taken a razor blade and cut out the interior. A little glue and she had a camouflaged box she had filled with her emergency fund.

A bundle of US one-hundred-dollar bills was strapped in one hundred counts, so each bundle was ten thousand dollars. And her book held four. Or had. There was a little less than two and a half bundles now, but this qualified as an emergency.

Old Kate would have never done something like this, even the dutiful daughter. What kind of person was she turning into?

Trick question. She was becoming a super-villain.

While she suspected that many of them were sociopaths and psychopaths in real life, she needed to keep a clear head about this. Minimize the mistakes. Keep the greed in line. Never under-estimate. Or over-estimate. Always have a plan, and an escape.

Think like Thibault.

She didn't know the area around the airport all that well, but if she were in trouble here, she was trapped and doomed anyway.

She let that lesson sink in as she exited the bathroom and made her way to security.

Destiny or disaster awaited.

Kate almost missed Itala when the petite Frenchwoman came into view. Only her size gave her away.

Itala had dyed her hair a gorgeous, lustrous red-gold. Kate felt pangs of jealousy that her own black hair would never do that, without her first doing significant chemical damage. So absolutely not worth it, even for something that fabulous.

Secondly, Itala was wearing what was obviously a uniform of some sort. Khakis that were fashionable, but loose enough to let her move. A royal-blue golf shirt with some logo on her left breast. A matching jacket in royal-blue, with white lettering that Kate couldn't read from here. A cute, short-brimmed cap, almost a kepi or a pinwheel, made entirely of a cloth patterned with blue and gray static.

Instead of the backpack or purse that Kate was expecting, Itala had a professional-looking messenger bag slung over her shoulder. She walked through the security hallway with a deliberate set to her shoulders, a woman on her way *Somewhere Important.*

Kate smiled at the woman as Itala's face lost the serious reserve and split in two with a grin.

"Dr. Catherine?" Itala inquired formally, as if performing for an audience.

For a moment, Kate felt a spear of panic that she had been set up after all and was about to be arrested.

Destiny or disaster.

"Please," she replied with a lopsided smile. "Call me Kate. Or Kai Di, depending on the company. Occasionally, Dr. Peng. I can be many people."

"I understand," Itala replied as she swept back her beautiful hair. "My uncle frequently calls me the Doppelgänger because I'm constantly changing my look."

"Do you have luggage?" Kate asked.

On a whim, she reached out and hooked her arm inside Itala's left elbow and began to draw her towards the escalators to the baggage area.

Best mates on an adventure.

The Frenchwoman flinched briefly, and then relaxed and began to walk.

"I have an anvil case," Itala said. "It is insulated, and will need to be dealt with in the next twelve hours."

"You brought it on the plane?" Kate was astonished.

Itala reached up with her free hand and brushed her breast, the logo on her breast, to get Kate's attention.

"We are a licensed, bonded, international, courier service, Dr. Peng," she said with mock seriousness. "How else do you expect we would get our goods to our buyers?"

"You know," Kate thought out loud. "I've never really considered the technical parts of how you do what you do. I mean, afterwards."

She blushed, still staring at the logo, and Itala's breast. There was so much she just took for granted in this world, insulated by her family's money.

People had to make things work. That sometimes meant flying halfway across the world to deliver a simple package that could not be shipped any other way.

Downstairs, Itala turned Kate away from baggage claim and led her to a small office tucked back against the inner wall. The Frenchwoman seemed to know exactly where she was going, and why, so Kate let herself follow, even though Itala had said she had never been to Emerald before.

She watched Itala pull a sheaf of papers from her messenger bag and present them to the man at the counter with a friendly, "Good afternoon."

The man took a moment to scan the documents, and then smiled warmly at both women, obviously checking them out.

"Just a moment," he said, disappearing through an interior door.

Kate was content to wait, arm in arm with the woman she was beginning to think of as her co-conspirator. Now, if they could just avoid arrest. Étienne wasn't around to smooth out any misunderstandings or provide helpful bribes to petty officials.

The man returned a few moments later with a black metal box.

It looked similar to the case Miranda had kept Kate's flying suit in. Two-and-a-half feet wide, perhaps eighteen inches tall, and probably twelve inches deep. It latched securely in four places, with two separate locks attached.

Every surface was covered with bio-hazards stickers and warnings, partly out of regulation, partly probably to keep snoopers at bay.

Kate watched Itala sign for the case and lift it easily in one hand.

The man also delivered a smaller case, one with a single lock and no stickers that Itala signed for as well.

And then they were off.

No Federal Agents swooped down on them as they made their way across the concourse. No muggers jumped out of a darkened alley.

Kate leaned close enough to whisper in Itala's ear.

"I have cash to pay you," she said. "But I don't think we should flash that amount of money here. Is it safe to take that on the light-rail, or should we get a car instead?"

Itala weighed the options as they walked.

"I think others might be more comfortable not riding with us," she said judiciously, holding the biohazard stickers up as a shield against other pedestrians. "Let's get to someplace private to handle everything."

"Fair enough," Kate said, changing direction and leading Itala towards the area where black cars, the luxury private service SUV's, waited for passengers. Taxis were perfectly safe in Emerald, but she just felt better in the back of a private luxury car. And she could afford to indulge herself in little ways, as long as she was always careful about the big things.

鶴

Kate had largely emptied her refrigerator and freezer, just in case. The next step would be a private lab space in which to work, assuming she didn't just do it here in her kitchen like a home-brewer. But that was for tomorrow.

Risk and reward.

She had never really been sure she would get this far.

The normally-fussy Mr. Loh had not only allowed himself to be petted by Itala, but had actually crawled up in her lap and purred while she did so. For at least forty-five seconds, which was forty longer than Kate had expected.

Then he ran away madly into the bedroom, like a performance artist hard at work.

Kate took off her sweater and lifted her shirt to undo the straps holding the money belt to her belly-button. She placed the belt on the kitchen table and unzipped it.

"What was the total damage?" she asked innocently, holding a bundle and a half of hundred-dollar-bills in her hands.

She watched Itala's eyes light up with raw greed for the merest moment, before the Frenchwoman got serious.

Itala grabbed the messenger bag from where she had leaned it against her foot when she sat down, and flipped it open. She expertly withdrew a bundle of papers and presented them.

"Fourteen thousand, fifty-seven dollars, and eighty-one cents."

Kate smiled and pulled nineteen bills off the smaller pile, leaving them on the table and walking over to hand the rest to Itala, trading her for the invoice.

"Here you go," Kate said with an impish smile. "I don't need change."

Itala made a small performance of counting one hundred and forty-one bills into her lap before slipping them into a plastic freezer bag she pulled from her messenger bag and putting them away.

"Ready to tourist?" Kate asked.

Itala gave Kate a very serious look.

"I'm expected home in eight days," Itala said with careful gravity. "So we can't get too crazy."

Then Itala's face broke into a huge grin.

"What did you have in mind?"

鶴

Kate had already made the reservations at her favorite little bistro in Ballard. It was a quiet, wood-paneled joint, amazing French food produced by a tiny, middle-aged Vietnamese man and his elegant, Mauritanian wife who towered over him by nearly a foot.

The back corner had been reserved, and Kate and Itala had poured themselves into it and happily accepted wine.

Kate knew she was in good shape, and Itala was as well, but they had probably walked ten miles since they had left her apartment. They had done all of the Market, walked the entire length of the waterfront, joined the small crowds of tourists doing the Square and the underground tour, trudged up to the top of Capital Hill, and then finally come back down through the Mercer Mess.

At that point, Kate had cried uncle and gotten them a cab. She was exhausted.

Exhilarated, but wiped out.

She attacked the glass of red wine with almost as much gusto as Itala did.

They had a moment of silence as the lovely woman who co-owned the place, Tafalkayt, came over and took their order, her rich West African accent filling the otherwise quiet room like a song.

And then they were alone again.

Kate watched Itala's face grow very serious.

"I've been wanting to ask you for a week," Itala leaned forward and said with a voice barely above a whisper.

"Yes?" Kate leaned forward as well, drawing the room smaller and smaller.

"The package," Itala continued. "I know what you want with it, I think. And you told us why."

"But?" Kate prompted after a moment of silence.

"How?" Itala replied. "I looked up this person, the man, the hero in question. He certainly enjoys giving interviews. He even has his own comic book."

"He does?" Kate was surprised. But then, popular musicians had television shows and trading cards. It made a certain amount of sense.

Kate needed to add more research to her plans. She wondered how much of what was printed was truth, and how much a fable designed to obscure sordid or boring truths.

Miranda had always warned her that the more mysterious a man tried to act when hitting on her, the more mundane he generally turned out to be, especially in bed. Not that Kate had ever experienced a man in bed, against which to compare, but Miranda had seemed to be an expert there, so Kate was willing to trust her judgment.

"He does," Itala continued. "I brought several issues to read on the plane, mostly out of curiosity. My own, mind you. Thibault has very little of his own."

"Interesting," Kate observed.

"He appears to be much taller than you," Itala whispered. "Stronger, probably faster. He is an expert in several Asian martial arts, and…"

Itala stopped talking. Kate could see the fainted hint of blush, or excitement, or something creep up her cheeks.

"Go on," Kate prodded her.

Itala leaned forward even further, putting her forearms flat on the table top so that the two women were huddled, almost like lovers whispering in each other's ears.

"He is one of the special ones," Itala breathed. "One of the Modern Gods. Golden Tiger can throw *ki-bolts*. That's apparently what killed Miranda, once you boil away all the hype and noise. How will you fight him?"

Kate realized she was close enough to kiss Itala right now, both heads hunched down and turned together. The mad temptation flittered across her mind briefly, but this was a very serious moment.

She leaned back slightly. Not much. Enough to break the spark of magnetic energy flowing between them.

Kate, Kai Di Peng, daughter of Wei De Peng, considered her response, how her father would handle this.

"There are secrets I could tell you, Itala," she whispered firmly, hearing Wei De's tones come out of her mouth. "But in doing so, I would bind you to myself, to my clan, for the rest of your life. Are you prepared to cross the River Styx?"

Itala leaned back as well. Again, not much. Enough to change the emotional signature of the table. Her eyes grew a little larger, and then squinted a shade.

There were lines one could read between, but nothing firm. Nothing real. Nothing *true*.

Kate held her breath while the other woman considered her next words carefully.

"Bind," the petite Frenchwoman repeated in a serious murmur as she considered Kate's words.

Kate felt herself subject to intense scrutiny from across the table.

She sat perfectly still and waited. Wei De had always told her that she could not want something for someone else more than they wanted it themselves.

She wanted Itala's help, and her friendship. But she could only wait for the other woman to decide. As she had said, they might have arrived at the River Styx itself.

Kate had already willingly crossed, paying Charon his coin, seeking Miranda.

Itala might join, and she might not.

Vengeance on this scale was a mad thing, not undertaken lightly.

The silence hung between them like fog on a cold morning. Kate immersed herself in the lovely smell of Bảo's spicy cooking.

Before Itala could answer, Tafalkayt returned with bread, warm and steaming, fresh from the oven.

The woman's arrival pricked the balloon of tension that had been hovering above the table, letting all the air suddenly rush out.

Kate felt deflated. Itala looked it.

By silent assent, they attacked the bread and let the other things go.

For now.

Kate could see a reckoning with the other woman, questions yet to be asked, stories to be played out.

She contented herself with the dinner while she waited.

THE FIFTH POINT

Kate stared at the morning financial news on the nearly-muted television as she finished stretching. Mr. Loh watched from his supreme position atop his carpeted palace.

She was unsettled this morning.

Dinner last night had been greater than any of the superlatives her vocabulary encompassed. She wondered if Tafalkayt and Bảo had outdone themselves, thinking that one of their favorite customers had brought in a date for the first time.

Kate blushed furiously at the thought.

Rather than return to the previous conversation, she and Itala had kept things light and vague for the rest of the meal. Afterwards, Itala had gotten a cab and gone to her hotel, complaining of abject exhaustion.

Kate had to agree. She had been in bed by nine o'clock and slept like the dead until the little alarm clock in her head had gone off at four, like it did every morning.

This morning she was awake, but troubled. She felt as though she was on the cusp of change, like a butterfly preparing to emerge.

Would Itala walk away? Go back to France, or Italy, or wherever, and be done?

Or would her curiosity bring her back to finally ask that question that would seal her fate?

Kate realized that her sleeping mind had forked her grand plans around that woman's decision. In her imagination, she could see two stacks of 3-ring binders, the big, red ones they still occasionally used for physical checklists and references, since nobody wanted to risk chemical spills all over their pretty phones and computers.

Kate finished stretching and poked her head into the bathroom to check herself in the mirror.

Bright green running tights with reflective patterns. A skin-tight black top designed to wick away sweat and keep her warm. No makeup except health. Long, lean, wiry. Skinny.

She smiled at her image then grabbed her running shoes from just inside the front door.

"Be good, Mr. Loh," she said as she put the shoes on and added a rain-proof royal-blue pullover. She tied her hair back and added the knit cap, taking a moment to stuff her phone, wallet, and keys into appropriate pockets before she left.

Downstairs, Kate contemplated the rain. Emerald sat in the rain shadow of the Olympics most of the time, unless a big, cold storm was coming down from Canada, or a Pineapple Express was bringing a warm monsoon up from Hawaii.

Today was a mist almost heavy enough to chew on as she set out. Just bad enough that windshield wipers would be on the second-highest intermittent settings.

Drizzle.

She aimed east, to run down off the hill. The Fifth Point was becoming more and more of a habitual destination, a mid-point turn-around, for her morning runs. It was open this early, and served a heavy breakfast that gave her the energy to get through her day.

Kate smiled as she jogged, considering that her caloric intake had gone up twenty-five percent in the last three weeks, and she had lost eight pounds. She might even be able to get into her skinniest jeans pretty soon at this rate.

Somewhere near the bottom of the hill, as she began to enter City Center, her phone rang. She looked around and found a well-lit, sheltered spot to stop and answer it. The neighborhood was safe, but it was still five in the morning on a weekday.

She checked the caller ID.

Itala.

Kate couldn't help the smile on her face as she answered.

"*Bonjour,*" she said merrily.

"I didn't wake you, did I?" Itala asked carefully.

"No," Kate replied. "Out for a run this morning. Then breakfast."

"At that all-night diner/bar?" Itala inquired.

Kate blinked, then flashed back to last night's conversation. They had stayed on safe topics. Her usual morning routine was among them.

"That's right," Kate stated. "I'm surprised you're awake."

"It's mid-afternoon in Paris," Itala laughed. "This is frequently when I do get up, having been out dancing all night."

"I see."

Kate wasn't sure what to say. There were simply no words demanding to be spoken. She could wait and listen. It felt kind of odd, but she was getting used to being someone else from who she had been a month ago.

"Would you be adverse to company this morning?" Itala asked, still careful, deliberate, in her tone.

Kate smiled at that. Perhaps Itala had stuck her toes into the River Styx and not gotten them gnawed on by piranha.

"I would love some company this morning," Kate replied. "Fair warning, though, they do coffee by the slice here."

"Truck stop brew. The best kind," Itala said. "Be there in fifteen minutes."

If Itala walked fast, she was fifteen minutes away from the restaurant.

So. Already awake and dressed.

Kate let herself hope as she stuffed her phone in a pocket and went back out into the drizzle.

鶴

Kate was beginning to think of it as shift change, at least for the customers.

At this time of morning, the crew was getting used to seeing her. A few late-night birds were still fighting to keep going. Morning glories were just starting to emerge. The serious silliness would ramp up in another hour or so.

The bartender nodded at her and started a fresh pot of coffee as she made her way to an empty table.

Kate took a spot close to where a payphone had been removed, years ago, before she had ever eaten here, replaced by a simple glass mirror. The hardware had been gone the first time she had walked through the door, but at the time it had left a hole in the wall with wires sticking out and the outline of the device where it had been painted around.

It had required asking to figure out what used to be there. The waitress that day, who was old enough to be Kate's mother, had grumbled loudly about generation gaps after explaining what a payphone was and what it had been doing there.

Kate missed it. It was another sign that the Boylston neighborhood was gentrifying, as the world's largest online retailer expanded and brought in employees with money and education who wanted to live downtown and walk to work. But it was a much, much safer neighborhood than it used to be.

Kate's rhythm was fairly well known here. Someone dropped off a glass of water as she flipped through the menu already there, while everyone waited for the coffee to brew.

Itala showed up a few minutes later, just as the bartender was dropping off the first mug of coffee. Her arrival threw the man completely off as he staggered back to the bar for more coffee.

"Do you always get up this early?" Itala asked in the relative bubble of quiet that encompassed them. "Running, I mean?"

"Yes," Kate thought out loud. "My brain almost always wakes me up at four. And I probably run four or five days a week. Sometimes, I just don't have the enthusiasm. Especially during monsoon days."

Itala waited in silence as more coffee arrived.

And then they were alone again.

Kate wondered briefly at how it looked from the outside. Her only really close friend had been Miranda. She was friendly with others, but couldn't go drinking with co-workers even if she wanted to. And everyone at the lab was way too old for her to consider dating. And the rest of her life she had been wrapped up in school, dramatically over-achieving by sacrificing any hint of a social life. Just like almost every other student in shouting distance.

And yet, here she was, unemployed, having breakfast with someone she hoped would be a friend, in an all-night diner.

Weird.

"I talked to Thibault this morning," Itala announced suddenly. "Asked him about the schedule for winter and spring."

"And?" Kate asked innocently, watching the other woman close. Itala's face gave nothing away. Kate considered allowing hope to emerge.

"The holidays are always an interesting time," the Frenchwoman responded. "On the one hand, people are frequently away from home at parties and events. On the other, those events are frequently at places we want to be. It tends to cause a lull in our contracting work, until people start to gear up for spring travel."

"I see," Kate said neutrally.

She had never really considered the economic and social aspects of that sort of existence, a life of crime. But she had an expert handy she could ask.

It might be useful to learn to think like a career criminal, if she wanted to pursue crime as a vocation, for however long she did.

The waitress interrupted any further questions. She took their orders, smiled warmly, and left them alone again.

Kate let Itala proceed at her own speed. Again, it felt strange to not have to say anything, interject anything. She could listen, and answer questions.

Where had this level of composure, of self-confidence, come from? What had happened to the mousy little scientist with *something important to say?*

"Thibault suggested that a break might be in order," Itala continued after a time. "Especially after the last contract."

"It went well?" Kate asked innocently.

Itala rolled her eyes and shook her head, but smiled.

"Anything but," she said. "I think Thibault is finally losing his touch, but he would never admit it. Still, everyone got home safe. Eventually."

"Okay."

Kate wasn't sure what to say after that. This was not exactly the sort of joint to discuss a recent jewel heist.

"Are you still serious about combat training?" Itala pivoted the conversation suddenly.

Kate blinked and took the time to draw a deep breath and release it.

"I am," she drawled quietly. "But as I said before, you will have to swear oaths that carry great weight with them."

Itala grinned back at her.

"I'm pretty good at keeping secrets," the petite woman said simply, before her face turned serious. "Is it really that big?"

Kate looked into her steaming black coffee as if there were secrets to be found in the bitter dregs.

These last few weeks had been filled with soul-searching, but always, she came back to the rage that Miranda was gone. That she would never see her best friend again.

That someone had to pay.

Kate fixed the Frenchwoman with a hard stare for several moments. She felt like Medusa, trying to either taste Itala's soul with the snake's tongues, or turn the smaller woman to stone.

Itala neither quailed nor blushed under that gaze. That was good.

"Yes, Itala," she finally said. "Yes it is. You know the why. You know the what, to some extent. But the how will be comprised of secrets that you must carry to your grave, lest it be used for evil."

"What you plan isn't evil?" Itala whispered, gazing back just as hard.

"It is justice for Miranda," Kate quietly snarled at the universe, letting the anger surface, just a little bit, but not letting it aim at Itala. "It is an eye for an eye. He cannot offer me blood money. I will take his soul."

Kate shut her mouth and ground her teeth to keep more words from emerging.

Itala nodded back in sympathy.

They sat in silence as Kate fought to keep the daemons inside from overwhelming her.

She knew where the rage came from. She was most surprised at the indomitable will she had developed that could contain these daemons, bind them with iron and silver, tame them. That was something the dutiful daughter had never expressed.

Plates arrived and cut off all further conversation for a time. Kate spent her silence cataloging the anger, like she did everything, so she could understand it and tap it.

Had learning how to reach out and touch the power in the world transformed her into something different? Something greater? Nothing else made sense.

Maybe she was finally ready to admit she was one of the Modern Gods, and just had never realized it until now. Or maybe she was growing into it.

But now she could embrace this change, put it to use.

She would become The White Crane, with or without Itala's help. She would become vengeance itself.

She ate a huge breakfast as she considered her future. Itala ate maybe half as much food, aghast, watching Kate shovel it in.

Kate eventually paid for both breakfasts and led Itala outside, arm in arm like before, past a memorial statue of one of the city's founders, so they could talk in more privacy. They crossed the street to an open, brick courtyard of an office building where one of the local television network affiliates was housed.

The drizzle had let up finally. Things were gray and wet, but otherwise calm. The sun wasn't coming up for a while yet, but there was enough light that they could talk, plus there were people coming and going from the television station this early.

"I could be talked into moving to Emerald for a time," Itala began. "My visa paperwork is in order, so I could stay for an extended period."

She looked into Kate's face for a clue, and found it. She quoted Kate a monthly rate that would allow her to be here and be available to train full time.

The problem was, Itala had never been to Emerald, and clearly had no idea how expensive this city really was. She might be able to live in one of the worse neighborhoods for that amount, if she was careful and ate a lot of ramen.

"Would you prefer to have an apartment, or to convert a space into a training dojo and have a bedroom attached?" Kate fired back. She consulted both of the three-ring binders in her head for notes she had been making mentally.

Itala got a cagey look.

"What kinds of training will you need, when you do this?" the petite Frenchwoman asked.

"Strength and endurance," Kate responded. "That's probably a set of machines we will need to either acquire, or join a gym to access. I would prefer privacy. I want you to teach me Savate and Parkour. I did some research online. Being able to maneuver in three dimensions will be important. I will also need someone to train me in some of the southern Chinese martial arts, but I think I have a contact there."

"A private gymnasium would be better, then," Itala said after consideration. "We can talk and work without being overheard, and no men will be there trying to seduce one of us."

Kate did the math in her head. Jean-Michel really had been paying her more money than she knew what to do with, for a long time. Now she had a purpose for it.

And Wei De had taught her all the necessary business elements. She would start several small businesses, one a private dojo, one a research lab. Possibly a courier service, since that was how Itala seemed to get around.

"Then I will find us a building and convert it to your specifications," Kate decided.

She quoted an amount she felt would be fair, perhaps more than fair. It would let Itala live nicely in this town, especially if she was not paying rent and utilities.

Itala's eyes got big.

"That's too much," she whispered in shock.

"Itala," Kate said, leaning close and gripping her by the arms. "Listen to me. I have the money to do this, and do it right. So we need to approach it very seriously. I would rather you be settled and secure than worrying."

Itala nodded, mostly to herself, it seemed. She looked down for a bit, obviously gathering her thoughts.

Finally, she looked up. There was a mischievous gleam in her eyes.

"So," she drawled slyly. "You're going to become a super-villain. Would that make me your sidekick?"

"That depends," Kate grinned back at her. "I hadn't planned on you being there, being in a spandex outfit. I was initially planning something more like henchman."

"In a cute costume?"

"Absolutely," Kate began to giggle. "You have to do something like this completely over the top. Else, why do it at all?"

Itala caught the giggles too.

They let the laughter wash over them for a few moments before the Frenchwoman got serious.

"I will keep your secrets, Dr. Catherine," she said simply. "I know how much you want this. I can see how much Miranda meant to you. I will help."

Kate felt overwhelmed by a tide of emotion at the woman's words. She stepped close and hugged her, rather than trust that the right words would come out of her mouth.

It wasn't going to be easy, what she had planned, but it would be easier with Itala's help.

PART II: SUPER-VILLAIN

鶴

THE HIDEOUT

They hadn't come up with a really cool nickname for the place yet.

Kate had never really been into the sorts of popular culture fiction where evil overlords built monstrous semi-secret bases for the heroes to invade and destroy, so she didn't have a lot of experience with those kinds of names.

They had found a perfect spot, however, down the hill from her apartment, in the old industrial district northwest of downtown. Someone had built a brand new set of industrial lofts not far from the early-Twentieth Century fishing warehouses. Each one came with power, water, a bathroom, even a kitchen. It was cozy as an office, but it was absolutely perfect for them to turn into a small training dojo.

Kate unlocked the door and stepped in, careful not to bang her briefcase-sized anvil case on anything. She looked back once over her shoulder to make sure, but there was nobody around this late in the evening.

Itala had ended up getting a small apartment about a mile away after all, just around the curve of Queen Ann Hill, looking down on the canal. That meant Kate didn't have to worry about coming in early and waking her up. Although, frequently Itala had either been there all night training, or had gotten up just as early as Kate, still keeping Paris time.

Winter had passed rather uneventfully. Time spent finding this spot, then equipping it with a climbing wall; as well as hiring a handyman to turn the back half of the space, beyond the bathroom and kitchen, into a small, portable, and complicated Parkour obstacle course to Itala's specifications. The front half, when she turned on the lights, had a set of workout machines picked up second-hand from a local chain of yuppie gyms that had gone out of business.

Who knew that Itala would turn into such a street hustler? Apparently, not even her, until she had started to see the effect of turning on the charm, smiling, and her cute, French accent on the boys in this town.

Then she dealt it in spades, playing up her wiles for all they were worth.

Kate closed the door quietly and locked it. It was late in the evening, so most of the other spaces were dark, but she didn't want anyone knowing what went on here.

None of their business.

She stripped off her jacket and hung it from a coat tree just inside the door. It was cool outside, but she was only a twenty-minute walk from her apartment. Just enough time to get warm.

Tonight was going to be a complicated night.

She had spent all week working up the will to do this.

Four months of research and modeling. There was no way to test this theory on any animal successfully. She would have needed a whole tribe of bonobos just to come close, and that would have taken years she didn't have.

She turned a corner and came up short.

"What are you doing here?" Kate asked.

Itala was seated at the table, smiling up at her, apparently having been surfing the internet on her phone for news or something in the dark.

"Waiting for you," the petite Frenchwoman replied. "You're finally going to do it, but you weren't going to tell anybody."

Kate could think of a hundred things to say, but none of them didn't sound like a child caught with her hand in the cookie jar.

Which was the honest truth.

"How did you know?" she said finally.

"I've been training you at close quarters all winter, Kate," Itala let the exasperation show in her voice. "Strength and endurance six days a week. Mobility four days a week. Hours and hours of notes and spinny computer thingees daily."

Itala put her phone to bed and stood her five-foot frame up to stretch.

"Last week," Itala continued. "You found something. Your whole body language changed. You went from confident to unstoppable."

"You noticed?"

"Kate, you glowed like a woman who had just had the most amazing orgasm ever," Itala retorted with a smile. "I was jealous."

Kate blushed furiously.

Itala might know what that felt like, looked like, but Kate didn't.

Still.

One of these days, she would need to change that, too.

Add it to the list. After Golden Tiger.

Kate caught her breath.

"So what would you have done if I hadn't come tonight?" Kate asked.

"You didn't come last night," Itala leered at her.

"You were here?"

Kate was shocked. Was she really that transparent? That predictable? Perhaps Itala really was that good of a friend.

"I was," Itala nodded. "If you're going to do something stupid, somebody needs to be here, just in case, you know."

"It's not that dangerous," Kate snapped, perhaps harsher than she intended. Perhaps not. She knew what she was doing.

"Has it ever been done before?"

Kate caught herself before she replied. There wasn't even a theory, as far as she was aware of, outside her head. The only people that might research it were national athletics authorities, and what she planned would be impossible to hide from even the most basic blood tests.

That wasn't the point.

She needed to be the physical equal of a man. Worse, equal to a male Modern God who could tap the same power she could, do things that physics couldn't explain without a lot of hand-waving and the famous newspaper cartoon that said "miracle happens here…".

"No," Kate finally replied meekly. "Never. But it is safe."

"So it will either kill you in five minutes," Itala said, "or not until you're eighty?"

Kate considered the math, the model, the formulae.

"Itala," she said quietly, carefully. "If it works, some of us might be able to live centuries."

"Centuries?" Itala gasped. "How?"

"Not everyone…"

Kate stopped short.

If it worked, she might quite possibly live forever, but that was because she was one of *them*. One of the Modern Gods. One of the few who could grasp the power in the right way and turn it into immortality.

Itala was human. Merely human?

Was that a nice thing to say?

Still, incapable of tapping the power. That sucks. She might get decades, but I will get centuries, if I want them.

I wonder if eternity will be lonely.

Kate drew a deep breath and held it. They had danced around the topic for months without ever committing.

She couldn't keep the secret anymore.

"I'm sorry, Itala," she said, continuing the conversation in her head, rather than the one in the room. "This will work because I'm not really human."

"Not human?"

Kate took a deep breath.

"I am one of what the media calls the *Modern Gods*, Itala."

There. She had said it. Out loud. Committed herself to this thing, this difference.

She could see power that was invisible to others, do things that could not be explained.

Shape reality to her own needs.

"Oh, is that all?" Itala said, relieved. "I knew that already."

What? How? She had never shown her abilities around Itala, other than that one time when they both nearly got mugged.

Did the power manifest itself physically when I tapped it? Did my eyes glow or something? Bands of light I shaped with my hands? The cartoons are all hokum.

Kate had never been in a position to see if anything gave it away. Maybe they needed to experiment and have a camera filming the whole thing?

"How?" Kate finally sputtered.

Itala's face lit up with a tremendous smile.

"In four months, Kate," she began. "You've gotten almost as good as I am at both Parkour and Savate, despite the fact that I've been studying, practicing, doing, for fifteen years. And I've gotten better with you pushing me constantly."

Itala began to pace, nervous energy obviously making her jittery.

"On top of that," the woman continued. "You barely sleep more than four hours a night. You devour books and magazines at a speed that I find frightening. And it's high-level chemistry, not the latest bodice-ripper. I know how you invented the skin cream now."

"You do?" Kate was even more shocked. "How?"

"You think three times faster than anyone else I know, Kate. So you got the work done three times as fast."

Oh.

"So now what?" Kate fell back on the first conversation.

"Now?" Itala shrugged. "You'll mix the last batch of magical potion together while I make some coffee, and then we'll do the Dr. Jekyll thing, and hopefully you don't turn into Godzilla."

Dr. Jekyll?

Yes. Possibly. But he hadn't been able to edit out the dangerous parts.

Hopefully, she would still be Kate when it was done.

Only one way to be sure.

DR. JEKYLL

Kate looked at the kitchen counter with a smile.

This, right here, was why they had covered over every single ground floor window, either with a shade or by putting something big in front of it, as well as hanging a translucent awning below the skylights.

Nobody got to see this part.

They had installed a very compact chemistry laboratory at the other end of the countertop, away from the microwave. All the space normally used for plates and utensils was taken up by flasks and beakers and test tubes and assorted paraphernalia. It was like a miniature version of her old lab on the other side of town.

Kate felt a very small stab of guilt as she thought about Devereux Pharmaceuticals. Her leave of absence was going to turn into, at the least, a gap year, a wander year, when they were poised on the brink of so many breakthroughs. Still, they would do fine without her.

And if she failed, Jean-Michel absolutely needed to be without guilt, without culpability. Even his reputation wouldn't survive two daughters turning to crime.

Itala snuck up beside her and sat down a fresh mug of coffee, done just right. It was well after midnight at this point, but neither of them was likely to sleep any time soon. Kate giggled.

"What's so funny?" Itala breathed from close by.

"If we were twelve, this would be a sleepover and we'd be making chocolate chip cookies," Kate replied whimsically.

Anything to break the tension at this point. Everywhere she looked, Kate saw Miranda. Or smelled her perfume. Or heard her laugh.

At times, it was almost unbearable. Right now, it was oddly comforting to think of Miranda watching over them as they did this.

"I could go get us cookies," Itala grinned back at her.

"No," Kate decided. "I want you close. Here. It won't be long now."

Kate checked the thermometer, upright in the beaker in front of her, itself seated patiently on a small electric hotplate. She stuck a glass rod in and stirred the brown-ish fluid.

It looked like nothing so much as a nice oolong tea at this point. Even if the smell was somewhere between wet dog and rotted wood.

Kate pulled the stirring stick out and sniffed it. Not bad. Earthy. She had been afraid she would need to find an additional ingredient to make it palatable, but this didn't smell yucky enough to stop her.

And it should be about done.

Kate stuck out her tongue and touched it to the glass rod briefly. Just enough to get the feel for the essence.

A bit bitter and sharp, which was to be expected considering what she had used to break down some of the long-chain molecules the way she wanted. Titrating it had put it slightly less acidic than orange juice.

Underneath that, a warm taste she could only classify as *brown*. Something like the blackest English morning tea, without the jolt of heavy caffeine she would expect from that taste.

Other things swirled underneath that, like a layer cake of sweet and savory expectations.

"And?" Itala asked, standing close enough to catch her if something happened.

Kate held very still at the thought, then just turned her head.

She held out the stirring rod like a mixer blade covered with freshly-made frosting.

"Here," Kate said.

Itala leaned back away from it.

"Oh, no," the Frenchwoman said. "One of us has to be sober enough to drive us both home tonight when this is all done."

They both smiled at that. Neither drank anything more strenuous than coffee most of the time. Even for her twenty-first birthday, Kate had only had a single glass of wine with her former co-workers, while carefully avoiding all questions about what she had been up to.

And she hadn't been able to take Itala with her. Too many questions. And not the right kind, but people would pry anyway. The two of them had settled for a nice, late dinner with Kate's parents, Wei De and Yi Wen, in a very stuffy restaurant. They had each drank about a glass of wine with dinner as well.

Wei De knew most of the truth about the situation. Yi Wen had contented herself with confirming that her daughter hadn't turned into a lesbian, while making it clear she was accepting of the thought of mild, youthful experimentation.

Kate blushed some more. It had been a little awkward, Mother thinking Itala might be her date, instead of a business partner or criminal henchman.

Still, everyone had survived dinner. For the most part.

Kate smiled and nodded.

Carefully, she picked up a smaller glass beaker and poured off a small amount calculated to be enough to show effects, this time, but not enough to make her go full Henry Hyde if something went wrong.

She couldn't imagine an error in the formula, re-written three times, just to be sure, but anything was possible.

The rest went into an oversized Erlenmeyer flask and got corked. That would go into the refrigerator if everything went well. If not, it got mixed with kitty litter and discarded with the organic composting detritus. That should be safe enough.

"Ready?" Kate asked, a touch breathless as the weight of the moment caught up with her.

"Are you?" Itala replied seriously. "It's not too late to put the glass down and walk away, Dr. Catherine."

Kate fixed her partner with a hard stare, but there was nothing in the woman's face except concern for her.

Could she walk away?

Miranda had been a super-villain. The consensus online was that she had played with fire and gotten burned.

Live by the sword…

No. Miranda needed a better memorial than being a failed criminal who got splattered trying to rob an armored car.

She was family. Golden Tiger had insulted the entire clan, both clans, in killing Miranda. Had he offered something better than "whoops, I tried to save her," that might have helped.

But no, the man had been rewarded by society, lauded for repeatedly using lethal force at the drop of a hat. Lionized for killing a common criminal when the authorities were all wrapped up in the red tape of *Process*.

She remembered her father's saying once that a liberal was just a conservative that had been arrested. Up until that moment, no law was too strict, no punishment too excessive. As long as it was meted out on *someone else*.

There was always a someone else.

What Golden Tiger had done, for that segment of society, had made him a hero.

Kate would have his head. It would look good on a stick somewhere, as a warning not to mess with her family.

Guanxi. Debts between family members. *Civilization*.

Kate took a quick breath and slammed back the warm mixture like she would have a shot of whiskey.

Don't think. Don't drink. Back of the throat and swallow as fast as you can.

It burned all the way down, just like people said the high end spirits did. The taste was nasty. Medicinal. She would have to find a tea she could brew around it to flatten out the complex volatile traces.

The glass made a hollow thunk as she slammed it down.

At least the mix didn't kill her immediately.

Still, she couldn't help but screw up her face in disgust at the taste. Some water about now would be nice, but she had to wait at least fifteen minutes on an empty stomach for her blood to absorb everything correctly.

At least the first time.

Later, after she understood the effects, she could dabble around the margins. Make it something to look forward to in the morning, rather than something to be endured.

Kate let go of the glass and turned to smile at Itala.

"So far, so good," she said.

And then down changed directions and everything went gray. The last thing she felt was her butt hitting the cold tile floor.

MR. HYDE

Kate looked at the ceiling tiles and skylight like they were some sort of bizarre mobile, moving very slowly clockwise in her field of vision. There was a hand on her neck. And then an ear in her nose. It was all a shade confusing.

"What happened?" she said.

From the look on Itala's face, the words weren't apparently all that coherent. But some of the panicked tension bled out as the woman looked down at her.

"Can you hear me?"

Itala seemed to be yelling, from the way her mouth moved and her neck tendons stood out.

Kate realized that her head was ringing in a manner similar to the time she got a concussion when practice sparring and she ducked instead of dodging, right into an elbow. Everything had that same far-away feel to it. And she was flat on her back again.

Kate blinked.

She felt six feet thick. And half a mile tall. And made of either feathers or bricks. It was hard to tell which. Maybe both.

She could smell the faintest trace of perfume from Itala's body wash, normally so faint as to be invisible. Today jarring, but in a pleasant way. Like Kate had stuck her nose into the bottle and sniffed really hard.

The ceiling seemed to be made of clouds. No, strike that, fog seemed to be rolling in.

Wait. I'm indoors. Fog can't do that. And it's not normally that shade of pale green.

Kate felt a band of tightness around her chest, like she was trying to put on a bra that was two sizes too small. She breathed in hard and flexed her side muscles outward.

Something broke.

Probably, it was outside her. She hoped. The elastic holding that imaginary bra let rip.

She could breathe again.

Kate pulled a lungful of air into her chest and held it.

The room made sense. Mostly. The floor was cold. Itala seemed to be on the verge of peeing herself in fear.

"Wow," Kate pushed out.

The words broke whatever spell was gripping her head.

Kate could think again.

The green fog overhead was how she normally saw the power floating in the air. Only she had never seen it that thick before. Or that much of it.

The room hadn't changed. She had.

Crap. How much had she drank?

The effect was something similar to the descriptions she remembered of the man who had accidentally isolated LSD, once upon a time.

Mind-expanding.

"What happened?" Itala said, unconsciously repeating Kate's words.

"It went boom," Kate giggled. She felt a mile tall now, able to see either Rose, to the south, or Sapphire to the northwest. Maybe even Frasier, if the winds were just right.

Kate put her hands flat on the floor and pushed against the frigid tiles.

Itala held her down.

"No, I'm okay," Kate said. Well, slurred.

Gods, she felt drunk.

Was that it? Too much power was like too much alcohol?

Kate let her senses unfocus and reached out a mental hand.

The fog, power writ physical, was like cotton candy.

Instinctively, she took a mouthful and bit down.

B
O
O
M
!

Yup. Drunk.

Kate giggled some more and let Itala hold her down. Gods only knew what she could do right now if she stood up. Safer to let it bleed out slowly.

"I'm drunk," she giggled some more.

"Drunk?" Itala was perplexed. "On testosterone and adrenaline?"

"Nope," Kate slurred some more. "Power. Those are just the keys. It's like an acid trip."

"How long?"

"Dunno. Gotta ride it out."

Itala seemed really worried now. But her training was kicking in. She grabbed a blanket off of a nearby chair and spread it on the floor before rolling Kate carefully over on top of it.

WARM.

Gods. The sensory overload had to be the worst part.

Kate let herself be mothered over. Not that she had much choice, but at least she had the presence of mind to not fight as Itala found another small blanket to cover her legs.

MORE WARM. GOOD.

Kate let the energy run for a while, until a stray thought struck her.

She didn't want to just be a victim of the power. Her purpose required that she master it.

Kate looked deep inside and found a pulsing red spot. It felt like her heart. Could be her soul. Maybe her Name.

She reached out and wrapped both hands around it comfortingly. Her soul felt warmer, calmer.

She looked up, smiled at Itala, and mentally reached past her.

Power flowed inwards. More than she had seen any of the times she had tried this before. Maybe enough to drown in.

Kate panicked for a moment, and then crushed that by thinking of Miranda's laugh. She visualized the power flowing through her veins. It felt like lava. Burned like it, too, but she refused to believe that the universe could best her.

She squeezed both hands into fists. Toes, too.

The pain was suddenly enormous. It felt like she was on fire, but her eyes were open, hoping to catch a glimpse, to see herself light up.

For a moment, she did.

The room seemed like a supernova, but Kate would not quail. She screamed in pain, but would not let go, like a bulldog with a bone.

She sensed, more than saw, as Itala leaned back, breaking physical contact to shield her own eyes, lest she be blinded.

The lava turned cold as she squeezed. Kate felt a mountain take hold in her chest, swelling outwards like a volcano. She sucked a hard breath deep and centered around it.

She could not stand to do the movements of Tai Chi Chuan, but she let her mind fall into the familiar, calming rhythms.

Meditation in motion.

Calm took root at the base of the flame.

The mountain grounded itself in her reality.

Kate snarled her defiance once last time, and then the pain passed.

Gone, like a soap bubble on a summer afternoon.

She blew out the breath she had been holding.

The room had stopped spinning.

Kate sat up and held out a hand to Itala.

"How long?" she asked quietly.

Itala pulled out her phone and checked the face.

"About three hours," the petite Frenchwoman whispered, obviously in awe.

Kate felt like she had just run a marathon in that time.

Her breasts hurt. No, her whole chest hurt. Kate looked down as the blanket fell away.

"Oh, shit," she muttered.

The buttons on her shirt had all popped off. And her bra had simply disintegrated.

Once upon a time, it had been a lovely, little white lace number. It hooked in front because it didn't need to do much, there not being much chest to contain.

But now the bra's wire hook had been torn asunder, as if some guy had grabbed both sides and pulled really hard.

And her breasts had swelled up at least one whole cup size, from small plums to oranges. They were hypersensitive, right now, but that would pass.

She hoped.

Kate flipped the rest of the blanket away.

She had ripped her pants as well, from hip to knee, right down the front of her thighs, because she had thighs now. Muscles everywhere.

At least her expensive shoes had survived.

Kate looked at her hands, at her arms. Her forearms were larger. Wired with power and swollen. Her upper arms as well.

She stood with Itala's help.

Thank God. She was still the same height. Good nutrition and hard exercise could explain the rest, but growing taller would be impossible to hide.

Itala just stared at her, open mouthed like a fish lying on the dock. Open. Close. Open. Close. Nothing came out.

"What are you?" Itala finally asked, on about her fourth try.

Kate had no answer.

Instead, she walked to the bathroom. Itala trailed helplessly behind.

The mirror told her no lies.

Her shirt had shredded because her chest was more than two inches wider now, latissimus muscles suddenly broad and defined where there had been almost none before. And her breasts had grown larger. Not large, but more than before. About a good boob job worth. At least her stomach was still flat.

And there was no hair on her chin beyond the fine, downy, peach fuzz she had yesterday.

Kate blew out her breath.

Not Henry Hyde.

Not some big, green monster raging.

Just Kai Di Peng. Dr. Catherine. Kate.

She scowled.

No. Strike that.

She was become Death, the Destroyer of Worlds.

She was The White Crane.

AFTERMATH

Kate focused on a cup of Itala's fresh, steaming decaf as she thought.

This evening had not been what she had been expecting. Thank God Itala was too stubborn to have left her alone when she was going to do something stupid.

Before, Kate had been built like a short fashion model, petite in all directions. Not particularly long, but extremely skinny.

Itala had been the one with muscles, wiry and carefully hidden most of the time under baggy clothes, but there to show off on the few times she had dressed up for dinner.

Now, Kate looked like a gymnast or a swimmer. Broad. Muscular. And she was certainly never, ever, getting in her skinny jeans again. Hell, at this point, a whole new wardrobe would be necessary, up at least a whole size, maybe two, depending on the designer.

She looked down at the spare you-dub t-shirt and gray sweat pants that had been on a shelf just in case. This probably qualified, considering it was a total fashion emergency.

On the table, one slightly mangled shirt. Shredded pants. Utterly destroyed bra.

Wow.

"So now what?" Itala asked quietly.

Kate shrugged. Where the hell did she go from here?

No, that was unfair. Kate knew exactly what the next step was. She had peeked over the precipice. The chasm was still a mile wide and an eternity deep.

Kate sipped some more coffee and looked up.

Itala looked terrible. Bags under the eyes. Bottle-blond short hair running every direction.

Haggard. Worried.

"Are you certain that you still wish to do this thing?" Kate asked.

She couldn't help the formal cant to her words or her tone. Things had gotten very, very serious in her head. Itala needed to know what she was getting into, even at this late stage of the game.

"In for a penny," the blond replied, exhausted but still flippant.

"It's more than that, Itala," Kate stated flatly. "You only know about half of it at this point."

Kate watched the other woman's eyes grow big, like in a Japanese cartoon.

"Half?"

Kate just nodded.

"In for a pound, then."

Good. Kate wasn't really sure she could have done this on her own. At least not this successfully, this soon. She had never had a friend like Itala. Miranda had always been too flighty.

"Thank you," she whispered, emotion loading the words.

"For?"

"Everything."

Itala just smiled and reached out a hand that she sat on the back of Kate's. Some amount of warmth flowed back and forth. And Kate's skin no longer felt sandpapered raw and prickly.

Ahead, the precipice still beckoned.

"Miranda Devereux was known to the world as the Scarlet Titan," Kate began slowly, looking inward and sipping her coffee. "She was an inventor, a genius, a mechanical engineer. A super-villain."

Kate paused and tried to find the words to sum everything up.

"She was my friend."

That was it.

Kate could talk about family, about *guanxi*, about many things. In the end, Miranda had been her friend. Her evil conscience that got her out of the dorm room, out of the lab, out into the real world. Who took her on adventures in exotic lands. Who kissed her when she was sixteen and never been kissed.

And now she was gone.

Gods, I miss you.

Kate looked up at Itala, letting the pain show in her face. Tears threatened, but Kate would not allow them to come. She had already cried herself out for Miranda.

"To avenge her," Kate finally continued. "I will become a super-villain as well. Not for long. I don't need long. Just long enough to kill that man."

"How?"

"Before she died, Miranda made a flying suit for me."

"A what?"

"A flying suit," Kate answered. "It's like a suit of light armor around my body, with wings that run past my fingertips and lifter/thrusters that let me fly."

"But how?"

Kate felt like she was suddenly a thousand miles away as the words came out of her mouth.

"We are Modern Gods, Itala," she pronounced, doom echoing in her tones. "The power has always been there, but very few people could tap it. A century ago, we would have been very few. They would have considered us sorcerers. Now we are many, born as heroes and villains."

"Power?"

"It does not obey science," Kate said simply. "It mocks it. Before this, I used my abilities to see, to understand chemistry at the molecular level, racing hundreds of steps ahead of everyone else to the outcome I wanted, and used my vision to see how to short-cut my way there."

Itala frowned. She pointed at a spot on the floor where two blankets were still roughly piled up.

"You're telling me that was just chemistry?" Itala asked skeptically. "That you on the floor, glowing for an hour like a lightning bug was just…what?"

Kate considered her words. None of them were adequate.

There might not be any.

"Magic," Kate finally settled on.

"That's crap," Itala responded instantly, hotly.

Kate could hear the raw anger under the other woman's words.

But she had a point, crude though it might be.

"It's been seventy years since the first atomic bombs went off," Kate let her mind wander back to the research she had done. "Burnham's theory is that cracking atoms blasted a whole new kind of energy, raw power, into the atmosphere. A bunch of it where there had only been trickles before."

"And?"

"And some people can use that power," Kate continued. "Can reach out with their mind and see it floating by, like a cloud of cotton candy. Can take a bite of it, pull it in, and then use it to change things."

"Magic."

Itala's voice dripped with all the sarcastic irony that only a Frenchwoman could manage. Anyone else would have just sounded petulant.

Kate held out her right hand, palm up. She closed it into a fist slowly, watching the play of new muscles in her arm as she squeezed.

She opened the hand after a second and picked up the tattered white lace that had been her bra, once upon a time.

"Itala," Kate said, barely above a whisper. "I've just added at least thirty pounds of mass, all of it muscle. Look at the wire hook here and tell me what did that."

"Magic," Itala repeated, much more disdainfully.

"Magic. Power. Something," Kate said with a shrug. "I can do things that your science cannot explain, Horatio. Glorious things. Or evil things. The limits are my will and my imagination."

Itala cocked her head sideways and pointed at the refrigerator where they had stored the remaining serum.

"Would that work for me?" she asked simply.

"Sort of," Kate replied.

"Sort of."

Truly, only the French could pack that much derision into so few words. Itala surpassed Miranda on that score.

"What I did," Kate began, looking for the right words. "Was to, for lack of a better term, edit the testosterone. Keep the anabolic effects. Leave out the androgenic. Increased muscle mass and greatly increased strength. Rapid recovery and healing time. Significant bone density."

"Really?" Itala dripped curiosity and mockery in equal parts.

"At the same time, if I did it right, none of the hair, or rage, or sexual characteristics of a male. It should work on you, as well. Sort of."

"Sort of," Itala sneered nicely.

"You can't unlock the power, Itala," Kate tried to placate her. "You can't transform yourself overnight into something else. Not like that."

That. How to encompass everything that they could infer by pointing to a pair of blankets, or a mutilated bra?

"Still, I can make you stronger. Faster. Tougher."

"What about roid-rage?" the petite Frenchwoman asked. Her voice had finally lost some of the cat-like edges. Maybe, they had gotten past *That*.

For now.

"That's an androgenic effect," Kate replied. "It shouldn't affect you. You'll still be the sweet, harmless, little girl who beats up bad men in alleys."

Itala blew an ironic kiss at her across the table.

At least she was smiling finally. The last hour had left them both emotionally raw.

"I'm going to need a mask," Itala announced, suddenly sitting a little taller in her chair and holding out her coffee mug like a toast.

"A what?"

"You're obviously going to need a sidekick out there, taking care of you, woman," Itala smiled innocently. "Keeping you out of trouble. Maybe I can't beat up Modern Gods, but I can certainly destroy dumbass street punks. Especially with your help."

Oh, shit. She was serious, too.

What have I unleashed?

FLYING

The Tuesday weather forecast had been for overcast and mostly dry. Kate had insisted on driving, since it was her brand new, cute, little, lavender Japanese hatchback. She needed the practice.

Itala was already an expert driver, after all.

Winter was mostly over. Spring was thinking about peeking out in the lowlands now, but there was still snow in the mountains.

"Okay," Itala said, looking up from her phone. "The turn off should be coming up in a few hundred meters."

"What if someone's there?" Kate replied.

"If he's cute, he can stay."

"Itala!"

"What?" The Frenchwoman grinned back at her.

"Fine," Itala continued with an exaggerated, exasperated sigh. "I have four more campgrounds and hiking trails plotted out, just in case. They just won't be as good."

Kate slowed the car to a crawl. They were on a blacktop road, but well up in the middle of nowhere in the Cascades and hadn't seen anyone for several miles. Not since they left the highway and passed through the little town on the edge of the national forest.

"There," Itala said, pointing to a gap in the trees.

There? That's it? I'm supposed to drive in there?

Kate felt a moment of anguish at what the branches might do to her new car, but took a deep breath and exited the road. It quickly turned into a green tunnel with a dirt floor. Kate felt like a character wandering into a fairy tale. A bigger fairy tale.

Suddenly, she was through, into the forest's stomach, having gone down its gullet. A gravel parking lot welcomed them.

Kate turned to one side and parked next to the campground sign. It was an old one, with an ancient hiking map and what looked like bullet holes through it.

Welcome to the middle of nowhere.

Itala was already out as soon as soon as the engine stopped running.

Kate took a moment to take a deep breath first before she got out.

You can do this.

She stood and watched the smaller woman pop the hatchback and drag out the big anvil case that held Kate's flying suit.

Kate looked around, but there was nobody, nothing, except for one agitated squirrel chittering angrily at them from the safety of a tree. She wondered if it would see her as a giant hawk in a few minutes.

That thought brought a smile to Kate's face.

There hadn't been many smiles.

"You ready to show me?" Itala asked.

Kate bounced almost physically back down to the present. She looked down to see the anvil case patiently waiting, with Itala kneeling beside it.

She felt a pang of guilt.

Up until now, it had been almost a game. Something she could back out of, if it got to be too much to handle. She had changed herself physically, but she could always explain that away as good nutrition and lots of exercise.

Maybe.

This was the precipice.

Once she did this, once she went flying, here, with a witness, there would likely be no going back. At least not in her mind.

How had she gotten here?

Her potential henchman had morphed into a sidekick, and then a partner. *What had she said? In for a penny, in for a pound…*

Kate squatted down beside her friend and took hold of the anvil case, quickly laying it flat and pressing her thumbs onto the optical sensors pads.

She was growing more sensitive. She felt a quick surge of power around her hands, apparently the machine drawing its power from her, tasting it, and recognizing that it really was Kate.

The box popped open silently to reveal the strange, white-metal contraption that was the flying suit locked down in travel mode.

Kate stood and stripped off her jacket, leaving only brand new, lime-green running tights, a navy blue sports bra big enough to contain her new breasts, and a tight gray workout shirt designed to go under warmups and keep one dry and serene in yucky weather.

She still felt like someone else in her new wardrobe.

I am someone else.

Would the comic book artists draw her as Tisiphone, the avenging Greek goddess? She remembered artwork she had seen of that winged fury. A westerner would probably make that mistaken connection instead of the correct one.

Would it be better for her or worse if she corrected them? Every edge, every ounce of advantage would work for her. Even Americans had heard of Sun Tsu and his lessons on misdirection in warfare.

Kate took another deep breath. She placed one hand on the flying suit's palm-print plate. The machine grew warm in spite of the chill around her.

She stood up as the machine began to unfold, a magical, metal, origami spider wrapping her in warmth and protection.

Itala's eyes threatened to bug out of her head as the petite Frenchwoman watched the transformation.

It was one thing to tease Kate about her cartoon super-suit. It was something else again to actually watch it appear.

Down the legs and around. Darkest black leggings and boots.

Up her arms and across her back. Kate had a moment of panic that the suit would not fit her new chest or the larger breasts, but the metal flowed around them like water and encased her in solidity.

Across the backs of her arms, over her wrists, out another eighteen inches like blunt daggers.

And then feathers. Black from shoulder to elbow, purest white to wingtips.

Kate fought to relax as the chest piece swelled upwards, wrapping around her neck like hands, and then caressing her cheeks, her temples, and meeting atop her skull.

Kate hadn't thought about her braided hair before, but she felt it on the inside of the suit, under the armor, but not being pinched or pulled. That left only the crest of feathers for someone to grab in a fight.

"Wow," Itala whispered.

Kate could see other words, unspoken, in her friend's eyes. Perhaps the slightest tinge of jealousy, but there were mostly smiles to be had.

What must it be like to be confronted with someone so much…? Better was a bad word. It suggested superiority of birth. Aristocracy. Belittlement.

Kate was a Modern God. She had accepted that.

Itala was human. Not *merely* human. Perhaps *defiantly* so. Willing to work twice as hard as Kate for barely a tenth of the reward. She would never fly.

Unless…

Kate flashed back to that moment of pain that had gone through her like a spear when she first drank the serum. Something unexpected had happened to her. Something far grander, far more intense than she had calculated.

Was it possible to somehow reprogram a mere human to become one of the gods? To alter whatever it was that would let them caress the power?

Could anyone become Power?

Better, was there enough Power for everyone?

Kate had been thinking of herself as an artist, a genius.

What if anyone could do this?

She smiled under the mask. First, she would have to do some research, to see if it could be done. Only then would she mention it to her friend. Best not to get her hopes up and then dash them.

"The White Crane," Kate replied gravely, holding her arms out sideways and letting more than three meters of wingspan move gracefully.

The secret was hidden around her waist and up her back. Kate lacked the vocabulary to describe them as anything more than lifters and thrusters, based on their function, but because of Miranda, she could channel raw power through them, like light was lased through a gem, and transform it into something greater.

She could fly.

Kate let the world around her fade. This was not a skill you thought about, any more than bird did.

Instead, she let her senses expand out to see the power floating around.

She was getting better at this, or something. It was like watching low-flying clouds on an otherwise clear day. The kind of haze Miranda would describe in some of the seedier dive bars she had been, where they turned on the smoke machines for *atmosphere*.

Kate took a deep sniff. The smell of ozone was there from the machine's transformation, but underneath that was something else. She couldn't place the taste, but it reminded her of the smell of freshly turned earth, rich and dark, without the bitter tang of coffee.

She remembered Miranda's words.

"Just let go and fly," her friend had said that one time.

Nothing to it but to try. There was nobody around but Itala, who had already seen her at her worst.

Hopefully my worst.

The air was calm but chilly this morning. Overhead, a bright, blue sky beckoned.

Kate took two steps and threw herself at the sky.

Suddenly, that chittering squirrel was below her. Trees began to fall away as well as Kate climbed into the air.

Mountains appeared in the distance, where there had been only forest before. Birds took umbrage, but gave way to her greater size. Even the eagles took a different path as she gained altitude.

Kate banked to her left. Itala was suddenly hundreds of feet below her, head tilted back and one hand up shading her eyes. Kate could hear a very faint cheering as well.

Today, she truly felt like a Modern God.

This was what it was really about. Free flight.

This was power.

Kate felt warmth envelope her, flowing outwards from her shoulder blades and engulfing her, like laying down into a warm bath.

Even the cold air receded, just kissing her lips, even though she could feel the breeze on her skin, fully encased in the armor of her suit.

It was like flying nude.

Kate looked down, just to make sure that she really was wearing layers. It had been almost a year. It was possible that the magic of her flying had somehow consumed her clothes and she was showing herself to the whole sky.

Fortunately, there were only birds and elk up here. Itala had already seen enough.

But, no. Kate was still clothed. Or, at least, opaque enough for modesty. The suit appeared to be skin-tight on her nudity, in spite of the layers under it.

She felt like a Goddess in her sky chariot up here.

Or one of the Chinese Gods, traveling to *P'eng-lai Shan*, the Eastern Isles of the Immortals. She was a white crane, after all. It was appropriate.

She banked again, slowly orbiting the clearing where her car was parked. It was enough today just to fly.

Tomorrow, Kate would worry about the advanced mechanics of flight. Speed, maneuverability, stall. But all those things could wait for now.

It was enough to fly.

She wished Miranda could have been here to see it. Perhaps it would be enough for her ghost to watch over her now.

Kate could fly.

鶴

She needed to land. Kate let thought become action.

The machine seemed to sense that and guided her arms and her feet. She flapped just to maintain her balance, and it felt natural to do so.

The ground swelled up below her, Itala growing from an ant to a mouse, to a cat, to a woman.

One foot went down as the ground approached, the other came up, crane-like.

Kate's toes touched down with no more gravity than dropping two steps to the ground.

And she was Earthbound again.

Kate smiled down at Itala, but was struck by the scowl on the other woman's face.

"What is it?" Kate asked, nervous that she had done something wrong.

Instead of answering, Itala started to walk about her.

Kate turned to her right to follow.

"No," Itala barked, polite but mercilessly. "You stay in place. I want to see all the way around you."

Kate was eight again, standing on display as her mother made sure her outfit was acceptable for company. It had been fine, but that image was still fresh in her mind thirteen years later.

Weird.

Itala passed into her field of vision again. The face was less cross, but no less pensive.

She walked close enough to touch Kate on her left forearm.

"And you can feel that like skin, you said?" Itala inquired. Pensive had won out in her tone.

won out in her tone.

"Yes," Kate replied, no less confused, but less awkward, less embarrassed.

"That's good," Itala continued. "We need to build a new harness in the gym."

"Why?"

Kate was lost, but she trusted this tiny woman who had cut years off of her mad quest for vengeance.

Itala stepped back rather than answer immediately. She studied Kate like a side of meat.

Kate blushed anyway. She felt naked under that gaze. Not nude. Exposed.

"In gymnastics," Itala began finally. "A young aerialist will often begin her training with a belt that lets her jump and somersault in the air, as training for the vault and the floor. It's a safe way to get inverted until you know how to do it right."

She paused again, stepped twice to her right.

"Hold your wings out," Itala commanded.

Kate obeyed. She had to trust the expert, she told herself.

In for a penny…

"*Oui*," Itala finally nodded, mostly to herself. "You will not need to fight him inverted, but you will be elevated, kicking at his head below you, strafing him at speed. I had not truly imagined what we could do, until I saw you move. *Bon*."

"Tell me?" Kate asked.

Itala gestured with her two hands representing two figures fighting, or dancing.

"You will be flying, Kate," Itala said, swinging her hands. "Charging at him. And then you will swoop back and stall, and kick him in the head. It must become automatic."

The word came out of Itala's mouth as *OTTO-ma-TEEQUE* as Itala's excitement overrode her soft French accent.

"I will need to build a flying obstacle course," Itala continued. "And it must be portable, as well. We must make Parkour three dimensional."

"But it already is," Kate pleaded.

"*Non*," Itala barked back at her. "I am still subject to the grasp of gravity. You are not. You must fly over, under, and through. And you must do it while chasing, and being chased. And being shot at, especially by that smart-mouthed punk in purple with the bow and arrow set. And we must train out here, where no one can see you. Plus we must work at night. Can you develop a radar like a bat?"

Radar? She was a white crane, not a *flittermaus*.

But still, it was power. She could do anything, if it became truly necessary. Perhaps she could do that, one of these days, when she had the leisure of retirement from a life of villainy. She had already proven she could change the armor, if need was great enough.

If she survived, she would have the rest of her life to explore the limits of power. To dream.

What would life be like after vengeance?

TRANSFORMATION

Warmth.

Kate let the steaming hot bath water caress her skin and work its magic on her back, shoulders, and butt. Magnesium salts were a wonderful invention, since bubble bath soap tended to leave her itchy.

The lights were too bright.

She wondered if it would be too dark in her bathroom with the lights off.

Obviously, she needed to invest in some candles soon.

Kate gave up on coherent thought. Five days in a row, she and Itala had driven out to a different campground, or trailhead, or park, and practiced flying. Or rather, practiced dive-bombing stationary targets and maneuvering in three dimensions.

Becoming The White Crane.

At one point today, Itala had put handkerchiefs on her head and shoulders for Kate to fly by and pluck them off, while not getting smacked by a four-foot piece of pink foam tubing Itala had cut from a swimming noodle.

Kate was exhausted. She was beginning to wonder if all of this was worth the effort. The training, the serum, the everything. All the secrets she could never tell another soul except Itala.

She could hear Itala doing something in the kitchen, through the closed door, most likely being supervised by Mr. Loh, who would be expecting treats. She couldn't bring herself to care enough to figure out what the sounds were.

Kate concentrated on not drowning as she got as much of her new body under the hot water as she could.

The door rattled and opened. Itala entered.

"*Bonjour,*" the woman chirped merrily.

Kate was normally very shy about nudity. Miranda had always been the one in the skimpy bikini that just barely wouldn't get her arrested on most beaches, while Kate stuck with a modest one-piece.

Right now, she couldn't work up the energy to care that Itala could see all of her.

Itala was holding a tray. There was a cupcake on it. And a lit candle. Something.

Kate pretended to be a crocodile, nose-deep in the hot water and lurking. There wasn't much higher brain to engage.

"Congratulations," Itala said as she sat on the closed toilet seat and held out her tray like a war trophy. Mr. Loh watched carefully from the door, but maintained a polite distance from that much water.

"Uh…" Kate surfaced enough to grunt. Still not enough brain to brain.

"I did not manage to hit you today," Itala smiled. "Except the one time. And then I was cheating because I've fought you enough times to start to learn your bad habits. And we will fix those, soon. Tonight, we celebrate. Make a wish."

She held out the tray with its single, flickering candle.

Kate surfaced enough to put her arms over the side of the tub and get her head in the right direction.

It still took two tries to blow the candle out.

Right now, her wish was to sleep for twelve hours.

"Good," Itala continued. "You've been in there for an hour and you're getting pruny. Out with you now."

Kate watched her set the tray down and grab a big, brown, fluffy towel from the rack to hold out.

It had been an hour?

Kate looked at her hands.

Apparently so.

She braced against the sides and pulled her legs under her. After being skinny for so long, having muscles was strange, especially suddenly having thighs and a butt. The boobs she was mostly getting used to.

She felt Itala's eyes flicker over her nude form as she stood up, but really didn't give a damn at this point. She took the towel and began to dry herself off.

Itala moved to the door, leaving the cupcake behind.

"After you dry off, and eat that, I will give you a good massage and put you to bed," Itala announced.

Kate hurt.

The new regimen of the serum, the edited testosterone, was supposed to speed up her recovery from intense physical exertion, like it did for men. Kate looked deep in her soul and realized that this wasn't the bone tired of flying hard. This was what it felt like when she had exhausted all the power she could hold, and had begun to burn personal reserves instead.

There apparently were limits to what the Modern Gods could do. Or, at least, there were limits to how much energy they could burn through in a reasonable amount of time. Good to know.

Now she needed to see if that could be extended, like developing muscles, or if it was a hard limit.

But that was tomorrow. Or maybe after two days of sleeping.

She finished drying off and hung the towel on the rack to dry. She considered if she should wrap it around herself for modesty, but it just wasn't worth the effort, the ten extra steps to bring it back in two minutes after she had gotten dressed.

At least the cupcake would be good for a bit of sugar rush. She needed something right now.

And it was yummy. Messy, crumbly, sticky enough she had to wash her hands and mouth. But good.

Itala was waiting for her in the bedroom. The smaller woman pointed imperiously at the bed, with her other fist on her hip.

"Face down, young woman," she commanded. "We shall set you to rights."

At least Itala had laid out a beach towel over the bedspread.

Good enough.

Kate more or less fell onto the bed face down. Her new shape made her a little uncomfortable, but not enough to roll over. Instead, she turned her head to the side and watched Itala climb up and straddle her back, holding a bottle of lotion in one hand and pouring a bit into the other.

Kate noticed that Itala was still wearing the gray sweatpants from this afternoon, but only a thin t-shirt, and apparently no bra under it. It was one of the very few times she could remember that Itala's shape could be easily discerned.

She wondered if the petite Frenchwoman was even more modest. Kate had developed muscles and curves, while Itala's response to taking Kate's serum was to apparently grow even more wiry that before. She was still slender, but it was all muscle now. And her chest had not changed. Having been larger than Kate when they met, she was smaller now.

The hand cream was cool on her back, almost cold as it puddled on her spine, just above her bottom.

Kate was struck by how soft Itala's hands were as they dug into the muscles on her back and shoulders. There was a surprising amount of tension still back there, even after an hour submerged, but she felt it slowly bleeding out of her.

Kate wondered if she could still manage to fall asleep in the middle of everything the Frenchwoman was doing to her. She settled for trying to figure out how to purr instead, as Itala moved up to her neck and worked out the kinks and burrs with hard hands, like digging for ore.

Kate closed her eyes and sighed.

Then Itala went slowly down her back again, gripping and pinching like lobster claws relentlessly digging in.

Itala moved around somewhere, but Kate refused to open her eyes to see. Instead, she waited.

The woman started on her feet next, before slowly moving up the back of each leg, working the long muscles of the calf and then the thigh before changing over to the other. Back and forth. Kate felt like she might be a foot taller by the time Itala was done pulling and stretching her.

Her bottom got a good workout next. The morning yoga had kept the muscles limber, but Itala worked them to a new level of relaxation.

"Roll over," Itala commanded.

Kate did, only vaguely awake, and then blushed lightly as she realized the other woman was looking down at Kate's nude form. She told herself the room was chilly as she watched Itala's eyes roaming. Instead of commenting, Kate closed her eyes and concentrated on her breathing.

Itala started on her right thigh first, working the front and side just as she had the rear. Then the left thigh. Right hand and forearm and shoulder. Left.

Itala straddled her now like she might have if she were making love to a man. The petite Frenchwoman leaned forward and began to massage the muscles in Kate's shoulders and neck from the front.

Kate couldn't help but purr.

It felt natural to reach up with one hand and pull on the front of Itala's shirt, drawing her face close enough to kiss her. Itala resisted, so Kate reached a hand around her neck and tugged her down. They ended up nose to nose, both breathing a little heavier than they should have.

Kate pulled Itala into a kiss, soft and tentative. Itala kissed her back for a moment before she broke it.

"Are you sure about this?" Itala whispered.

"No," Kate replied softly. "I'm not."

"Have you ever done this before?" Itala murmured.

"No," Kate sighed. "You're only the second person I've ever kissed. After Miranda."

Itala leaned back, up, away.

"No boys?" she asked, surprise evident in her voice.

Kate caught Itala before she could get too far. She ended up with her hands wrapped around the smaller woman's back, under her shirt. It was all muscle there in a way that felt natural to hold her.

"It's not right," Itala muttered, apparently mostly to herself, as she tried to move and realized that Kate was stronger.

"Please?" Kate pleaded.

That brought Itala up short. She stared down at Kate as if from a dizzying height, a slightly-terrified raptor eyeing a dangerous rabbit on the ground.

"We shouldn't do this," Itala replied, barely above a whisper.

"If not you, who?" Kate asked softly. "Who else can I trust? Who will keep my secrets?"

She could see two sides warring in Itala's eyes, greed and lust lined up against her fear and caring. Under her skin, Kate could feel the tension surge and relax.

"If nothing else," Kate implored. "Please just hold me tonight?"

Kate let all her own fear and nervousness show. She knew she would never have done this if she hadn't already been so bone-tired as to let her guard down, and then so relaxed under Itala's tender touch.

So open. So willing to confront her fear, and overcome it.

It was yet another precipice between the girl she had been and the woman she could see in the distance.

Itala came to some conclusion.

Kate could feel it in the muscles in her back before she saw it in the woman's eyes.

Itala reached down and took Kate's cheeks tenderly as she leaned forward.

Kate closed her eyes as Itala leaned in, the two women breathing softly on each other. Kate let one of her hands trail down and hold Itala's bottom, while the other went up to her neck to pull her down.

It was a harder kiss this time. Still tentative, but the hesitance of new lovers learning each other's dreams.

Miranda had kissed her like this, at first.

They grew bolder as they stayed joined together. Kate let her hands explore the older woman softly, enjoying the play of the new muscles Itala had developed from her own serum, even as it had transformed her from a wiry Chinese girl into a comic-book heroine.

Itala broke the kiss and stared into Kate's suddenly open eyes.

"No more," Itala whispered. "Else I might not be able to stop myself."

Kate really didn't want her to stop. The feel of Itala's touch left fire on her skin. But she also didn't want to go too far with her friend and risk their friendship. Not over something like this.

What was it Miranda had always said? Men were a dime a dozen, but friends were rare diamonds.

Reluctantly, she let go as Itala leaned back and away from her. Kate wanted to reach out and touch the breasts she could see straining against the thin material of Itala's shirt.

She held her breath as the woman climbed off her hips and stood up beside the bed. Itala still had that strange, distant look in her eyes.

"Cuddling only?" Itala breathed heavily at her.

"Just hold me, please," Kate whispered across the vast distance of five feet. She could still smell Itala from here, lotion, the faintest perfume, sweat, musk.

"That we can do," Itala promised.

Kate caught her breath as Itala suddenly pulled her shirt over her head, followed onto a pile on the floor by the sweat pants, until she was standing proudly beside the bed wearing only Hello Kitty panties. Kate had grown larger than the other woman, but couldn't take her eyes off of Itala's skin and muscles.

Both women appeared cold this evening.

Itala grabbed the bedspread and pulled it down, sliding under the covers.

Kate rolled the other direction, pulling the beach towel with her and rubbing it quickly over her back and legs to wipe away any lotion still on her skin.

She crawled under the sheets from her side, and snuggled up against Itala's skin. She felt arms around her back and neck as she pressed herself against the woman's chest.

Itala kissed her once on the forehead as she shivered. Whether that was from the cold or the emotion, Kate could feel the warmth begin to seep into her bones.

All of the everything almost overwhelmed her for a second, but she felt Itala's hands on her back, holding her close.

She wasn't alone.

Maybe, just maybe, she could do this after all.

MODERN GODS

Kate woke in near-total darkness.

She did not open her eyes, but let her other senses expand out and identify the room as she lay still on her left side.

Mr. Loh slept against her thighs, alternately purring and squeaking slightly as he dreamed of mice.

She smelled the lotion on her skin, along with the faintest hint of Itala's perfume.

With a start she suppressed, Kate realized that Itala was purring in her ear. It wasn't a snore, but not quite her kitty's squeak either.

Itala was asleep behind her, breasts pressed against Kate's back. One of Itala's arms was under Kate's head like a pillow, holding her left hand, while the other was wrapped around her side, cupping her breast warmly as they both slept.

It felt lovely, but Kate really had to go to the bathroom.

Carefully, she untangled herself from the other woman, working slowly so as to not wake her. Itala continued to purr, even as Mr. Loh chirped at her once to angrily scold her as he moved out of her way, and then slithered into the warm spot against Itala's belly as Kate stood up.

Nothing hurt. That was amazing all by itself.

The clock read seven thirty, hours after Kate normally woke automatically. There was a rim of light around the outside of the curtain

She pulled a shirt from a drawer and pulled it on against the chill in the air, and then added her running tights as well.

She leaned down and kissed Itala lightly on the forehead. The woman purred once in her sleep but did not awaken.

Kate eventually found herself in the living room, with her laptop open, sound off, and a dozen tabs open. Stories and news articles about the man she stalked, the Golden Tiger. The first dozen issues of an officially sanctioned graphic novel series. Fan art pages. Anything.

Eventually, she decided it was necessary to go back to the source.

If she was going to be a Modern God, she needed to truly understand what she was, what the others were.

Others had written about the topic over the decades, from dry-scholarly tomes that made chemistry textbooks look exciting, to educational Japanese Manga, to silly American comic books. But only one person had truly captured the zeitgeist of the age.

Yukiko Yamanaka had been born in Edo, Japan in 1940.

In the *Era Before*.

In the *Era After*, she had been left an orphan by the war.

Her mother, Natsumi, later married a US Army Occupation officer, Lt. Col Everard Maddox Burnham, who had adopted Yukiko as Charlotte Yukiko Burnham, the name under which she had written her first runaway best seller, *Gods Walk Among Us*, as a young college professor and professional historian of the modern age. The period of history when atomic energy unleashed magic on the world.

Yukiko was not the first of the Modern Gods, but she had given form to the understanding of the world that it had become, when humans could suddenly shape power into dreams, and vice versa.

Burnham did not fly. She could not summon demons or angels. Heat beams did not come out of her eyes on demand. In fact, nobody was sure what power she might express, beyond a gift with metaphor and storytelling that compared favorably with Shakespeare. And very few others.

However, Kate watched a video of this tiny, seventy-four year old woman as she threw out the ceremonial first pitch at a major league baseball game last summer. Somebody had the wit to turn on the radar gun when she did.

How many retired female college professors could throw a ninety-three mile-an-hour split-finger fastball that dropped off the table just shy of the plate?

There were reasons that Modern Gods were not allowed to play professional sports, once their powers were known. They truly were a breed apart.

Kate was several chapters into the most current edition of the book. It was obvious to her what Charlotte Yukiko Burnham was. Only someone who had seen the power floating in the air above her, had tapped it, had transformed herself with it, could write about it so accurately. Nobody else would be able to judge.

Kate had held it in her hands like cotton candy. Tasted it. Swallowed it like the finest cognac. Used it to set the world on fire.

Charlotte Yukiko Burnham-Lambert was her cousin. That much was sure.

Golden Tiger was as well.

Kate finished the first twelve issues of the man's supposed origin story. How much of it was outright fabrication would be hard to judge. Had he truly been raised as the only westerner in a secret monastery in the high reaches of the Tibetan plateau? How many tropes of modern adventure fiction did that hit? Was it possible to fight a tiger hand to hand and win by forcing the great cat to bow in defeat? Seriously?

Kate was absolutely sure about the golden flames the man could summon. There was video of it on several occasions. And she knew how to do it as well.

Similarly, the ability to fire the *ki-bolts*. That was his signature move. They apparently came in several flavors, depending on how tough, how armored, how invulnerable he thought his target was.

Miranda had seemed bullet-proof in her battlesuit. So he had used the one that could kill an armored tank. It had gone through Miranda like a bullet.

According to the reports, he claimed to have been unable to get her out of her armor in time to keep her from bleeding to death internally.

Kate saved a picture of the man to her laptop, him standing on a sidewalk in Angel City, with Miranda's blood literally on his hands. She felt a growl growing in her chest.

Every time she considered whether or not she really should do this, it came back to him.

According to Burnham, heroes and villains in the sixties and seventies had fought with a different code of honor. While many of the craziest lunatic villains might go in for threatening to poison a reservoir to draw out a hero, almost invariably those actions were just traps to catch the hero, and not serious threats to kill everyone.

Nobody had ever backed an explosives-laden truck up to city hall and blew it up in the middle of the day. If they were going to do that, it was at midnight, where they and their henchmen could capture the few lonely security guards and get them safely away before committing their grand vandalism. And again they would taunt the hero with riddles beforehand to draw them out.

That very concern for innocent life is what usually caused them to be caught. It gave the hero too long to get there and thwart things.

But there were two sides to the coin. Heroes never killed. Even the most dangerous villain would be captured, disarmed, and turned over to the authorities. If a gang of henchmen eventually managed to break them out of prison or the insane asylum, again, casualties were limited or non-existent.

It was almost a kabuki. In all the good ways.

And then, in the eighties, something changed. People, especially heroes, started carrying firearms. BFGs, in the slang of the time. *Big Fucking Guns* that could level buildings.

Deaths became inevitable. Collateral damage became acceptable. Villains did not always get arrested.

More and more frequently, they were buried instead.

It was getting harder to tell heroes and villains apart as a result. Vigilantes showed up and started firing. Innocents were often caught in an inescapable crossfire.

Death became commonplace, instead of something exceptional. Especially as the first generations of heroes retired to obscurity and let the kids have the keys to the mansion.

The world appeared to be going to hell in a handbasket. And here she was, planning how to ambush one of the most famous costumed heroes of the day and kill him. She wasn't even sure that people would rate her a villain. She might be just another vigilante. Golden Tiger certainly had enemies other than her.

If Kate had been going to make a career out of this, she would need to plan differently. But for now, The White Crane would only be around for a little while, and then she could put her away and go back to being Kate. Or Kai Di, a person she rarely impersonated much anymore.

"I'm hungry." A voice brought her back to the present.

For a moment, she was utterly lost. Why was Mr. Loh suddenly talking now?

Kate looked up. Itala stood in the doorway to the bedroom, wearing nothing but a t-shirt and her Hello Kitty panties.

The whole night came back to Kate. Warm. Soft. Safe.

She was so happy they had stopped when they had, where they had, how they had. That she had a friend, and not a lover.

Miranda had been right. She usually was.

"Fifth Point?" Kate inquired with a warm, encompassing smile. "Need a run this morning?"

"How can you run after yesterday?" Itala questioned her. "Last night, you were on the verge of exhaustion. I expected you to sleep all day."

Kate looked inside. That place where the fire had been guttering weakly was bright enough to light a star this morning.

"I have a very good friend," Kate replied impishly. "She takes amazingly good care of me, body and soul, when I need it."

Itala yawned and ran a hand through her messy, bottled-blond hair.

"Fine," she said. "Whatever. I need a shower."

Kate watched Itala stagger into the bathroom and close the door. For the briefest moment, she considered offering to scrub the woman's back, but decided that it could wait.

She had a lot of planning to do, now that she was almost ready to face this man, this villain, this hero.

SIDEKICK

Y ou need a costume," Kate whispered as the waitress took their order, topped off their coffee, and went around behind the bar to attack a computer with their order.

"I told you that, already," Itala sniped back, just as quietly.

Kate wondered if they looked like two young lovers to others in the joint. It was far later than normal for her today. People in here were on their way to work, or just coming in for a coffee on a break. The kitchen was going full bore. They would need to talk quietly.

"No, I mean now," Kate volleyed. "We're almost ready to head south and start getting serious."

Itala leaned back in surprise to stare at her. Maybe the other woman hadn't been expecting Kate to move this quickly.

"Well, I can't fly," Itala retorted.

"No," Kate was thinking out loud at this point. "But if you had a staff, I bet you could do some fantastic acrobatics. Add some ass-kicking boots, some fighting gauntlets to protect your hands, and add a masque to some basic spandex and *viola*, bitch on wheels."

"Huh."

Itala leaned back and sipped her coffee. Kate could see her eyes on a distant, invisible horizon, flickering back and forth.

Kate waited. She watched people come and go instead. The Fifth Point was far busier than she was used to. This would be one of the places she missed most, but she needed to be down at the south end of the coast for what was going to happen next.

"Quarterstaff?" Itala asked suddenly. "If we're going to be fighting people like you, I'm going to need something more than just a stick. Maybe a spear."

It was Kate's turn to lean back and think.

"*Ji*," she said.

"Huh?"

"It's a Chinese word," Kate explained. Perhaps Kai Di explained. This went back to her childhood and stories her mother's maid, Wu Ren, would tell her. Ancient tales about gods and heroes in the family homeland.

"And?" Itala prompted her.

"It means halberd, which is a type of spear," Kate explained, keeping her voice low. "But it also means luck or happiness. Ancient artwork often show halberds that way. But I'm not sure a spear would be all that useful against someone like Golden Tiger."

It was Itala's turn to smile.

"It will for what I have in mind," she smiled serenely. "I need you to give me some cash. This is not something that should show up on a credit card statement."

Kate tilted her head to the side to look at the woman somewhat askance. On the one hand, that was smart thinking. On the other hand, what they were planning was conspiracy to commit murder, and the murder itself. Maybe she needed to convert entirely to cash at this point, so as to not leave a trail of electronic evidence behind.

"Probably two grand and a ticket to Nice," Itala replied, her eyes out of focus and a smile creeping up on the corners. "I can get him to make it for me in a week or so."

"Are you going to tell me what?" Kate whispered.

"Nope," Itala grinned at her. "But you'll have a sidekick with her own bad-ass motif and regalia. It'll be awesome."

The food arrived before Kate could go any deeper, but she suspected that Itala wouldn't tell her any more than she had already.

Had she just unleashed her own super-villain on the world?

MARAUDER

Kate pulled into her favorite campground and found a parking spot in the most remote corner to back into. This training ground was the one farthest away from her apartment, well out on the main highway headed east and up in the foothills. It also had the best clear space to fly, away from everyone, in a little pocket valley with steep slopes on three sides that created pockets of thermals and ripping crosswinds that kept her on her toes.

The lot was empty today. Rainy Tuesdays in May tended to be like that. Folks might stay an extra Monday off work, possibly Tuesday as well, but they would have headed home by mid-day, leaving her to herself.

Itala was in the south of France so she didn't have to spar, or practice, or maneuver.

Today, Kate just wanted to fly. To absorb the smell of the mountains and clear air before she headed south and had to learn to breathe air she felt like she could chew.

And it was brown down there, most of the time.

Yuck.

She was getting good at this. Kate backed into the space and popped the hatch open. She quickly stripped off her jacket and tossed it in beside the anvil case. Pulling her flying suit out seemed faster than usual. Perhaps it wanted to fly as much as she did.

Kate powered up and let the suit embrace her, truly the only lover in her life right now, touching her skin-on-skin and becoming one. She closed everything up and chirped the car alarm, just in case. She threw herself at the sky.

The power was thin today, but she had been recharged by her activities the last three days, even if it had involved sending Itala off on her errands. The days had felt empty without her friend around.

That was part of the reason she had come out here. She felt more alive in the air than on the ground these days.

Still, Kate took care to draw as much of the power as she could hold into herself. She was experimenting with charging up her own personal battery as far as possible, extending reserves for the time when she wouldn't be able to stop and think about it.

She felt alive. She felt like she was becoming The White Crane in fact, instead of just theory.

Movement caught her eye as she soared back from the face of the rock, dancing on the updrafts with eagles and hawks. She felt like a raptor spying a rabbit in the grass.

Someone was standing next to Kate's car, her car, leaning on the driver's door. Someone she didn't know. Someone who had been waiting.

Without Itala around, White Crane could just fly away, but that was their car, their baby. If that bastard scratched the paint, there would be hell to pay.

The White Crane swooped lower. Enough to get a good look, not enough that he could touch her. The flying lessons with Itala, snatching a piece of cloth from the other woman's head while avoiding the pool noodle, kept her limber right now.

It was a man. A big one, too. He felt close to two meters tall, and broad, with his arms crossed on his chest as he watched White Crane circle.

This was not a random stranger on a day hike. They would be waving. People in the Pacific Northwest were friendly like that.

This had an ominous feel, like a man waiting for a much smaller woman to come into his reach, a trapdoor spider lurking. She wondered what he would have done with Itala around, if two small women would have intimidated him.

White Crane didn't think so.

Enough. He was alone, he wanted to deal with her. She had been studying Savate with Itala, and various forms of southern kung fu, the animal forms but mostly crane, with Master Daniel. And she was a Modern God, if push came to shove.

She pivoted in the air and began to hover, settling slowly towards the ground while she watched the newcomer. The suit handled the complicated tasks autonomously, letting her flap the great wings to maintain stability. It really was like swimming.

White Crane came to roost softly, never taking her eyes off the stranger.

He had a mean sneer. And three-days brown stubble. And greasy hair. From the ground, he was dressed like an Anglo biker from a bad B-movie, with knee-high leather boots, torn blue jeans with grease stains, a black leather vest with some logo on the left breast and nothing under it but hair.

And bad tattoos. Ugly blue ones that looked homemade.

"Nice rig," he growled at her.

Even his voice sounded like a badly-tuned motorcycle.

"Can I help you?" White Crane asked. She kept her distance. Ten meters was far enough to talk without yelling, but not close enough that he could surprise her.

"You sure can, little lady," he smirked at her. "We gonna do this easy, or hard?"

"Do what?" White Crane replied. The words confused her.

"Gimme the suit," he commanded harshly, standing up from where he had been leaning against the car and taking a step towards her.

Kate might have backed up. The White Crane didn't back down from any man.

"No," she snarled back at him.

He might think he was tough. White Crane was tougher.

The man stopped, smiled, and nodded at her.

"Good enough, little lady," he said conversationally. "GIT 'ER, BOYS."

Something sounded behind her. Kind of a twanging sound like a giant guitar.

Inside, White Crane cursed silently. Itala would have never fallen for such a trick.

Suddenly, she felt something wrap itself around her.

White Crane looked down in a momentary panic. Someone had dropped a net on her, thick nylon lines woven together, with the rim alternating between weights and hooks. Inertia and spin slung it over her like a giant blanket, trapping her arms against her body and forcing her to her knees.

She looked back and saw three smaller men emerge from cover, dressed in green camouflage, one of them holding an object that looked like a giant crossbow, something from a Saturday morning cartoon. The other two looked to be carrying baseball bats.

Not good.

A crunch of gravel brought her head back around. The big guy had rushed close.

She watched in slow motion as his right fist closed, cocked, and seemed to catch fire for the briefest moment, glowing faintly. At the speed of thought, The White Crane realized why the energy was weak in the air this morning. Someone else was using it, feeding on it.

She could not move, could not block, trapped in the heavy weight and tangles of the net. She could only try to roll with the blow as that fist grew large and pistoned into the side of her head with a savage ringing, bone on metal.

White Crane saw stars when she blinked. She was on her side in the gravel, coated with a gritty dust that tasted like chalk.

Movement was hard. Thinking was hard.

"See, boys," she heard the man brag. "Just like a woman. Whomp her once and she'll do whatever you tell her."

White Crane heard harsh laughter answer him.

Her own answer started deep. He was her cousin, a Modern God. And he was a bully, probably a rapist, from the words and tone. A predator on women.

The White Crane was a Modern God. And a woman. A small woman. The kind men like this would hurt, given the opportunity. She had seen the statistics, read the reports. Felt the rage. She let it smolder in the deep recesses of her soul as she caught her breath.

Rough hands grabbed the net, grabbed her, lifted her upright. He breathed stale tobacco smoke in her face and shifted all of her weight onto his left hand.

"Nice tits," he growled as he ran one coarse paw over her breast, squeezing it painfully as he laughed.

The White Crane was a Chinese symbol of longevity and wisdom, an emblem of the Gods themselves. It did not allow assault by common brigands.

There would be no rapine, no pillage.

Anger became rage.

Rage became fire.

Fire became power.

White Crane tapped the power within and transformed it. She felt herself engulfed in a pure, red flame, the Chinese phoenix, symbol of The Empress of all birds.

She became an Avatar of Death.

White Crane opened her eyes and focused on the man holding her off the ground. His face was scarred and pitted under the stubble. The first hints of fear flickered in his eyes, reflecting the soft red flame that had engulfed her.

White Crane snarled out loud and kicked him in the balls with all the rage, all the power, all the fire at her command.

His eyes bugged out and lost focus. He lost his grip on her nipple, let go of her weight, dropped her.

White Crane fell six inches to the gravel, standing like Aphrodite emerging from the sea.

The net offended her.

She pushed her fire outward, driving it down her arms and feathers and transforming them into razor-sharp vengeance. Arms went straight out from her sides, parting the net like spider web as she howled. It blew away in the winds of her anger.

Eyes left, eyes right. Three men.

Merely human.

Utter, slack-jawed shock. Good enough.

White Crane took a step to one side and pivoted. Big, Bad Bully was on his knees now. She drove the heel of her boot into the side of his head like she was going through a locked door.

He fell with a hollow, ugly thump, like a melon dropped from a third floor window.

Movement.

One of the men with the baseball bats took a step towards her.

"You bitch," he screamed as he swung.

White Crane became Rage.

Became Death.

One arm flashed out at the aluminum stick as it came down towards her head. Razor-sharp feather blades sheared it off in his hand, leaving only four inches of stump above his fingers. She began to spin in place, turning with the momentum of her first strike.

Her feathers struck the man like a pair of giant broadswords, two meters each of silver blade, wrapped in red fire, honed to perfect sharpness, driven by the anger of a small woman about to be raped by four big thugs in the middle of the forest, power augmented by rage.

White Crane came out of her spin and looked at the two men still standing. She felt the first man's blood dripping from her wingtips.

Vengeance howled. Flames danced down her arms, her feathers. She was The Empress. All women fell under her grace, her aegis. Men were become wolves howling at the door, foxes scratching at the henhouse.

The second man raised his baseball bat and stepped forward, swinging wildly.

White Crane leapt backwards and up, letting the strike pass below her as she flipped in the air and swooped down on the man. She considered a kick as she went by, but these men had chosen to play for higher stakes this morning when they got out of bed.

So be it.

The blade slashed down instead. It should have caused her to stall, but the rage drove the edges through the man like a bandsaw.

More blood. More rage.

White Crane danced to her left, twenty feet in the air and poised to pounce. The last man, the one with the crossbow, had not moved. Even from here, she saw the stains on the front of his jeans where he had pissed himself in fear, smelled the rank ammonia wafting off of him.

She landed in front of him, ten feet away, the Angel of the Apocalypse descending.

His eyes tracked her, but really didn't focus. He was frozen.

That alone saved him. Movement right now would have gotten him eviscerated, the man with the net gun hunting flying birds.

That was the greatest insult imaginable to The Empress.

"Do you wish to die?" White Crane enunciated slowly.

She was rewarded with a blink.

She stepped closer and repeated herself.

This time, the faintest shake of the head. No.

Good.

"Drop the crossbow. NOW," The Empress commanded.

The device fell to the gravel. His hands twitched. His whole being began to shiver.

"Please," he whispered, his voice coming up from whatever depths of hell she had plunged his mind into with her violence.

The Empress would not be denied.

"Kneel," she snarled.

She could tell the man was operating unconsciously at this point, a poorly programmed robot, a marionette with tangled strings.

He dropped to his knees with no more sound than the gravel crunching.

She was close enough now to smell the bacon and eggs he had eaten for breakfast.

"You are mine now," she murmured, reaching out her right hand to caress his cheek.

He flinched at the sight of the blood-drenched feathers, gleaming razors, so close to his neck, but held perfectly still otherwise, like a rabbit frozen by the hawk's call.

After a moment, the man bowed his head, both a nod of acquiescence and expecting the headman's axe.

White Crane reached down and lifted his jaw, turning his face up to stare into her radiance.

From here, the man looked Hispanic. Black hair cut short under a baseball cap, black eyes, skin a rich brown without the yellowish tinge of her own. It was a round face, fleshy on a man who was barely an inch taller than White Crane. He looked to be older as well, perhaps in his late thirties or early forties, with strands of white appearing around his ears and temples.

"What is your name?" The Empress demanded. Her voice was quieter now, almost intimate in his tones. She would calm the wild animal with her voice, now that she wanted to.

"C-C-Carlos, ma'am," he murmured.

His eyes were all whites and pupil now.

"Carlos," she repeated calmly. "I own your soul, Carlos. Do you understand me?"

"Yes, ma'am," he said.

She felt him tense, but it was an expectation of death, not preparation for violence. There was no violence left in the man at this point. The fires had purged it.

"Would you like to live, Carlos?" she continued.

"Yes, señorita," he whispered.

She moved to one side so she could point at the biker bully who had started all this. The man lay on the gravel with his head at an unnatural angle.

"Who was he?" she asked.

The voice was polite, but The Empress would not be denied.

"The Marauder, he call hisself," Carlos said. His voice was beginning to come back, if not his mind.

She did not recognize the name from her research, but she could really only name a few hundred of the men and women who had put on costumes and tried to change the world. And there were far more villains than heroes.

White Crane wondered what that said about the state of things.

"And?" she prompted, unsure where to take his thoughts.

Up until now, she had been entirely in the moment. First, flying just because she could. After that, fighting for her life in an ambush from men set to do her harm.

And where had The Empress come from? It was one thing to be The White Crane. That was an identity she was familiar with. She had spent months thinking about her. But this had gone someplace larger, someplace darker, someplace bleaker.

"I was in charge of weapons for the gang," Carlos said, oblivious to everything around him as the shock of violence set in. "Tommy and Joe were just cheap muscle."

"Weapons," White Crane locked onto that train of thought.

"Sí," he said, seemingly edging back to a human place. "Build things for him. Occasionally invent new gadgets. Maintain vehicles. Mr. Fix-it."

"You have done evil, Carlos," The Empress intoned severely.

"Sí, mistress," he agreed, bowing his head again.

Clearly, he did not expect anything but a fast death.

White Crane heard a sound in her mind. At first, she thought it was Kate trying to get her attention. But when she listened, it was Kai Di, the scholar, tapping her on the shoulder.

White Crane listened as Kai Di whispered hurriedly in her ear.

The Empress smiled in her mind.

"Carlos," she said firmly. "Look at me."

He resisted her hand for a moment, but relented to look up again at his executioner.

"I will spare you," she said. "If you will serve me. I am The White Crane. I am supreme. What will you choose?"

The words sounded so awkward and stilted coming out of her mouth. It sounded like something out of one of the comic books she had been reading. How writers thought people really talked in this sort of a situation.

"I will serve, mistress," Carlos swallowed past a dry tongue.

In her mind, White Crane receded a bit and let the scientist take charge. They needed clear, logical thinking at this point. There were three dead men back there.

Questions would be asked. She could plead self-defense, if she was willing to come clean to the authorities about what she was up to.

Who she was.

And give up any hope of getting her revenge.

In for a pound.

"How did you get here today, Carlos?" she asked brusquely.

"Marauder, he rode on his Deathcycle," Carlos replied. "The rest of us came in the van."

Hmmm. Two vehicles. Three with hers. Two drivers. And she couldn't ride a motorcycle. Itala could, but she wasn't due back for a few days.

Boy, was she in for a surprise.

White Crane leaned back and looked around. From the air, she remembered a steep ravine downhill from here, where this little canyon debauched onto the wider valley and the main road further up into the mountains. Maybe she could throw them down there.

"Body and soul, Carlos," she glared down at him.

The man actually crossed himself and kissed his thumb, almost white with fear.

"The three of them must disappear."

"I have a shovel, mistress," he offered quietly. "It is in the van with the gear."

And the man was practical, at a moment when her thoughts had turned fancifully-exotic.

"Show me," she commanded, regal in victory.

This was not the day she had planned. Maybe better. Certainly stranger. Another precipice.

CARLOS

Marauder's Deathcycle was something of a letdown when White Crane finally saw it. She was expecting something more grandiose, befitting a name like that.

It was only when she got close that she felt the chopper tug at her with wispy, psychic fingers. It was another machine like her flying suit. Powered by will and personal fire.

She studied it more closely. It had started life as a standard two-stroke American engine, what one of her now-former co-workers had once called a rumbling ass-pounder. Exaggerated handle bars for a big man with long arms. Long forks on the front end. Navy blue and chrome everywhere.

White Crane moved close enough to touch it, but kept her hands and feathers clear.

She saw where Marauder could make the machine light up with flames if he pushed himself hard enough. On a dark night, it would look like he was flying low to the ground on a pathway of living fire.

Probably intimidated the hell out of the punks and bikers that were his usual stock-in-trade.

Welcome to the Bush Leagues, punk.

Dead punk.

That man would not be missed. Probably not even by his friends.

The van was a late model panel truck, painted navy blue and with the name and contact information of a furnace repair company on the side. Good disguise. White Crane wondered who would answer if she called the number. She memorized it, just in case.

Carlos pulled a shovel from a strap of tools just inside the back door.

He smiled tentatively at her and waited for instructions.

White Crane considered the clearing where the vehicles were hidden. If nobody found the dead punk Marauder, they could leave the motorcycle here until Itala could come back for it. Or maybe rent a trailer to haul it away.

White Crane gestured for Carlos to precede her back through the underbrush.

"Gracias, señorita," he nodded and skittered past her.

The rain had never gotten to be anything heavier than an annoying mist today, so the blood had mostly pooled, but not drained or been washed away.

White Crane stood to one side as Carlos picked out a spot under some bushes, well away from the trail and the gravel parking lot, and began to dig industriously.

In her head, the argument raged.

Kate was aghast that they had killed three people and were calmly going about the business of hiding the bodies.

Kai Di took a very clinical approach, laying out all the steps of forensic science and how they needed to cover each in order to get away with killing in self-defense. To her, it was only murder in the sense that these bastards had really stood no chance once she got angry. But that was always the risk when picking a fight with a stranger.

White Crane considered what to do with her new henchman. If he was any good at technology, especially if he had been responsible for the motorcycle, she could put him to use.

This had gone beyond simple vengeance a long time ago. Now she had payroll responsibilities.

And Marauder probably hadn't operated in a vacuum. Perhaps Carlos would have connections to other criminals, maybe other super-villains.

It wasn't like there was a manual on how to do this. Or rather, the one she had considered buying on-line looked more like a gag gift for the holidays, and less like a serious tome. Not that she was planning to sit down and write one, one of these days.

Probably.

"Mistress, is done," Carlos called, breaking her concentration.

How far down the rabbit hole had she been? The man had opened up the earth three feet deep, six feet wide, and eight feet tall while she sat and gathered wool.

She gestured for him to accompany her. They quickly grabbed Marauder and carried him to the grave before placing him in it. Joe went next. Tommy was last.

Carlos buried them industriously, crossing himself when he was done.

"Did they have any family?" Kate asked. Both White Crane and Kai Di were surprised at the question, but curious as well.

"Tommy, he had a wife," Carlos replied mournfully. "But Marauder and Joe, no."

"What about you, Carlos?" Kate continued.

"Sí," he said. "Ex-wife, down in the Bay area. Three little ones almost grown up. Esmeralda, she married again and rarely lets me see them."

How did one have a family when you were a criminal, or a hero? Double lives? Triple lives? Maybe more. Easier to be alone, or to have a gang.

Suddenly, she had a gang. But she could use a man like Carlos.

THE OTHER BASE

Back in Emerald, Kate waited in her cute little lavender hatchback for the light to turn green. Carlos had actually pulled over to the side of the road when the light changed on her after he had crossed the intersection. It was either a very elaborate trap, or the man was utterly cowed.

She had seen a whole new layer of shock, back up on the mountain, when she had collapsed the flying suit and stood before the older man in her running tights and silks. She had felt almost naked without some sort of masque.

But he had driven the van into town in a perfectly normal manner. Kate had followed him down from the mountains, onto the interstate, and down into the city and beyond. Good timing, too. Kate was expecting traffic to get stupid busy, pretty much right behind her, all the way. And it had, according to the real-time map on her smart phone.

The light turned green. Kate zipped after the panel truck as he pulled out into traffic. They were in the industrial suburbs south of Emerald, down where the valley opened out along the Green River and warehouses seemed to have been planted in nice, orderly rows, like corn.

Carlos signaled and turned the big truck into a driveway. They were in one of the seedier areas. Old. Post-war architecture and kinda run down.

This was an old concrete and steel box building with two bays on the front and lot of storage to one side.

Apparently, there was a garage door opener, because one of the two doors suddenly wound itself up.

Carlos drove in and continued deep enough for Kate to follow.

Inside, it was a vast cavern, big enough for an overhead crane, with an ancient spur of rails where a couple of railroad cars could be backed up into the building and emptied, covered from the rain.

There was almost nothing here now. Just a workshop with a variety of tools carefully organized. A kitchen area that looked clean. Spare motorcycle parts stacked and organized off to one side. There was even a bivouac area with what looked like four military-surplus cots and a variety of footlockers.

Everything a super-villain gang on a shoestring budget needed to scrape by. It had obviously not been a terribly profitable enterprise. That was where she and Itala had an unfair advantage on most. At least, on anybody without a reasonable licensing deal.

Kate parked and got out. Carlos was standing to one side, halfway between the van and the workshop, hung on twin poles of indecision. The Empress Bird wanted to reinforce her lessons, but Kate could see it wasn't necessary.

"Who else knows about this place?" she asked as she got close enough for the conversation to be personal, instead of yelling across the space.

"Nobody," he said indifferently. The shock seemed to have worn off, leaving a dull numbness.

It was a feeling she knew well.

"Well, no," he continued. "Boss rented from someone big. Another one like you."

"Like me?" she asked, confused.

Kate could not wait for Itala to get back. She was operating too much in the dark here.

"Si," Carlos agreed. "Uhm…the Northern Dragon King. Sí. El Jefe."

Northern Dragon King. That was a name that had resonance on the internet and her research. He was one of the first tier of super-villains, tangling mostly with the biggest heroes: Provost, Starchild, and Wudan. That was a connection worth exploring later, when she needed help tracking down Golden Tiger.

Who could have imagined that the criminal underworld was so robust and interconnected?

"How soon until Marauder is missed?" Kate asked seriously.

"Marauder no be missed, mistress," Carlos replied. "No by anyone. But we have lease through end of the year. I handle all the paperwork for the boss. Is good."

If this man did book-keeping, too, she was absolutely keeping him. Even after she put away the cowl and went straight.

"Then I can claim all this for myself?" she thought out loud.

"Sí, jefe," he agreed. "Is all yours. Please no kill me."

She turned to study his face.

Fear. Bone-deep fear that she had saved him just long enough to show her the base.

She was not a black widow spider.

"Carlos, listen to me," she commanded, hearing the tones of The Empress take control.

He stopped shivering. Or maybe shivered a little less.

"Yes, ma'am," he murmured.

"I have no plans to kill you, Carlos," she said clearly. "You'll do for me what you did for him. Good henchmen are incredibly hard to find."

At least, they were in all the comic books she had consulted. Villains always had to make do with the bottom of the barrel, plus one chief of staff type who was either found to be incompetent, compromised and blackmailed, or trying to take over himself. At least, those tropes were the most common.

Probably just human nature writ large.

"Oh," he said, suddenly at a loss. "Okay."

Seriously, was he just expecting to die here?

"All this will stay here for now," Kate decided. "I have an assistant, a sidekick, who will be back from her current mission in a few days. You will take orders from her like you do me."

"Okay," he said. "The pretty blond girl?"

So, the group had been spying on them for a while. Kate wondered how long they had been there, waiting for the right moment to strike. Itala being gone would have been a golden opportunity. Or so they had thought.

Morons.

"Yes, Carlos," Kate said. "Her. She can kick your ass almost as easily as I could."

"Is good, boss," Carlos agreed. "You ride motorcycle, or should I look to sell it off when we get it back?"

And there, right there, was the basis of the saying *no honor among thieves*. Carlos was wasting no time mourning his comrades. Or maybe, he would do it when she wasn't around. Certainly, she had taken over as his pack alpha. Maybe he just needed a strong personality to direct him.

She had known people like that. Give them a concrete task, and they worked miracles. Leave them alone, and they would flounder their way into crime and mischief. Many did.

"Do you have any money?" she asked

"A leetle," he replied evasively. "Boss was burning everything on the expectation of a big payday when they sold your suit off."

That made sense. Marauder didn't strike her as the type who was deep into planning and analysis, especially from what Carlos was saying.

Kate pulled money from one of the side pockets on her running tights.

"Here's one hundred bucks," she commanded. "Treat yourself for dinner, get some rest, and tomorrow, start cataloging everything here. We'll be back in three days and decide what to keep, what to sell, and what to move to my base. And maybe, we'll move everything here instead. Be flexible."

"Sí, jefe," Carlos grinned as he took the wad of bills. "Mostly done anyway. Not long to fix."

Kate nodded and walked back to her car. Carlos followed enough to pop open the garage door from the van and watch her with a slight wave as she backed out and turned around.

Hell, she was turning into a real super-villain at this rate.

ITALA RETURNS

Kate waited on pins and needles.

She had offered to pick Itala up at the airport, but her friend wanted to get to the workspace before they talked. So Kate had waited, patiently.

Sort of patiently. Maybe.

She had considered running the obstacle course again, or hitting the weight machines to work on her legs. In the end, she settled for something midway between yoga and meditation.

A key in the lock brought her back to the present. The door opened, closed, locked.

"You here?" Itala yelled into the hollow space.

"In back," Kate yelled back.

"Good. Stay there. I want to show you a surprise."

It had already been a bad week for surprises. What was one more? Kate untangled her limbs and stood up, more or less relaxed. She couldn't see the front of the space from her spot on the mats next to the kitchenette. She waited.

Shadows moving were the only thing to indicate Itala's approach. The woman moved in total silence today.

And then she turned the corner. At least it looked like her. It was the right height, the right silhouette, the right motion.

And it was a female, but it was in a costume.

Navy blue bodysuit with a crimson belt and belt pouches. Matching, heavy-duty, red leather boots with twenty rings, and oversized gloves, the kind with a flare at the wrist that went almost halfway up the forearm. Old school.

A single crimson stripe, about as wide as Kate' palm, from the woman's left knee to almost the top of her left shoulder, straight up and over her left breast.

In one hand, she held a black quarterstaff that looked like graphite that had been dipped about a third of its length in fresh blood.

The face was hidden behind a mask that covered her neck all the way around, like a balaclava, and came up over her ears and across her forehead, with a mesh of some sort over her eyes and fabric across her nose that left her mouth uncovered. The top was open, letting her blond hair puff up and over.

The hair gave it away. For a moment, Kate had been afraid that one of the local costumed heroes had heard about what she had done to Marauder and had tracked her down here.

"Like it?" Itala asked with an impish grin.

"Love it," Kate replied, stepping closer to engulf her friend in a hug. "I'm pretty sure I can still top it with my news, but it will be a lot closer."

"Really?" Itala asked sarcastically. "Better than this?"

"I think so," Kate said. "Better than…what do you call yourself?"

"I am *Redlance*," Itala announced grandly. "Crimson Ji. Villainess extraordinaire. What have *you* done to top that in the two weeks I've been gone?"

"Sit down. This might take a while," Kate smiled and gestured to the table. "Let me tell you about a man named Carlos, and a motorcycle."

鶴

In the end, Kate had to acquiesce when Itala demanded that they go retrieve the Deathcycle before they did anything else. She certainly couldn't drive it. At least, not yet.

That was why she had hired a wheelman in the first place. Once upon an eternity ago, when she was just looking for a little help.

And Itala looked like a child, perched atop a bike obviously meant for a man a foot and a half taller. But as Kate followed her back into town, she had to admit that Itala handled it like a well-trained horse.

Maybe they should keep it, repaint it, and turn it into Redlance's transport. White Crane obviously could fly all by herself.

Weird.

But no weirder than waking up one morning, deciding to put on a super-cowl, and seek a bloody revenge on a total stranger.

Kate pulled into the parking lot of the dingy warehouse where Marauder's gang had hung out first, unsure what to expect. Itala was following, with her nasty stick handy, just in case.

It didn't matter.

Carlos had heard the bike from more than a block out, if he already had time to open the office door and peek out at them.

She could see the relief on his face as he recognized the Deathcycle, and the woman riding it, and Kate in the lavender hatchback.

Had he thought that Marauder had dug his way out of a grave and come back to get him?

Of course, nobody ever really died in comic books. How often was that the truth when dealing with Modern Gods?

What were the limits to power?

The garage door rolled up invitingly. Kate rolled in and looked around, halfway prepared to run someone over if she had to, to keep her secret.

When had she gotten so bloodthirsty? That wasn't her.

No, that was The Empress Bird talking. And The White Crane backing her up.

Still, the place was empty.

Carlos came out of the front office and waved. Itala rumbled loudly into the space as well and shut the bike down to coast into place.

Kate was struck by the innards of the warehouse. Before, it had been spare and relatively clean. Now, she could see how messy the other three men had lived, because Carlos had apparently done nothing but clean and organize for three days.

It showed.

She got out of her car and smiled to put him at ease.

What must his last three days have been like, waiting to see what his own fate was going to be?

"Good morning, mistress," Carlos smiled and corrected himself. "Mistresses."

Apparently, he had already settled into his place in the pack. That was good, too. Itala shouldn't have to put him there forcibly. Not that she couldn't.

Kate pushed White Crane and The Empress back in her mind. She needed Carlos to want to work for her, as opposed to fearing her rage. She needed to work to control that over-arching rage, she was finding.

"Carlos, this is Itala," she introduced them. "In costume, I am The White Crane, and she is Redlance."

Carlos nodded to Itala as she dismounted, snapped the kickstand and looked up at him. She bristled at the man for about a half second, until she apparently realized that he really was no threat. Especially if there were no police waiting for them.

Another one that was apparently in for a pound.

"Mistress Redlance," Carlos semi-bowed.

He looked up and smiled at both of them.

"Should I rebuild the Deathcycle so it fits you better?" he asked earnestly.

Itala was taken back. Kate had rarely seen that look of surprise on the Frenchwoman's face. It felt good.

"Can you?" Itala asked.

"Sí, is easy," the man smiled broadly. "I haff many of the original parts. They fit you better. Move the grips in, lower the frame, adjust the clutch and transmission for a lighter load. Much better. Do you need it to make flames?"

Kate watched Itala's face go slack. She hadn't shared her theory on the Deathcycle's special effects, nor on her thoughts as to how a human might possibly be transformed to use them.

That would make a lovely present later, or a secret she took to her grave.

She would not hurt Itala.

"Not for now," Kate stepped in. "But keep it, just in case."

"Is good," Carlos grinned.

He stepped back and studied Itala closely.

Kate hadn't been able to convince her otherwise, so Itala was wearing the Redlance costume under a cute, short, black leather jacket, with the cowl pulled down around her neck like a scarf. The Lance itself separated into two pieces with a locked screw setup, and was in something Itala had called a rifle holster on the left side of the bike.

He blushed suddenly and turned to Kate in grave seriousness.

"I'm sorry," he said. "I no mean to stare. Need to figure out measurements. We keeping the base, boss?"

Kate turned to Itala, caught the faintest hint of a blush on the smaller woman's face at being stared at by a man who looked old enough to be her father.

"Thoughts?" Kate asked.

Itala walked around in a small circle, eyes in the air.

"You could probably fly inside, if you were careful," she observed.

"I thought of that," Kate replied.

Carlos fell utterly silent and watched. His hands, down at his sides, were making some strange motion that took Kate a second to identify. He was unconsciously dismantling the bike and changing out parts while he listened to them plan.

"And it's not in your name, in case we need to hide better," Itala continued.

"Yes," Kate agreed.

"And the lease is paid?" Itala turned to Carlos.

"Sí," he nodded. "Through the end of the year."

Itala turned to Kate with a look as serious as doom.

"When do we start Phase II?"

There it was.

Another precipice.

Three days ago, she had killed a man. Several men. Self-defense, sure, but she could have just flown away. White Crane always had that option.

Not that the thought had crossed her mind at the time. In the moment, White Crane had transformed into The Empress Bird and demanded death.

In the three days since, she had wrestled with her conscience.

Westerners, Christian Anglos, frequently were raised with the concept of over-arching guilt. Killing was supposed to be wrong. Kate had those twinges.

Kai Di Peng was sixth-generation pure Cantonese, blood and culture, that just happened to be raised in America instead of the mother country. Marauder had been sexually assaulting her, planning to rape and kill her, when she kicked him to death.

She was reminded of the old Texas legal defense. *"Yer Honor, he needed killin'."*

Marauder had it coming.

Civilization just might be coming apart, if you listened to the folks on the Sunday morning talk shows go on about crime and bad behavior. Certainly, Kai Di Peng, instead of accepting that Miranda Devereux had died in the act of committing a crime, was intent on going after the man who had killed her, who had the imprimatur of law on his side, vigilante that he might be.

It was going to be an eye for an eye.

"Phase two, boss?" Carlos asked, lost.

"We're going to Angel City this summer, Carlos," White Crane replied. "We're going to kill a man much like Marauder."

"Sí?"

"Sí," Itala chimed in.

"Hokay," he agreed. "You want trade hide-outs? I know a guy in Ramona. Outside Angel City. Maybe a little too barrio for nice, white girls, like you. But *muy* safe. They come up here for a while."

Nice, white girls? Probably close enough for a man who was, at most, one generation removed from Latin America.

White Crane turned to Redlance. A moment of silent negotiation covered all the bases.

When had the two of them gotten that close, mentally?

She turned back to Carlos.

"We need two weeks to get everything packed and ready, Carlos," she decided. "Then we'll need a car trailer, a bike trailer, and a second box truck to haul our stuff. You figure out how much it will cost and let me know."

"Got it, boss," he said, turning away from them and already apparently cataloging the warehouse for shipment. Kate wondered who had really been the brains of Marauder's gang.

He turned back just as suddenly.

"I need your phone numbers," he said.

"Right," Kate said, reaching for her phone.

Itala's hand stopped her.

"No," Redlance said, fierceness under Itala's soft scowl.

"No?"

"No, you keep your phone, but we'll all three have burner phones that are secured. In three days. Feds might already know your number."

Kate turned a quizzical eye on her friend. A light bulb went on.

"Black sheep?"

"Black sheep."

"Okay," Kate said. "Then there's only one task left to handle."

She smiled at Itala.

This would be the last major step before they set out to kill a man.

FATHER

Sunday night. Approaching seven PM. Kate hadn't always been able to make it to dinner at her parent's house, but this was one she could not miss.

She parked her hatchback half a block up, amidst all the other yuppie cars, and got out. Itala was slower, until Kate peeked in the window.

"Is this really necessary?" Itala asked plaintively through the glass.

"Yes," Kai Di commanded. She could feel White Crane standing in the background of her mind, fierce and proud. "Yes, it is."

"Fine."

Itala opened her door and stood up. Tonight, she was wearing a long skirt and a flowing, loose top, both in a rich emerald. Her hair even managed to be well-controlled this evening, rather than the crazed mess it frequently was. If she looked close enough, Kate could even see hints of makeup on the woman.

Not much. Lips slightly more red. Greens and blues above the eyes. Possibly some blush.

Itala was making a statement about finally being a grown woman, rather than a tom-boy, if Kate had to guess.

Kate had chosen to make her own statement. Tight leggings in dove gray tucked into her favorite boots, the ones with the crane bangle still on the ankle. Blood-red silk sleeveless tunic that almost covered her bum, belted and tight enough to show off her new muscles. Black shiny mock-turtleneck that made her arms look even more powerful.

In the recent past, dinners with the parents had been an affair where she dressed in baggy layers, trying to look as much like the girl she used to be as possible. They probably suspected that Kate had put on weight and was trying to hide a muffin-top.

They would be right about the weight, and wrong about the location.

She had left her own long, black hair down tonight. A slight breeze ruffled it. The fading sun made it glow.

She felt like a Modern God.

Kate took a moment to eye Itala as they walked, making sure everything was in place and gorgeous. The Frenchwoman wasn't here as a girlfriend, but as a dear friend who was becoming family. They needed to understand that.

They would understand *guanxi*. They lived it.

Kate took a deep breath and knocked.

Wei De opened the door quickly.

Kai Di stepped close and hugged him intensely. After a moment, he let his arms wrap around his daughter and return the hug.

She leaned back and watched his eyes grow big. But he said nothing.

Itala stepped close as well.

He was less surprised this time, partly because Itala's transformation wasn't as severe, partly because he was expecting something. But it was there in his eyes.

"After dinner," Wei De commanded serenely.

"After dinner," Kai Di agreed.

鶴

Father's study hadn't changed, Kate noticed. But then, it hadn't changed at any point in her exceptional memory.

Dinner had been proper, with Yi Wen asking about their lives and prospects for boyfriends, none too subtly. Mu Ren had outdone herself with the food. It was a proper reminder of Kai Di's childhood in this home. Father had remained stern and taciturn, as befit the modern Chinese Patriarch.

But now they were upstairs, Father, Kai Di, and Itala, the good brandies in hand. The smell of the expensive alcohol blended well with the jasmine and sweet oils in the background, nestled deep in the cloth.

Father eyed them both for several seconds, as if reading their minds and their souls.

He smiled abruptly.

"Both of you, it seems," he began.

Kate felt her face go slack for just the slightest second, but Father just grinned.

Itala suppressed a sputter, mostly.

"Oh, no," he continued. "Not that. Although I see hints of it as well."

He swirled the caramel liquor and took a sip.

"I see you have *both* decided to become hunters."

"How can you tell?" Itala asked bluntly.

She did everything fairly bluntly, except when negotiating.

"Kai Di has developed muscles no woman would normally possess," Wei De observed. "You, too, other daughter, although not as much. Still, far more than you had in the winter."

"And from that you conclude?" Kai Di inquired quietly.

"You have decided to take up the cowl," he smiled warmly. "As we discussed, so long ago. Your enemy is a hero in a mask. You will become villains to fight him. It is a proper motif, a well-balanced tao. Kai Di has discovered a bio-chemical breakthrough, but it will only work somewhat for you, Itala, for reasons we all understand."

"How would you understand, Father?" Itala asked. There was just a hint of uncertainty under her voice now.

Wei De smiled at the two woman and held out his left hand, palm up.

A small flame came into being from nothingness. It quickly transformed into a very tiny fire pixie with big eyes and a larger mouth. It grinned at both women for a moment, winked, and then disappeared in a flash of light.

Itala gasped. She turned to Kai Di, wordless.

"Yes," Kai Di agreed. She had never seen him do anything of the sort, but she was not that surprised. "Father as well."

The room fell heavily silent.

"What will you need?" Father probed.

Kai Di called on the flexibility of Kate, the firmness of White Crane, the power of The Empress Bird to support her.

"Only your blessing, Father," she said. "We will depart for Angel City in a few days, and not return until we are successful."

Wei De nodded gravely at both women.

"Go then, with my blessing, daughters," he intoned, very much the Patriarch on his throne.

Kai Di expected a bell to toll mysteriously in the background. It always did in the movies.

"I would greatly appreciate that man's head on a stake," Wei De continued. "Jean-Michel would as well, although he would never ask for it."

"That is the plan, Father," Kai Di replied. "That is the plan."

PART III: CITY OF ANGELS

鶴

RAMONA

Brown.

Summer in Angel City was brown. Kate could think of no better way to describe it.

The hillsides on the north and east of her were ten thousand shades of brown. The sky was another dozen more. At least it was breathable, these days. She had seen pictures from the early Seventies, when the smog was so thick that the mountains disappeared on a bad day. And heard stories from the early Nineties, when the haze was still thick enough to be apparent on a bad day.

Already, she missed Emerald.

At least a few Modern Gods, and some seriously brilliant humans, had turned their talents to making SoCal a better place. In her lifetime, it might be green again.

Of course, they would still have to find a way to get rid of half the people in order to make the freeways passable. And no way in hell would she trust these folks with flying cars, until someone worked out a safe auto-pilot that couldn't be overridden. When someone did, he'd be the next tech zillionaire.

Until then, Kate let Itala drive the rental van.

Carlos was immediately in front of them in the blue truck, hauling the modified Deathcycle on a trailer under a tarp, while they had Kate's hatchback on a trailer.

It was slow going, but at least they were off the freeways and down on the side streets of Ramona.

Mr. Loh was perched carefully on the dash, supervising their every move and occasionally adding his running commentary on other drivers to go with Itala's.

On the one hand, Kate was struck by the overall poverty of the neighborhood they were in. But there were no boarded-up store-fronts, and lots of people going places, mostly on foot, or driving ancient cars, sometimes older than their drivers.

And there were smiles on the faces she saw.

Carlos pulled into a parking lot in front of what looked like it had been some sort of factory, light industrial, half a century ago. There were still faded advertisements for cigarettes nobody even remembered these days, twenty feet tall, on the near bricks, slowly bleaching out under the California sun.

Carlos honked twice and then climbed down from the rig.

Itala pulled alongside and they waited. Kate had locked her door, but Itala had the charged end of her lance in one hand, out of sight. She recognized the kind of neighborhood, apparently.

After a few moments, a woman emerged from a side door of the building. The newcomer took a moment to study the two vehicles, and then called something back in through the half-open door.

Moments later, she emerged into the sunshine.

"Carlos?" she called. "Is that you?"

"Sí, Tori," Kate heard him yell back. "Is good to see you."

The woman, Tori, took a moment to study Itala and Kate in the other truck.

"What happened to that loser?" she asked Carlos as she walked close enough to talk instead of yell.

"Traded up," Carlos replied with a laugh.

Itala opened her door suddenly and got out, leaving the stick behind, for now, so Kate did the same, leaving Mr. Loh to guard the van.

Up close, Tori was short and pudgy, barely five feet tall and kinda roundish. She reminded Kate of the kind of method actor you would get from Central Casting if you asked for a middle-aged Mexican peasant woman, with the first strands of gray in her otherwise black hair, and crow's feet around smiling eyes.

She smelled like garlic and freshly-baked bread.

As Kate approached, Tori held up a hand.

"No names," she commanded, before pointing a thumb at Carlos. "Him I know. Him I will work through if you need anything. We've cleaned everything. Keys are on the desk, along with my phone number."

Tori stopped to check first Kate, and then Itala, top to bottom. It was a professional appraisal. She turned back to Carlos.

"Sí, muchacho," she said to him before she smiled at all of them and walked to an ancient green sedan parked a little ways up the street. Two men emerged from an opening garage door and ambled over to the car. Everyone piled in and the car rumbled down the road in a fog of black diesel fumes.

Kate looked closely at Carlos. He blushed.

"Friend of my first ex-wife," he half-explained.

Itala had refrained from commenting, and headed towards the open door.

Kate followed.

They had made it this far. They had a hideout, and now they just needed a plan.

After all, it wasn't like they could just call the man and invite him to his own execution.

Inside, they found an office, where the original business had managed shipping and receiving. Two desks behind a four-foot-tall wood counter with stains from old glasses and burns from cigarettes. The walls were mostly blank, except for one Motivational poster that simply said "*There is a difference between wanting and committing.*"

Someone had taken a red magic marker and added "*Fifteen to life.*" underneath that.

Through the inside door was the factory floor. The space beyond was vast and empty.

White Crane automatically looked up. The ceiling was fifty feet away, with a row of rafters ten feet below that like ribs on a giant whale.

Would that make her Jonah?

At least there were hollow gaps up there. That would be useful practice, climbing up and slaloming through the spaces at speed. Risky, but necessary.

The rest of the volume was vacant. There was a kitchen against the office wall behind her when she turned around. Three garage doors, plus space where half a dozen more could have been put in. A machine shop with one of those old-fashioned lifts where you grabbed a chain and pulled hard, plus a pit to get under a truck while working on it.

Carlos smiled a mile wide.

"I build in a small apartment for you there," he said, pointing to the corner by the bathrooms and then the opposite corner. "I put me in a room over in the far corner. We *bueno*."

Kate nodded. It felt a little like sleep-walking. She had never really considered how much effort there must be to being a villain. The logistics alone were confusing her.

Fortunately, both Itala and Carlos had experience at this sort of thing.

Still, weird.

"Kate?" Itala called from the office.

Kate walked back in there and saw Itala holding an oversized, ornate, linen envelope in one hand. *The White Crane* was hand-written on the front in metallic gold ink.

Kate took the envelope and turned it over. It had been sealed with wax and marked with a proper Chinese chop. She could make out a stylized dragon, the western kind with great wings, rather than the wingless Chinese *loong*. The Mandarin characters for Northern Dragon King, or Dragon Emperor, were worked into the design, as well.

She peeled the wax carefully, saving it so she could send a picture to Wei De later and ask him to do some research.

Inside was single piece of paper, the size of a wedding invitation and made from very heavy stock. It had a time printed on it, five thirty in the morning tomorrow, a set of coordinates, and his signature chop again, this time dipped in vermillion ink.

Seriously? Vermillion?

Kate punched the coordinate numbers into her phone and let it map the place.

"Carlos, do you know where this is?" she asked after it settled.

He studied the map closely for a few moments and then grinned.

"Sí," he said. "Prado. Chino Creek Park. Been there."

Carlos touched the map just enough to move it a little. A new icon appeared just northeast of the park. The Chino Residence Hall, a medium security women's prison.

Well, that was a subtle message.

"Carlos," White Crane came to the fore. "You'll ride with me in the hatchback tomorrow morning. We need to think about a low-profile sedan with tinted windows for you. Cheap, old, but runs well, so I can get close and get into costume. But that's later."

She turned to Itala.

"You'll come in on the bike?" she asked. "What do we call it? *Deathcycle* is so tacky."

"*Cheval,*" Itala grinned savagely at her. "Chevalier needs a warhorse to ride into battle and joust, no?"

"*Cheval,* it is," Kate agreed. "Sleeping bags and cots tonight. Up early. Tomorrow, we'll start to build the place out, if everything goes well with Northern Dragon King."

鶴

White Crane spent the evening watching videos on her phone with the headphones on. About two weeks ago, Northern Dragon King had attempted to rob a precious metals storage vault downtown by strong-arming the place.

Alarms had gone off.

Starchild had been close enough to get to the scene before the Dragon and his fashion-matched gang got anywhere significant.

Apparently, the whole setup had been a trap to try to capture the woman who passed herself off as an alien hero sent to Earth to protect us from villains and other aliens.

Five minutes of bad dialogue and collateral damage later, the Dragon had armed a super-bomb of some sort, with hostages tied up close by, and fled with his crew when Starchild had to choose between the hostages and the criminals.

Another Thursday in Angel City.

Kate flipped to a video website and watched as the man, who called himself the Northern Dragon King, turned from a human into a giant, flying lizard with fire-breath. He wore a simple mask, but she had no doubt the man was Chinese. Probably ABC, American Born Chinese, because if he had been in China, he would have either been killed young, or turned himself into a major warlord.

And it wasn't like his name left any questions about his ego, either, portraying himself as one of the deities from classical Chinese literature.

He would expect *guanxi.* That might be his right, being one of the biggest super-villains out there, and one who routinely fought with the biggest heroes.

Plus, he was providing the warehouse they were using. Granted, it had been paid for, but the lease was technically in the name of a dead man.

Whatever.

If he was truly Chinese, or even ABC, he was going to be in for a surprise when he decided to lord it over The White Crane or The Empress Bird, to say nothing of Dr. Kai Di Peng.

Try me.

THE NORTHERN DRAGON KING

False dawn peeked over the hills to the east.

White Crane had her new phone with her, in a pocket that was either inside the flying suit, or outside, depending on her mental needs. She still wasn't sure how the suit managed it, but it did. Good enough.

She had left Carlos across the valley, safe on the other side of the creek, parked outside a small airfield that apparently served middle-aged men with remote-controlled airplanes. It was so quiet as to be abandoned this morning, which made it a useful place for him to wait. Plus, nobody would be driving by in a car on the way to this meeting.

White Crane couldn't do anything about giant, flying dragons, except hope he arrived in a limousine this morning.

The morning was already warm, to a girl that was used to flying in Emerald in a wet spring. The air this far south was dry and gritty. She found herself wanting to shower more frequently than daily, just to get the grime off.

Itala assured her that the feeling would go away in a few days.

White Crane couldn't decide what was worse, being dirty, or not caring.

She brought her focus back to the present with a harsh word to her subconscious.

There was nobody in the air this morning. Well, there was a news helicopter well southwest of her, out over some Orange County freeway where there was a faint pillar of smoke, but she was on the other side of the hills from all that commotion and staying low. Hopefully, if anyone had radar on, she looked like an eagle.

No, she was too far south. Condor.

Two vehicles were pulling into the parking lot, below her and to one side. Several men piled out of an oversized, blacked-out, black SUV and took up positions guarding an identical vehicle behind it. Most of them had guns.

She was more concerned about the one guy who didn't. He was dressed in a bright red bodysuit, trimmed in black. His face was a blank mask of cloth, with two black ram horns coming out of his temples.

News reports called him *Devilback*. One of the Dragon's chief henchmen.

White Crane was clear of the trees, coming in out of the northeast so she was not coming at them out of the sun. She could hear *Cheval* rumbling angrily as the bike approached.

She circled the parking lot once, looking for someone hiding in ambush. Marauder had succeeded in exactly one task. He had taught her to be more paranoid when flying.

This park was unlike the Cascades. There was almost no brush at ground level.

White Crane landed as Redlance drove into the lot and circled around behind her. Itala had killed the engine and coasted in with nothing more than the crunch of gravel, before she dropped the kickstand and dismounted.

White Crane didn't have to look back to identify the sound of the Redlance snapping together and resting on the ground. Her friend, her backup, her partner was about five feet behind her and about the same to her left, in case something went wrong.

She counted four men with guns, and one with a costume. The Empress Bird growled, just below the surface of her mind, but that was in response to any man right now, rather than these.

The rear door of the second vehicle opened.

A man emerged, dressed in an honest-to-goodness costume from the Ming dynasty, ankle-length black robes with extra-long, baggy sleeves and a belt. On his chest, an image had been embroidered showing two white cranes flying. It was from a famous portrait of a Ming Dynasty minister. Kai Di remembered the picture, but couldn't place a name to it without looking it up later.

If it mattered. She probably would, anyway, but more out of curiosity than need.

The second man to emerge was the one she was concerned with.

He also wore traditional Ming robes, but these were gold and trimmed in red. He was a big man, especially for being Chinese. White Crane guessed he was a shade over six feet tall, and lanky, but with muscles.

His build was similar to her own, she decided after a moment. Not the hulking brute that some men achieved with steroids and repetitions, but a long strength. Useful in a man who could turn himself into a dragon the size of a semi-truck and trailer.

"You really are a white crane," the Northern Dragon King observed quietly with a touch of surprise. He said it in Mandarin, apparently unconsciously, maybe to himself.

"No," she replied, also in accentless Mandarin. "I am *The* White Crane."

He seemed taken aback for a moment, as did his minister, but both men smiled quickly.

"And your associate?" the Dragon King continued smoothly. He had a rich baritone voice, obviously used to dominating conversations.

He would have been awesome as a radio DJ for a nighttime jazz station. She wondered what he did in his secret identity, if he had one.

"Hóng Jì," Itala answered immediately in Mandarin as well, before switching to English with a fierce, French lilt. "Redlance."

"I see."

The distance between them and the men was still more than twenty feet, but the Dragon King did something that made it feel more intimate.

It took her a second to recognize that it was simply the man's raw charisma being unleashed. It wasn't just looks, although he was very good looking, either a mature thirty-five or a very-well preserved fifty.

No, his entire body exuded charm and confidence. It almost felt like this was one of his powers, projecting his dominance, his surety, his charisma over the space like a mist.

White Crane felt herself responding to him like a woman would to a man. It was a new experience, since most men she had ever known had failed to match up to her own Father, or fathers.

This Northern Dragon King fellow just might.

"A man named Carlos works for you now," he continued in Mandarin after a second. It was a question, even if he didn't phrase it as such.

"He does," White Crane agreed. That much. Nothing more.

If the dragon was Chinese, even ABC, he shouldn't expect much detail from her. Even if he was a man addressing a woman.

Reticence was a cultural thing.

They studied each other across an invisible chess board for several seconds.

"And that used to be Marauder's Deathcycle," he continued with a nod. "I recognize the sound of the engine."

"Past tense," Redlance agreed sweetly.

White Crane fought to keep a smile from her face. A Chinese man, even American-raised, would not be used to Chinese women who failed to be properly subservient. Especially to someone who styled himself after one of the great Gods of Chinese history and literature.

Tough luck, bubbles. Mandarin makes you a northerner. Down south, we consider your kind steppe barbarians.

She would never say that out loud, but the attitude was high in her thoughts. That Itala could pass herself off in Mandarin was just a bonus, since the tiny, blond Frenchwoman was subservient to no one.

Apparently, Northern Dragon King was satisfied that he would get no greater answer.

"Angel City is mine," he said firmly.

White Crane felt the full force of the man's charm and charisma behind those words. It was almost solid. She would need to research this man to see if his other powers included doing to women the sorts of things he was doing to her.

Or if it was just her.

"We will only be here long enough to kill a man," she answered coldly.

Suddenly, several of the guns were pointed at her and Redlance.

White Crane smiled coldly.

"Not one of yours," she continued. "I want Golden Tiger."

The Dragon King smiled paternally at her.

"He's bush league," the man announced, identifying himself with the Americanism. "Why him?"

White Crane considered several answers. Most of them gave away too much. If she let this man learn who she really was under her mask, she might never escape his clutches.

She had no plans to grow old as a super-villain, even if a few chose to.

"The Scarlet Titan," she said finally.

She watched the man nod knowingly and study both of them closer.

"She was one of mine," he purred.

Miranda worked for this man?

Kai Di came to the fore at that point, pointing out strange little comments by her best friend, and observations that made more sense in that context.

The joys of a near-photographic memory.

White Crane was impressed by the association with the Northern Dragon King, but not overly so.

"What is your connection to her?" he continued.

Again, any word might give away too much. There was, however, one word this man would understand. It would encompass everything nicely while retaining her secrets.

"*Guanxi,*" she replied.

Ties of familial duty. They could reach across cultures, generations, continents. It could connect a brilliant, young, research chemist on a mad revenge quest with a small-time jewel thief from France. It could have them travel two thousand miles from the lovely, green northwest to the arid, semi-desert hells of southern California. It could bring her to a park in the middle of nowhere, talking to one of the biggest super-villains on the west coast as the sun was rising.

Moments of silence passed.

"I see," he said finally, waving his hands at his men like a conductor. The guns were pointed elsewhere again. "I remember a quote I read once. Something along the lines of this: *A story about revenge is usually just a story about forgiveness, redemption, or perhaps the futility of revenge.*"

"That would be for the squeamish," White Crane responded with a challenge in her tone.

"Have you ever killed anyone, girl?" he answered back. It was soft, quiet, and yet razor sharp.

The Empress Bird smiled wickedly.

If she had Wei De's powers and gift, she could call forth an illusionary image of that moment, the sound of crunching bone, the smell of freshly-shed blood, like copper in the air.

Her voice had to tell the tale instead.

"Marauder won't be back for his bike," she observed, just as sharp.

"And how will you kill this man, this Golden Tiger?"

She could see the power of the dragon lurking in the background. Even from this distance, she could tell that his eyes had changed, had gone from circles to slits for pupils.

White Crane wondered how close to the surface the great wyrm might be. The Empress Bird was close enough to color her thoughts.

Maybe all the Modern Gods went mad, eventually. She could imagine the pressures, the potential, the power itself overcoming anyone's will. There were times it threatened to drown her. She had to keep a tight rein on it.

She suspected that many of her kind didn't bother. It would explain their behavior better.

"We've not been here a whole day, *Ao Shun*," she shrugged lightly, using the name of the Dragon of the Northern Sea from the ancient tales.

She heard the mandarin standing next to the dragon draw in his breath with a soft hiss. Apparently, he knew the tales, as well.

You aren't dealing with ignorant Anglos today, boys.

"It might be fitting," the dragon growled. "If that man died on that same street, trying to stop another woman from robbing that same armored car, full of someone else's money."

White Crane considered the man, the offer, the apparent sincerity in the voice.

On the one hand, it would cut short months of surveillance and planning to find the man, track him, ambush him.

On the other hand…

"At what cost, *Ao Shun*?"

The man smiled. It was a triumphant, predatory face. On most men, it would probably look petty and sneering. Here, he truly looked the part of a dragon king.

"*Guanxi*, White Crane," he replied.

AT WHAT COST

Kate made sure to sit very still on her cot as Itala raged and stomped in the open space of the warehouse. She had never seen the woman so angry.

"Do you have any idea what that man might demand?" Itala growled as she finally came to a halt, standing squarely in front of Kate, nearly close enough to reach out and touch.

Kate had put away the flying suit and was sitting in her running tights and top. She really needed to buy a color-coordinated outfit for under the white wings. Maybe with a masque of some sort.

But right now, she needed to pay attention. Better attention.

Itala had at least lowered her mask, leaving her petite, angular body distracting, but with what looked like a scarf around her neck.

Again, Kate fought to bring her attention back to Itala's face.

The woman was just flat mad. Angry. Stomping.

"*Guanxi*," Kate replied calmly, quietly. It was like talking to a spooked horse or an angry cat.

"Ha!" Itala stomped some more.

Carlos was trying to pretend he was invisible, seated on a chair he had pulled from the office last night. At least he was out of the line of fire. Mr. Loh was hiding under a shelf in the corner.

"*Guanxi* means favors, Itala," Kate continued. "There is a scale of appropriate behavior involved."

"He's going to help us kill a man," Itala countered. "Will we help him kill someone else?"

"We might," Kate replied. "That would zero the ledger book. It might be preferable."

"To?"

"To him asking for little things that build up over time," Kate said. "To drawing us so deep into his web that we might never escape."

"What if he wants more?" Itala shifted the conversation abruptly. "I saw the way he watched you. What if he demands you?"

Itala took a half step forward. That put her in reach to poke Kate in the sternum with one hard finger. It hurt, just a little. Mostly surprise.

Kate was taken aback. She had been concentrating on the words and verbally fencing with the man. Had he been staring at her body?

She felt White Crane give a tiny thrill at the attention. The Northern Dragon King might be a worthy consideration.

"Well?" Itala demanded.

Kate snapped back to the present.

"Any man can ask. Any woman for that matter," Kate answered hotly. "That doesn't mean he gets to require anything. I make that decision."

"Good," Itala stepped back. "Make sure you know what you're doing before you do anything stupid."

Before Kate could answer, Itala turned and stomped off in the direction of the bathroom. The door slammed and Kate heard the shower start up.

What?

She turned to Carlos, but he was white-faced and trying to pretend he was tiny and invisible.

He did offer a shrug, but his eyes stayed huge as he got up and moved in the direction of his workshop. Apparently, he thought the storm was over.

At least over enough that he could work on *Cheval* without flinching. Much.

Even Mr. Loh was staying out of sight.

Kate tried to think of something useful to say or do.

Itala's rage had been like a rabbit suddenly growling and hissing. She knew the Frenchwoman had it in her, but had never seen it aimed in a friendly direction.

Kate wasn't sure how to handle it.

Retreat sounded like a good idea. Let Itala have a shower and get clean and composed. There had been no time to get groceries, so they would need to head out for breakfast at some point, unless they grazed on things bought for the road.

Kate decided to do some shopping. Then she realized that anything she wanted to purchase would be delivered to Emerald, instead of Angel City.

She needed a post office box or something down here.

How did villains do it? Did they have a chain of drop points, like they did hideouts and hidden bases? At least she had cash. A dance studio store or outdoor outfitter would probably have enough of what she needed, and she could always ask Carlos to ask Tori for the rest.

More *guanxi*.

It was interesting how quickly she could fall into the patterns of favors and horse-trading in a way that transcended Chinese culture. You had needs, and either provided services or paid cash, and other people made things happen.

What would *Ao Shun* demand for his help?

A tiny part of her experienced a jolt that the man might find her attractive enough to make those kinds of demands. She had always expected that her parents would eventually try to find her a proper husband from one of the correct clans and families back home, or, more likely, one of their pureblood but Americanized cousins.

How would they feel about having a Han God for a son-in-law? Even if he did turn into a dragon.

Kate smiled secretly and called up a new website on her phone. The flying suit normally fit into an anvil case, but had shown itself to be amenable to transformation if her need and power was great enough.

Perhaps she needed to convince it to fold itself into a backpack she wore at all times, and she could add a stylized white crane costume out of something tight and sexy. The kind of thing like Itala wore as Redlance.

The kind of thing that might turn a man's head.

"Carlos," she called quietly across the space, waiting for him to turn and look at her. "Do you know a good seamstress down here?"

She stood and pointed at her tights and top as the man considered his response.

"I need a better costume for under the suit."

"Sí, mistress," he nodded. "I talk to Tori."

"Thank you, Carlos," she said.

There was a whole new day ahead. Get some food. Unpack the trucks and set up the obstacle course and weight machines. Start familiarizing herself with the flying landmarks of Angel City.

Figure out how to kill a man.

THE COURIER

Kate wasn't even aware that the new hideout had a doorbell, until someone rang it. It had been two quiet days. The interior space was almost configured the way they wanted it. The refrigerator was full. The three of them were settling in. Itala had calmed down.

For the briefest instant, Kate's brain spun images of neighbors throwing a surprise welcoming party, but then she remembered where she was.

Most prior tenants of this warehouse had probably not been friendly. And future ones probably wouldn't be, either. The neighbors would rightly be very, very wary.

She turned and caught a glimpse of another side of Carlos's personality as he opened a small metal case that had been resting on a nearby shelf and pulled out something that looked like it belonged in a science fiction cartoon. But there was no doubt in her mind that whatever it was fell under the rough rubric of *Gun*.

Carlos signaled for her and Itala to stay back as he made his way into the office. Neither woman was in costume, or anything close, but Itala had the Redlance in one hand, all set for mayhem. Kate prepared to throw a chair or something.

She stood just outside the door to the office and listened. Whoever it was had a male voice. Calm, succinct, professional.

The door closed.

"Is safe," Carlos called quietly.

Itala was still through the door first, anyway.

Carlos had set his blaster pistol thingee on the desk, next to a small wooden shipping crate, a box a little larger than one foot by one foot by two feet.

"Package from big boss," he said, pointing at the symbol of the Northern Dragon King painted on the front.

"Do we know what?" Itala inquired.

Carlos just shrugged.

"No too heavy," he observed.

"Is it safe?" Kate asked.

Carlos shrugged again.

Itala popped the two latches on the front that held it closed and flipped the lid back carefully.

Inside were two devices Kate couldn't place. They were obviously metal, matching gray hemispheres with a red button marked *Arm* and a green button marked *Danger*.

Someone had a sense of macabre humor. Or at least irony.

There was a manila envelope on top. Itala lifted it, glanced, and handed it to Kate.

For The White Crane had been handwritten on it in Mandarin, in a man's hand, apparently in vermillion ink.

That limited the options to three people. And Father's calligraphy was a whole order of magnitude better than this. So, *Ao Shun*, or more likely his minister *Jiang*.

It wasn't particularly overloaded, but there was something inside about the size of a smart phone, only much heavier. Kate opened the envelope and carefully poured out the contents into her hand.

The device thingee was a light metal, possibly aluminum. It had a button, a light, and what looked like a count-down timer clock from the movies. The sort that was always wired to the bomb for the hero to cut and save the day.

Kate stayed away from the button.

The rest of the contents was paper. Maps, schedules, diagrams, lists. Meticulously detailed notes about the daily schedule of an armored car service and the two men who would be riding in it starting three days from now. She even knew their phone numbers now. If she cared.

The bomb timer thingee was, according to the notes here, a *Getaway*. USB charger cable included. Again, someone with a sense of humor.

Kate wasn't an expert on nuclear physics, but had read enough papers in her time to understand what an electromagnetic pulse generator was, even if she had never heard of one smaller than a loaf of bread. This one would slip easily into the back pocket of her jeans.

As she weighed its mass in one hand, Kate felt the device tugging at her soul.

So. Another gadget that was intended to be fueled, at least to some extent, by a Modern God pushing power through it.

She read closer. There was an entire addenda hand-written in Mandarin.

By itself, the Getaway could jam cellular and radio signals over a two block radius reasonably well. With a *push*, it could either go much wider, or shut down anything electronic, or even electrical.

Or both.

Where there is a will…

Kate came out of herself and looked at Itala and Carlos.

"What else do we have?" she inquired.

"These two are booms," Carlos pointed at the other devices. He sounded like an expert, in spite of the excitement in his accent. "Short-range plasma lance. Put one on hood, blow engine. Put other on back door, blow open. Probably nobody killed. Is very good stuff."

Guanxi, indeed. She would owe the man for this. But it would let her get back to her own life sooner.

Kate laid out the pickup schedule and the map.

"We'll need to scout this," she said. "I don't trust that everything will work out just like this. Mondays are the busiest days, and the ones where they are the most paranoid. Thursday would be best. That lets us do a dry-run Wednesday. What do we need?"

Carlos raised his hand.

"New paint job on truck," he observed with a wry smile. "Maybe a plumbing contractor this time?"

Kate nodded.

She could begin to see light at the end of the tunnel.

WEDNESDAY

In the movies, stakeouts were always portrayed as being far more exciting than watching paint dry or mold expand.

Kate considered having a word with some Hollywood types to complain. At least the Cult of the Mermaid had infiltrated southern California, so she had someplace to sit and sip coffee while she stared out the window at traffic.

Itala leaned next to her at the standing shelf that ran around the outside window, far less fidgety. She might have had more practice at this sort of thing, considering her previous life as an apprentice jewel thief.

Carlos had a table with a good enough view. If all went well, he was just going to drive up in the van, open the back, and drive off with The White Crane hidden inside.

She might be dripping with Golden Tiger's blood at that point. Getting away while not leaving a trail would be important.

Late morning, the coffee shop was going through a lull. It never actually got quiet, but it did mostly empty out. The staff took the opportunity to rotate shifts as the only other people inside were a real estate lady chatting on her phone and a lawyer meeting with a prospective client, from the looks of the two.

Itala nudged her with an elbow and leaned close.

"Time," she whispered.

Kate checked her phone. Two minutes early, but inside the pickup window.

A heavy, steel box on wheels rumbled up and squatted in the loading zone on the far side of the street.

The back door opened and a man climbed down. He had a gun, a bullet-proof vest under his shirt, and the beginnings of a pot belly. Kate could also see interesting ink sneaking a peek over his collar and past his cuffs as he moved. He carried a heavy-looking courier bag in his left hand, looked around carefully, and walked into the store across the street.

This wasn't the last stop for these men before returning to the depot, but it was the last big store they needed to visit. The back would be close to full. They ought to be looking forward to being done.

And it had been nearly a year since the Scarlet Titan had tried to rob them and ended up dying on the pavement to Kate's left and down about half a block.

Kate felt her teeth grind.

Itala leaned close and wrapped an arm around her waist for a quick hug. That helped. Kate remembered to breathe.

Seven minutes. The man emerged from the front door with three bulkier bags in his hand. He was wary as he stepped into the sunlight, looking left and then right before crossing the sidewalk and standing at the back door.

The man inside apparently popped the lock, or the door. The first guard reached up, pulled the door open and used the leverage to climb up inside, closing the door behind him.

Twenty seconds. The vehicle signaled and lurched out into traffic, waddling off to its next destination.

Kate considered the logistics.

A generation ago, before modern conveniences like credit card readers, the store probably had to offload a hand-cart worth of cash every day. Now, the truck came Monday, Wednesday, and Thursday and the bags were light enough to carry in one hand.

Armed robbery of grocery stores and similar places had gone way down as well, there being so much less cash money to actually steal these days because everyone used plastic.

Of course, this wasn't an armed robbery, but an assassination. Still, they needed to make it look serious.

Kate drank the last of her chai and watched the truck disappear from sight.

She had begun to associate the earthy, cinnamon tastes with vengeance itself.

THURSDAY

In Emerald, a day like this would be cool and cloudy. Possibly drizzly. Mid-sixties. *Home.*

Kate was beginning to develop an active hatred of the dry, gritty heat of the southlands. Of the implied need to shower three times each day if she ever wanted to feel clean.

Itala didn't seem to mind, but she didn't much show her emotions. She might be seething with homicidal fury over a topic, and Kate might never know.

And Carlos was from Ashland, in the Bay area, originally and seemed to enjoy the heat. Plus, he had spent significant portions of his adult life down here.

Philistines.

White Crane had her perch. She had noticed that humans tended to be two-dimensional creatures unless pressed or trained otherwise.

The coffee shop from yesterday was on the ground floor of a five-story office building, the tallest on the block, or any of the surrounding blocks.

Most of the architecture around her were two- and three-story walkup office buildings that dated to the era of the hard-boiled detective novel.

She was looking down. Nobody was looking up.

At her feet were both of the bombs from the Northern Dragon King. There was no way to test that they would work, except by using them. The instructions had said attach and activate. Hopefully, they wouldn't blow the armored car and all the loot to flaming shreds scattered all over the street.

She wasn't here to kill anyone except Golden Tiger. It would be unethical to kill random bystanders who had the unfortunate luck to be walking by on the street today.

There.

Two blocks down, a big, gray slab of armor just turning onto the street.

White Crane heard the dull rumble of *Cheval* approaching as Redlance got into position and costume close by. Nobody would notice White Crane up on the roof if she was still. A woman in spandex with a mask, riding on a loud motorcycle, might get attention. Less, since she was wearing a helmet and a leather jacket, but enough.

The truck pulled to the curb below her like a cruise ship docking, slow and majestic.

Twenty seconds passed.

The rear door popped open and one of the guards got out, looking both ways.

Merde.

That was a woman, instead of the pudgy, tattooed guy White Crane had been expecting. Hopefully, she was just as casual about things as he had appeared. White Crane only had one way to determine if her flying suit was bulletproof, and didn't want to test it today.

The Latina guard was short, but heavy. Maybe a size 12, maybe less, depending on what kind of bullet-proof vest she was wearing over what looked like over-inflated breasts.

The female guard closed the door, one small, heavy satchel in her right hand, and crossed the sidewalk with a direct stride.

White Crane reached down and picked up both bombs. She already had the Getaway stashed.

Things were about to get sharp.

Redlance would be around the corner on White Crane's right, behind the armored car. That was the safe place. The bike, and the woman on it, would be a quick speed bump if she accidentally got in front of the monster truck making a run for it.

The timing would be tight, but not impossible.

White Crane pushed with her mind, and felt herself levitate from the roof. Not much, but enough that she could fall forward into a dive and swoop without having to leap up or out.

All that training on the three-dimensional obstacle course.

She waited for the right moment.

The door to the store opened.

White Crane paused just enough to confirm that the female security guard was the one exiting, and dove headlong off the roof.

The bombs were heavy, but not enough to redirect her flight. Perhaps four pounds each. Less than the barbells she lifted frequently.

Five floors. Six, since she started on the roof.

Free-fall.

Robbing an armored car in broad daylight, in Angel City.

Seriously?

She would ask how it all got to this, but every step had been a deliberate choice. She just could not let her vengeance go, as many times as she thought about it.

Swoop.

The woman below had a sixth sense, apparently. Something caused her to look up.

Fortunately, her brain stopped working at the sight of the giant, white raptor plunging at her.

White Crane grinned ever so slightly as the woman's jaw fell open in shock and her pupils got as large as silver-dollars.

White Crane swooped down hard and leveled her flight six feet off the concrete sidewalk. The neighborhood was old enough, and warm enough, that they had never bothered to string the power-lines underground.

It never snowed in Angel City.

That just meant a tangle of hawser-thick wires to fly under and around.

Piece of cake. Probably.

White Crane was so focused on the vertical she lost track of the horizontal. There was an ancient barber shop next door, with a candy-cane striped pole out front. It shattered into about a zillion pieces as a wingtip caught it going by.

White Crane almost turned turtle with the sudden torque before she stabilized herself. She looked up.

She had almost flown past the female guard in her surprise and maneuvering.

White Crane reached out her left foot and kicked the woman in the shoulder. It wasn't enough to knock her out, but it did knock her down.

Hopefully that would be enough. The other guard was likely to be reacting right now.

White Crane had to stop him from doing anything stupid.

She pivoted in the air like a ballerina, feet first, and stalled her flight, landing exactly next to the front wheel of the big truck, like she had planned it, instead of just getting lucky.

She slammed the first bomb onto the hood a little harder than was necessary. It had magnets, after all. It would hold.

She left a dent anyway. The *spang* of impact was probably audible blocks away.

Shit happens.

White Crane flipped the switch up to arm the device. It also uncovered the button to fire it.

She held her breath, pushed it, and dove backwards towards the rear of the truck as fast as she should, floating like a butterfly caught in a headwind.

She knew what a plasma lance was from watching videos on the internet. And how it was supposed to work. But those were big ones. Anti-tank shells designed to go through a glacis plate and kill a really big battle tank.

She really hoped *Ao Shun* had taken into account the target when he sent her the bombs.

Boom.

The hood of the truck shattered. She would have said melted, but that implied something like an ice cream cone that had fallen on a hot sidewalk on a summer afternoon.

This was more of a hypersonic retort, like ten thousand angry dragons all snapping their fingers simultaneously.

The front end of the truck recoiled hard enough that the wheels were in the air briefly.

Okay. One truck disabled.

White Crane turned around.

The female security guard was at her feet, stretched out and kind of glassy-eyed.

White Crane didn't want to hit a woman, but she really didn't want to get shot.

She chopped the woman hard behind the ear with the back of her wrist. All that training in the Crane style came out now. Her feathers flowed flat and soft, like fabric, as she did, so she didn't draw any blood.

Good. She's out.

White Crane looked up. The back door of the armored car had a thick window. Also bulletproof, but transparent. A man was standing there, looking out.

Shocked out of all rationality by the scene before him.

White Crane wondered if this man had been here the day the Scarlet Titan died.

She saw a radio in his hand, calling for help.

Good. Hopefully Golden Tiger was close enough that he would get here before any police could arrive, and they could settle this properly.

Still, she wanted the guard neutralized, but didn't want to kill him.

The idea that popped into her head like a light bulb was so rude she nearly laughed out loud. Or so evil.

Certainly, mean.

First, White Crane pulled the unconscious guard's gun and tossed it down a gutter.

Safer that way.

She walked to the back of the truck and looked up at the man three feet away. There was a little slot in the door he could open to fire his gun out, if he dared, but she was wearing a costume and could fly.

He didn't look stupid. Or suicidal.

Time to find out.

White Crane attached the other bomb to the door, right below his face and smiled at him. She wasn't sure if he could hear her, so she spoke slowly and clearly. If nothing else, he might could read lips.

"Surrender before I blow the door open," she said loudly.

She had to pay some level of attention to the man, in case he did something crazy right now, but she also needed to be listening and looking about, in case Golden Tiger was about to pounce on her.

Redlance watched from the alley, all set to ambush the hero, but that one was a Modern God with unknown powers. White Crane needed to be able to help her friend, instead of being a liability that needed to be protected.

The guard was wavering.

White Crane held up one finger where he could see it.

He blinked.

She held up a second one.

The eyes got big.

She held up the third finger and reached for the bomb. If the guy in the truck wanted to be a dead hero at this point, that was his choice.

He got to the door before she did.

"I give up," he screamed in a high-pitched tenor audible through the armor. "Please don't hurt me."

That he had a gun, apparently forgotten on his hip, she let pass.

"Come out slowly," White Crane ordered. It was mostly The Empress Bird in command right now. Certainly, they were working in tandem.

It came out as the Voice of Doom. They were all okay with that.

"Yes, ma'am," he said, popping open the door and scrambling down the steps with his hands over his head.

This was the part that was a little fuzzy in the plan. What to do with the two guards? Knocking them unconscious had seemed good. They were technically the enemy, after all.

And witnesses.

And possible collateral damage in a fight.

White Crane let him pass and slammed the back of his head hard enough to knock him silly, but not to hurt him, a little concussion notwithstanding.

He went down like a sack of potatoes.

White Crane caught him with one hand, pulled the gun from the holster with the other, and tossed it down the same gutter as the first one.

She dragged him over to the side of the building and propped him up in front of the barber shop. The patrons inside were all at the window watching, but everybody had the sense to stay indoors today.

White Crane grabbed the woman and pulled her next to her partner. They should be safe here from what was going to happen next.

Except nothing happened.

White Crane looked around. The pedestrians on the street had all fled for cover when she nuked the truck. There was no traffic on the roadway, either. Even the legendary sanguine nature of people in Angel City wasn't enough for them to just keep walking in the middle of a small war between Modern Gods.

She had the street to herself.

And there were no sirens closing, either.

What the hell was wrong with these people?

White Crane scowled professionally at the entire street. It cowed before her.

If she was that kind of person, this kind of power would be awesome. Probably addictive. It might explain criminal Gods.

Still, no Golden Tiger.

And nobody else either.

Damn it.

White Crane grabbed the three currency bags the woman guard had dropped. She tossed them into the street by the back of the truck and climbed up inside the rig itself.

Inside, she found boxes and pigeonholes and piles of more bags. She grabbed as many as she could and tossed them out the back door, daring someone to do something to stop her.

Nobody did.

Where is he?

She grabbed more, opening every bin there was and tossing everything after the first.

Only the really heavy ones got left behind.

Who wanted two hundred pounds of nickels, anyway?

The inside of the truck looked like a rabid Chihuahua had gotten loose.

Nothing.

White Crane gave up.

She peeked carefully out the back.

Nobody there.

She dove out the back door hard and fast, just in case her intended victim had snuck up on the roof and was perched to strike when she stuck her head out. She landed beyond the pile of bags and looked back.

Nothing.

Merde.

Fine. Phase Two.

White Crane held up her right hand and signaled with a loud whistle, two fingers in her mouth.

A block away, a plumbing truck pulled from the curb and rumbled up. Carlos smiled at her from the driver's seat.

He stopped the big panel truck even with the armored car, threw it in park, and climbed out, wearing a simple, white domino-style mask. Enough to hide his face. Nothing fancy.

Carlos pulled open the back door of the truck and started heaving bags in. White Crane helped a little, one eye always to the sky and the street.

Where is Golden Tiger? How was he going to attack?

Seconds passed.

The pile of currency bags vanished.

Carlos looked nervous, finally. Up until now, he'd been on autopilot, too.

"Sí, boss?" he asked.

"Drive," she commanded, taking two steps to grab the unexploded bomb from the armored car and making sure it was disarmed.

The panel truck's engine purred smoothly to life.

Okay. Now is when he'll strike.

White Crane braced.

Nothing.

She reached down into a suddenly-existent pocket on the thigh of her flying suit and pulled out the Getaway. She pushed the red button to Arm it and looked both ways, just in case.

Nothing?

Damn it.

She pushed the green button marked Danger and watched a clock-timer appear with four and a half minutes. It started to count to zero as she climbed up in the back of the panel truck and pulled the door closed.

Carlos dropped it into gear and took off. For a big truck, it handled like a sports car.

White Crane looked out the back window.

Stunned bystanders. She kept expecting a mournful barking dog or something.

What had failed? Where did we gone wrong?

She saw Redlance emerge from the alley on *Cheval* with a roar of acceleration. The folks emerging from storefronts cheered, like Itala was a hero giving chase.

How much of these superhero battles were just public perception, shaped by Madison Avenue after the fact?

Food for thought.

White Crane studied the device in her hands. She felt it tug at her soul and let her perception expand to enter the device. At the same time, she reached out for more power and pushed it into the machine, like she did with her flying suit.

She felt a cloud of energy emerge. It was invisible, but felt like warm, soft cotton candy in her mental hands.

She cast it into the air, carving out two hollow spots in the middle, one for the panel truck and another for *Cheval*.

Cars stopped moving around them. Cell phones rebooted. For people deeply wedded to their technological toys, human civilization ended, at least until she got out of range and physics started to behave again.

The timer sped to zero quickly, but that was fine.

White Crane took one last look back at Redlance and an empty road as they jumped up on the freeway. She powered down the flying suit and tried to figure out where everything had gone so desperately wrong.

What the hell was she going to do with all this money?

GETAWAY

Kai Di was still deep in her analysis of yesterday's debacle when Carlos looked up and whistled softly. She had gotten up and dressed this morning as White Crane, knowing no better way to approach things, so she was in the new white spandex costume she wore under the flying suit, with a masque loose around her neck, similar to how Redlance dressed.

She came back to the present and studied the table in between the two of them.

Carlos had separated the bills from the robbery into two piles, roughly the same size, although the one on the left seemed to be all ones and fives, and all the big bills were on the right.

She raised an eyebrow at him rather than speaking. He smiled serenely.

"One million, two hundred thirteen thousand, eight hundred, fifty-three dollars, boss," he preened, gesturing to the extremely well-organized pile between them.

One point two million dollars? What the hell? How had they managed to steal that much money? Where was that damned hero that was supposed to stop them?

"Why two piles, Carlos?" she inquired, trying to keep the rage out of her voice. It wasn't directed at him. Everything had gone exactly as planned, as far as he was concerned.

He gestured at the pile of small bills.

"Twenty percent for the big boss, the dragon," he replied professionally. "The vigorish. They always get the little bills. Way easier for them to launder, less for us to carry around."

He seemed very proud of himself.

Kai Di wondered how frequently Marauder had been reduced to robbing convenience stores and ATMs for spare change, instead of having big scores like this.

Okay, that was rude. But he deserved it. Jackass.

"Okay," Kai Di replied. "I'll let you handle the money, while we figure out the next step."

She slid her chair back and stood up, letting her muscles relax from their tension. Her anger was bone-deep right now.

Apparently, she just wasn't cut out for a life of crime.

"Boss?" Carlos began as she turned away.

She stopped and turned back. Carlos was a godsend as an assistant. Maybe she should give him most of the money when Golden Tiger was dead? Let him retire in style and obscurity?

"Smart money would be to leave town for a while," he continued. "Is what happen with people we trade leases with. They hiding out in Emerald. Realize we're not done."

He got a pained look on his face.

"Maybe you get lucky and good guys show up now," Carlos opined. "Maybe we booby-trap the place, just in case?"

White Crane and The Empress came suddenly to the fore. Kai Di was research and analysis. Kate was social. The other two did warfare.

"That's a great idea, Carlos," she said. "Please use five percent of our take to get supplies."

"That's fifty-four thousand dollars, boss," he replied, aghast.

"Ten percent?" she asked, lost at the possible costs to hero-proof a warehouse.

"One percent, mistress," he finally said. "That's ten grand. We can get stupid for that money."

"Do it, Carlos," she commanded. "I have powers. Redlance can take care of herself. You need to protect yourself. You're too valuable to me to lose."

Really? Did I just say that out loud?

Carlos replied by blushing furiously.

Apparently she had. Maybe she had just inherited another uncle? Or a mischievous cousin.

Guanxi.

"Sí, boss," he said quietly, ducking to hide his blush and starting to gather the piles of bills.

Kate retreated to the kitchen, letting Kai Di and the others drift into the background and relax.

Itala had slept in this morning. She had just emerged from the shower, dressed in her Redlance spandex costume. Right now, the Frenchwoman was just fixing some tea.

Itala quickly grabbed a second mug as Kate approached and filled another sleeve with loose tea from a tin. She poured the rest of the hot water over it and studied Kate's face.

"That bad?" Itala asked.

Kate shrugged.

"We'll have a little over one million dollars net," Kate replied sourly.

Itala's eyes bugged out in surprise, and then got small as avarice overrode everything else.

Kate decided that she would need to divide the loot two ways when it was done. Itala had never had the kind of security and peace of mind that serious money could bring. It would be nice to take care of her.

What would happen when they got out of the revenge business? Or, when White Crane retired? Would Redlance continue? And would she be a hero or a villain?

"Wow," Itala finally whispered.

"Apparently," Kate smiled wanly. "Crime pays."

"So now what?" Itala asked quietly.

If this was a cartoon, Kate would have seen dollar bill signs in Itala's eyes. She held the giggle at that image inside. Nothing to ever hurt her friend.

"Carlos thinks we might get lucky," Kate continued. "Golden Tiger might track us down and attack the hideout."

If you could call that lucky. She didn't suppose most villains would agree.

"Thought of that," Itala said, touching her costume and pointing to the lance, resting on the counter within easy reach. "Figured I'd be prepared today."

"You suppose we could ask Tori to leak our whereabouts to the good guys?" Kate was thinking out loud at this point.

"Maybe," Itala agreed. "Figured out what went wrong yesterday."

"Oh?"

"Somebody tried to hit a gold repository downtown Wednesday night," Itala said with a grin. "Read about it on my phone. News wasn't sure who stopped them. Golden Tiger might have been up all night fighting crime and slept in yesterday."

"How could he be so inconsiderate?" Kate laughed. "Didn't he know we had a date for brunch?"

Itala laughed as well.

"Maybe we should hit something at night, next time?" Itala wondered.

The doorbell interrupted Kate's response.

She was so keyed up right now that she was actually able to watch Itala vanish into the being known as Redlance, in slow motion. It was like instant replay on a close touchdown call.

Both hands came up and pulled the Redlance mask into place in a single, fluid motion, flipping her blond hair up and back. A beat later, both hands grasped the lance, locked it together, and powered it up with the faintest hum.

Where her best friend had been a heartbeat ago, something primeval had appeared.

White Crane came to the fore at the same moment.

She pivoted and sprang two steps to the new backpack that she had taken to carrying for the flying suit, pulling her own masque up as she did.

The suit seemed to be almost alive this morning. The device read her intent before she even reached it and was unfolding into the origami spider, flowing towards her across the open space.

Was it alive, in some strange, pseudo-magical sense? Certainly, she was beginning to wonder with the three devices she knew: the flying suit, *Cheval*, and the *Getaway*.

White Crane turned to Redlance. Two seconds had passed.

Carlos was already holding his ray gun pistol close to his body, like a professional cowboy.

White Crane nodded at him and leapt into the air. There was a rafter over the door with just the perfect vantage to pounce on someone entering the warehouse through the office.

She watched Redlance shift to the left side of the door, where she would be attacking someone's right as they came through.

White Crane approved. Most humans were right-handed. Most close combat forms blocked with the left arm. It would leave them open and off-balance to defend themselves cross-body, and she would land on them like a ton of bricks when they did.

Who the hell would be ringing the doorbell this morning, anyway?

鶴

White Crane listened carefully as Carlos shuffled into the office and approached the front door. He wasn't thrilled, that was obvious, but he was the only one without a secret identity to protect.

Hopefully, he understood how much she valued him and that she would hammer the living shit out of anyone who tried to hurt him.

She heard the door open noisily. Carlos had been adamant that they not fix the jarring screech of the hinges. Said it made it almost impossible to come in that way secretly.

White Crane had to agree. Even up here it was sharp.

Silence for a heartbeat. Whoever it was, it wasn't the sort of casual pedestrian that rated a door just slammed in their face.

"Mistresses," Carlos called. "Is safe. Is big boss."

The door closed solidly.

Big boss? Ao Shun? *The Northern Dragon King? Here?*

White Crane leapt backwards off the rafter and looped longways around the space to get a better view as she flew closer. There were two men with Carlos. From the colors alone, it was most likely *Ao Shun* and the man dressed in the Ming Court costume.

She had taken to thinking of the second man as Jiang, named for the famous man in the classic picture she remembered. It was good enough, until someone told her otherwise.

She landed well back from the office, considered her options, and powered the suit back down into her backpack with a wish. If he was the ambush, things were going to get very, very messy inside here, but why would he want to do anything?

Why was he even here?

Carlos came into the warehouse first, followed by the Dragon King in his own spandex costume, all gold and red, trailed finally by the other man. Redlance had unsnapped her weapon back into two pieces and relaxed, though she still had her masque up.

White Crane was no longer winged, but kept her masque in place as well.

She nodded formally to the man, a mark of respect to an elder. Angel City was his home. She was just visiting.

Ao Shun indicated Carlos with a tilt of his head.

"Does Carlos speak Mandarin, yet?" he asked politely in formal, almost stilted English with a hint of Oxford accent under it.

What? Carlos? Huh. Not necessarily a bad idea.

"No, sir," White Crane replied. "There hasn't been time for him to master the tongue."

Did he even want to?

"Very well," *Ao Shun* continued in English.

The man who would be a dragon king began to pace absently, shifting to a track parallel to the office wall in such a way that he remained a polite distance from both women.

"I was saddened to hear that your mission to attack Golden Tiger was unsuccessful, even if you did manage to make off with the contents of the armored car and not hurt anyone."

He paused, more or less in front of White Crane.

"What is your next step?" he continued.

White Crane was torn inside.

Ao Shun was a Modern God. She knew that. He had power. He also had charisma. Something.

He turned in on now, focused it on her like a spotlight.

Neither Kai Di nor Kate had enough experience with men to know if this was an artifact of the man's personality, or if he had some subtle superpower that affected her psychically. Certainly, it had not worked on Redlance to discombobulate the French woman, like it had White Crane.

Of course, he hadn't been concentrating on Redlance, only White Crane.

It was hard to judge.

Kate watched the way the man's muscles rippled under his costume as he moved and wondered what he smelled like. Could sexy be a super-power? It might explain some things.

Kai Di understood that this man standing before her had a very Confucian view of the world, with himself at the pinnacle of a social hierarchy as the Emperor of Angel City. Possibly of the entire West Coast. A case could be made, considering who he usually fought.

The Empress viewed this barbarian pretender with disdain, though she would never say it out loud.

"Hunt him down, possibly at night," White Crane finally enunciated clearly, shushing the others in her head so she could think. "We've studied his movements over the past two years, what of it we could. There are a handful of other places to look."

There. Leave it at that. Never tell a master criminal more than you need to.

"I see," the dragon purred intimately. "And after you have finished him off?"

Somehow, the man had gotten close enough to breathe on, when White Crane wasn't paying attention. Kate didn't mind. Kai Di cataloged his cologne. White Crane held perfectly still. The Empress located him for a swift kick to the balls if she had to.

White Crane shrugged, ever so slightly. They were torn, these women.

Guanxi demanded that Dr. Kate Peng return to Emerald once her revenge was complete and return to her life as a mousy research chemist.

On the other hand, she was bound to this man now. Also, *guanxi*.

How to square that circle?

She resisted reaching out to touch his arm. Nothing more than that. Just human contact. Fingers on his muscles. Safe, right?

An awkward moment passed.

The Empress broke the silence.

"That remains to be seen," she said augustly. "What does Angel City offer?"

Ao Shun, the man known to the world as the Northern Dragon King, smiled benevolently at her.

She watched his nostrils flare. Not much. Just the faintest twitch. He was smelling her.

White Crane found herself warm. Almost uncomfortable. Scatter-brained. Even Kate couldn't offer any useful advice.

"Much that can be stimulating," the man purred. "Much that can be rewarding."

He was almost close enough to kiss, if one of them took a half step. She wondered if she would stop him, if he tried. Most of her wanted him to.

Everything around them moved in slow motion.

She watched his eyes. They flickered down, across, back.

She realized he was staring at her breasts. These were much larger, more impressive than the ones she had borne six months ago. She felt them grow tight under his stare as the warmth in her belly crept outward.

Men had never noticed Kai Di Peng as an object to lust after before this.

He smiled at her. It was a half-smile, a flickering grin, gone almost as fast as it appeared.

White Crane licked her lips, tried to swallow past a suddenly tight throat.

Ao Shun broke the tension first.

He stepped back. Not far, enough to shift his shoulders, to rotate so that he also faced Redlance, standing back and to one side patiently.

White Crane glanced over. Itala's nipples weren't poking out of her costume.

White Crane remembered to breathe.

"Carlos," *Ao Shun* said with his commanding tones as he looked over at the table. "I see that you have anticipated our arrival. Marauder didn't deserve your talents. Thank you."

White Crane watched her left-hand-man blush furiously under the praise. Carlos and Jiang moved to the table and began carefully stacking piles of bills into a gym bag while the other three watched.

White Crane walked closer to the table, but in a circle to her left, putting Redlance between her and the dragon.

It felt safer with the other woman there, interrupting.

Ao Shun smiled at her discomfort.

He studied Redlance first, briefly, but no more than necessary. His gaze was more lingering on White Crane. His smile was warm and promised hot, tender kisses.

White Crane blinked, came back to the present.

Stop that. Super-villain. Bad guy. Unfortunate ally at present. Nothing more.

"We will speak again," *Ao Shun* commanded her intimately. "Perhaps in a week."

He again studied both women. Appraising them, perhaps.

"Dinner would be a good time to talk. To plan your futures."

And then he was gone.

Three long strides had put him at the door to the office.

To White Crane, it was like a searchlight had gone out. Or a cloud had covered the sun while she lay on a towel sun-bathing.

Her skin got all goose-pimply, and not just her nipples.

Carlos followed the two men out.

The door screeched open. Closed.

Redlance turned and faced her with a harsh scowl.

"I thought you two were going to need to get a room," she snarled softly, her French accent ramping up with the anger in her voice. "Certainly, the cots wouldn't be big enough. And you'd've had to move all the money to do it on the table."

What?

"What?"

"You're wet right now, aren't you?" Redlance continued, harsher.

White Crane was glad that her masque covered most of her blush. Not that she could deny it.

But she had never had a man look at her like that. Never responded to a man like that.

Never craved touch.

Even with Itala, or Miranda, it had been a softer reaction. More feminine. Sharing, instead of being conquered.

Where had this come from? Twenty-one and never been kissed?

Itala, Redlance, was as close as *Ao Shun* had been. The fire was nearly the same in her eyes.

Carlos returned from the office and stopped dead in his tracks.

"I go," he volunteered meekly.

"You stay," Redlance commanded. She pointed at the table. "Sit right there."

"Hokay."

He appeared to be trying to disappear into himself. It was like watching a mouse try to hide in the shadow of a blade of grass. The Empress offered that observation. White Crane was still in combat mode.

Redlance rounded on her. Again, almost close enough to kiss.

But where *Ao Shun* had offered a warm fire, Redlance was all supernova.

"We've never talked about it," Redlance said abruptly. "What happens after we kill him?"

The snarl wasn't gone. It was dialed back to just a harsh rasp on White Crane's skin.

Oh.

A little light bulb went on in White Crane's head.

She bit back the first words that wanted to come out of her mouth.

Itala hadn't said *No* that night. She had said *Not yet*.

There had been an implicit, unspoken suggestion that they might yet, someday.

Perhaps. Afterwards.

And then a man seemed to be coming between them.

Could she actually make Itala jealous? Her? Mousy, little Kai Di? No, White Crane.

Or was Itala afraid of losing out on everything she might have gained?

Kate had never been very good at lying. This didn't seem like a good time to try.

White Crane let Kate come to the fore. This was not a time for flight vectors and combat. Itala was a friend.

One in pain.

Pain she had caused, however unknowingly.

"I had hoped to give you and Carlos all the money," Kate said quietly. "Then the three of us could retire. Carlos could go visit his ex-wife and his kids. I'd go home to Emerald and go back to being boring."

"And what about me?"

Itala was there now, instead of the harsh warrior Redlance. Her voice had become…younger, more fragile. Pained.

Kate couldn't imagine an Itala that was afraid of anything.

"I don't know what you want, Itala," she whispered. "So I don't know how to make you happy."

"Oh."

Itala relaxed suddenly. She began to breathe again. Or perhaps breathe at a normal rate.

Itala was close enough to caress, to kiss. All four of her considered it. If they had been alone with her, they would have reached out and pulled the Frenchwoman close.

All four of her craved that intimate touch that they had never had, but had come close to with this woman. The warmth. The security.

But in the back of her head, White Crane could also feel *Ao Shun's* hands tangled in her hair, pulling.

Perhaps it was best Carlos was there, as much as he was trying to be invisible.

Who wanted to watch their parents fight?

Itala took a half step closer, put a hand on her arm.

"All the money?" she whispered in shock.

White Crane was listening the hardest. She heard the tones of anguish in the woman's voice, at war with avarice and jealousy three ways.

Kate was the one who reached up and put her hand on Itala's, holding it tight.

She nodded, unwilling to trust her voice or her words.

"What about us?" Itala whispered as she moved closer.

Kate reached out and put an arm around her friend, pulled her close.

Itala was short enough to lean her head on Kate's shoulder as she wrapped her hands around Kate's waist.

Kate ended up hugging the smaller woman close, soothing her.

Carlos looked like the fourth circle of hell might be a pleasant alternative. Kate waved him off to escape somewhere, anywhere. He vanished gratefully.

"What do you want?" Kate asked softly, patting the Frenchwoman's back.

"I don't know," Itala whispered back.

Kate could feel tears starting in her friend. She kissed Itala lightly on the forehead and rocked slightly.

"I saw the way he looked at you…" Itala started.

Kate let the words tumble off into space. She had seen it, too.

Felt it. Wanted it. Craved it.

Craved the man's hands on her body, roughly, touching her in new places, new ways. Things promised that neither Miranda nor Itala could offer.

But she didn't dare say it out loud. Not now. Never to Itala.

White Crane came to the fore.

"Shh," she whispered soothingly. "He styles himself as the Northern Dragon King of Chinese legend. He sees me as a simple sexual conquest, nothing more. A notch in a bedpost."

"Moron," Itala huffed back.

White Crane smiled down at her friend, an inside joke shared by any two women at the expense of any man. They never seemed to get past a woman's tits and consider her brains. At least, not the dumb men.

Still, some tiny part of her thrilled at the thought of being desired, if she could find a man worthy of the effort.

Was he that man?

INTO THE DRAGON'S DEN

Are you ready for this?" White Crane howled into Redlance's ear over the roar of *Cheval*. The evening air was warm and dangerous. She had her hands wrapped around Redlance's stomach as they rode too fast, too loud on the beast's back.

More than once, White Crane had considered letting her hands drift north as she held onto the smaller woman's waist. Grabbing hold of her chest while the Frenchwoman's hands were busy holding the bike steady. The night had that kind of wild, gonzo feeling to it. And Barstow wasn't *that* far away.

They were both in spandex tonight. Both wearing black leather jackets. Redlance had a full-face helmet, while White Crane settled for just a bowl helmet and her masque.

At speed, they would look like any two women on a big, gnarly bike, out for an evening spin. You had to look close to see the Lance in its holder, or the flight suit's backpack. And they would be gone if you did.

"Never," Redlance yelled back.

"Good enough," White Crane laughed. "Turn right at the next light and down a half-block on the left."

Redlance was apparently feeling dangerous tonight. She took them low and hard into the corner, almost skidding the rear wheel on the gravel before she opened the throttle back up with a howl like Godzilla approaching.

Their target was a shipping warehouse, a long, bland building in a row of them, along a boring stretch of industrial Generica.

White Crane had often wondered how a large, successful, criminal enterprise might hide from the authorities. And from hyper-present heroes. Apparently, the answer was in noise and static.

Statistical chaos.

You could build a fantastically expensive secret base in an active volcano on an island in the southern oceans, but it wouldn't be secret long, and someone would come along and blow it up. Plus, it was probably a bitch to recruit competent help if they had to hang out in the middle of nowhere and not go into town on Saturday night.

If you were in Angel City, you had the extra hassle of stupidly expensive real estate. Better to lease a warehouse temporarily and convert the innards to something useful. Only a villain like the Wombat could easily use his powers to dig new underground bases quickly.

Kai Di wondered if that man wouldn't be better off going legitimate and just becoming a tunneling contractor. He would probably make several times as much as he ever would as a villain.

And quickly be bored out of his mind.

She could see the draw of using power, and doing things well outside of your comfort zone. Of being a hero, or a villain.

She was in Angel City, wearing a spandex costume like it was nothing, after all. The life might be addictive.

Redlance braked savagely enough to screech the tires and snap the big warhorse up the driveway and into the old parking lot, dodging ancient potholes and spurts of grass.

A man stepped from a doorway at the front and approached them politely. He was dressed in black slacks, white shirt, and a gold tie, with a neutral smile pasted on his face.

Even super-villains needed parking valets for their parties.

Redlance killed the engine and coasted in his direction.

White Crane was wearing her mask under the helmet, so she just popped it off and fixed the man with a hard stare, daring this poor Angelino to say something stupid. Men down here had a reputation as sexist pigs.

"Good evening, ladies," he said with a quick half-bow. "You are right on time. Would you like me to park your bike?"

Apparently, *Ao Shun* had hired good help.

"I'll put it where I want it," Redlance growled back at him, hard and a touch surly, but not mean. Perhaps feeling the mad energy of the warm night.

White Crane certainly was.

He nodded back, and turned to point to a spot close to the door beside the warehouse, just before the first of twelve bay doors running down the side.

"Would this be acceptable?" he asked simply.

"It'll do," Redlance answered him and hopped off the big machine.

White Crane followed, and started to lean on the rear fender to push, but Redlance already had it in motion.

Kate occasionally forgot how strong Itala really was under that spandex. The serum might not have transformed her utterly, like it had Kate, but it had helped the smaller woman turn into something far grander than she looked. Far more dangerous. Far more awesome.

White Crane followed, stripping her cute new leather jacket off and laying it across the seat with her helmet atop it as the bike came to rest.

Redlance hung her jacket from the upper grip, and then put the helmet atop that like a skull impaled on a stick. She snapped the Lance together and rested it by her foot.

Bad-ass chick ready for a party or a rumble.

The two women turned and surveyed the empty parking lot, the weeds, and the valet who had followed them.

"Would you like to leave the keys, ma'am?" he inquired politely.

"No," Redlance growled.

White Crane smiled.

Itala's humor had gotten a little better over the last few days.

It was strange to have someone jealous over you. Kate had never been in that position, wasn't even sure how to handle it, except to pay extra attention to her friend and keep her own lustful daydreams about dragons to herself.

Tonight would be different. Dinner with *Ao Shun* and his cadre. A celebration of a successful heist. Planning for the next steps in stalking Golden Tiger.

Summertime in Angel City.

White Crane took the lead, walking towards the door to the warehouse office and entering, Redlance a stride behind her, prepared for a small war.

Inside, the building had been transformed.

It had started out as the belly of the giant whale, all concrete floors and giant steel ribs. That was still there, but someone had rented out a party warehouse for a nice wedding, or retirement party.

It was not crowded, but there were people everywhere, mostly in one of two matching liveries.

Either they were hard men and women in red pants and tunics, trimmed in gold, or they were wait-staff of various types in black slacks, white shirts and black aprons.

White Crane did a quick glance and saw nearly one hundred fifty people around her.

There were a number of tall round tables with stools to her right. Comfy for three, crowded for four. One larger round table, low and perfect for six. Two long tables for catering food, able to handle a buffet line down both sides, no waiting. An open bar had been set up to the left.

An expert string quartet entertained the room from the center beyond the grand table. They were just loud enough to soothe the savage beast, but not so loud that you had to yell over them.

How weird would it be for your band to be hired to play at a super-villain's dinner party?

Jiang rose from the big table and walked towards them with a friendly smile on his face.

"Good evening," he said in flawless Mandarin. "Welcome."

White Crane was struck again by the man's robes. They were long, like a judge's, with baggy sleeves. But what caught her eye, as always, were the two white cranes embroidered on his chest. Just like that of his original namesake.

It was a Ming symbol, indicating the man was a minister of the first rank.

She wondered how he felt about encountering a true white crane, symbol of the Empress of China.

Jiang indicated the bar and the food with grand gestures.

"*Ao Shun* will make a grand entrance shortly," Jiang continued. "Then we will eat, socialize, and eventually strategize. Can I get you anything?"

"No, thank you," White Crane replied mildly. She walked towards the bar first, with the other two trailing.

She had no intention of drinking anything alcoholic tonight, beyond possibly a few sips of wine after she had eaten. This was just a scouting trip.

The bar had a few bottles of liquor, and a choice of red and white wine, but most of the space was given over to soft drinks, fruit juice, and bottled water.

Probably best to not mix powerful strangers, unknown egos, and free booze.

She grabbed a bottle of orange juice from an oversized bucket filled with ice. Redlance grabbed a flavored tea that had been largely hidden underneath.

Jiang hovered close in his role as host and escorted them to the big table.

Two people, men, were already seated around the head table. White Crane recognized Devilback from her first meeting with *Ao Shun.* He still wore the faceless mask with the great curling horns, but had pulled it up enough to reveal his mouth as he sipped white wine from a glass.

White Crane was surprised to realize that the man known to the world as Devilback was black under the costume. She knew from her research that most people assumed he was either white or ABC. Interesting.

The other man was in green. She couldn't tell much more about him than that, as he wore a strange hood, pushed slightly back from his forehead, but not all the way back around his neck. His face was obscured by something that looked like an ancient gas mask, with two, big, bug-eyed lenses protecting his eyes.

Weirdly, he was drinking a can of soda pop from a glass, through a straw tucked into a purpose-built hole in the mask.

Both men nodded politely at them as they approached.

Because she couldn't see eyes, White Crane could only assume the men were staring at her body and ogling her as she got closer.

The thought brought a thrill to her stomach.

Nobody had ever noticed scrawny, little Kai Di Peng, except social misfits she didn't find interesting to begin with.

Was this growing up? Or were these new feelings and lusts a side effect of the serum? Had she missed some crucial bit of editing with the testosterone? There had been no extra growth of hair, no uncontrolled rages. But she was certainly noticing men noticing her more often.

It was unsettling in both good and bad ways.

Rather than sit, White Crane nodded back at the two men and continued on to inspect the buffet. It was purely accidental that she walked in such a way that both men, all three men, got a very good view of her bottom as she went by. And the little extra wiggle was just her keeping stretched out and warm.

Right?

The food ran the gamut. Three kinds of salad: a cobb, a green, and a chicken caesar. Eighteen kinds of steamed, stewed, or casseroled veggies to pick from. Steak in a brown sauce or chicken and cheese in a red sauce. Individual dessert pies or puddings to pick from.

The smells were lovely. Not home. Mu Ren would have done something entirely else here, and done it better. But still, yummy.

Someone had put a lot of thought into it. And a good amount of cash.

Of course, she had just given the man nearly a quarter of a million dollars a week ago. She had probably paid, however indirectly, for this spread. She might as well enjoy it.

A sound caught her attention, behind the murmuring and conversations. Almost hidden beneath the string quartet. Nearly lost under the general hum of the building.

If asked, she would have said it was the sound of wings flapping. Her own didn't, but she became a bird goddess every time she took flight, and some of that had wormed its way into her soul.

Apparently, Jiang heard it as well. Or was responding to some other signal.

He turned and clapped his hands together once over his head to get everyone's attention.

"He's here," Jiang called out.

There was a rustling as everyone stood up or came still, and the room got silent, except for the sound the green man's chair made as he pushed it backwards across the concrete and came to his feet a touch later than everyone else.

White Crane had her back to the food. Redlance had ended up on her immediate right as they had turned around.

At the far end of the warehouse, two hundred feet away, a garage door quietly wormed its way open with an electric hum. Warm, chewy air floated in on the evening breeze, cutting through the chilly air inside.

A man stood in the doorway, just finishing the transformation back from a giant, flying, golden dragon as White Crane watched.

The string quartet suddenly changed songs to something White Crane instantly cataloged as *Entry Music*. It wasn't *Hail To The Chief*, but it was in the same vein. The same *Ego*. It sounded like a riff on Handel's Messiah, or the opening to Beethoven's Ninth.

Certainly not Copeland.

The man considered himself Emperor.

We'll see about that.

White Crane took the opportunity to study the man closely as he approached the party. Her father, both of her fathers, had taught her how much you could learn about a man, just by the way he held himself, the way he walked, the set of the eyes. It worked for women as well, but the messages were entirely different.

Ao Shun really did view himself as the conquering hero. That much was obvious from his stride, his stance when he got close enough to the two women to gaze down.

Of the group, only Devilback was taller, and that not by much. Jiang was perhaps an inch taller than White Crane, but she had no idea if he had platform soles under those robes to help. The man in green was average height, at least if he was white. Who knew what ethnicity the green might hide?

"Good evening, my friends," *Ao Shun* grandly announced. "Thank you for joining me tonight."

He turned and strode to the bar, where a very competent female bartender, with a very hard, if cute, face, was already expertly pouring him a whiskey from a new bottle.

Ao Shun took a good jolt from the highball glass and smiled benevolently over the crowd. He gestured with his open hand at the two tables of food.

"Dinner is served," he called.

White Crane watched as all the man's henchmen suddenly queued up politely for food, while Devilback, Jiang, and the green man sat back down at the big table.

She cocked her head at the dragon king, but he just smiled enigmatically back at her and indicated that she should precede him to the table.

At the table, he pulled back a chair for her, next to Jiang, and then seated Redlance next to Devilback, putting himself between the two women. Kai Di cataloged the behavior of the men around her, especially the four at the table.

Among the henchmen around her, the ratio seemed to be around nine to one male. And the Northern Dragon King was very obviously showing off two lovely women in tight costumes.

Harem kind of night?

Because she had missed it earlier, White Crane was surprised when a waitress emerged from behind a screen in one corner of the warehouse, with a stack of plates expertly running up both arms. Obviously, a professional.

She served *Ao Shu*n first, and then White Crane, then doubled back to Redlance, before winding around the table clockwise to serve Jiang last.

The food was interesting to look at. Someone had taken a steak and pounded it thin, laid a layer of pastry atop that, added a pinkish cream sauce of some sort, and rolled the whole thing up like a cinnamon roll before baking it. Kai Di had never had a Beef Wellington prepared this way, but it smelled divine, with a side of squash in various colors, steamed and then served in garlic and butter.

Her stomach rumbled quietly in anticipation.

Ao Shun had already dug in, so White Crane did the same. The others were on their way as well. Even the green man had stripped the bottom half of his gas mask off to eat. He was anglo under there, after all.

The food tasted just as wonderful as it looked.

One of the advantages of her serum, in White Crane's eyes, was that she burned calories like a top-level *male* athlete. Since she ate generally healthy food, she could eat a lot of it and not worry about her figure.

That was possibly the best part. There was a significant weight of beef here, and she chowed down.

All too quickly, the plate was clean.

Mu Ren will need to hear about this, so she can reverse engineer the recipe.

White Crane burped accidentally before she could cover her mouth. Jiang didn't bother covering his mouth.

Divine.

Ao Shun leaned back from his empty plate as the waitress quickly cleared the table and the bartender delivered another highballed whiskey.

He looked to his left first, at Redlance, and then his right, at White Crane.

"While I realize you have both only just arrived, you have already made a successful splash in Angel City," he began, those clipped, English tones under his words. "I would still like to welcome you."

He held up his glass in a toast. The others quickly joined in. The table was small enough they could all touch glasses and plastic bottles in the middle.

"I would also," *Ao Shun* continued, "like to welcome you into our broader criminal enterprise."

The Empress had been waiting for those words, or something like them.

Guanxi.

How could he fit these two strangers, these two young women, into the web of relationships and connections he had built up in this city? And how could they pay him back for the assistance he had already provided them?

The money was just a tax on their operations. Lubrication that went up the food chain.

A man who styled himself as a Chinese emperor would be counting the assistance he had provided–the bombs, the plans, the schedules, the *Getaway*–on his abacus.

What would he want in return?

Part of her thrilled when she saw his eyes stray down to her chest as he talked.

Would he ask her for something more intimate than just assistance on a raid? Would he make demands on her as a woman?

Would she resist?

Kate looked forward to the physical possibilities. Kai Di was a neutral observer, a scientist. White Crane saw him as potential. The Empress sneered at all of them.

Less than a heartbeat had passed. White Crane realized he was waiting for a response.

She raised her bottle of orange juice in his direction.

"While I do not intend to make Angel City my home," she began, just as grandly. "I would like to thank you for the help and the hospitality as we hunt down the menace who brought us here. To the death of Golden Tiger."

That brought a ragged cheer more like the growl of hungry hyenas. All of these men lived with the daily fear of being tracked down by one of the costumed heroes and thrown into a prison from which they might not ever escape.

She started to say something else when something about the room changed.

White Crane would not have been able to identify it alone, but Kai Di was watching.

It wasn't that the room got colder. It was quite warm with the bodies and the heat.

It got *more hollow*.

She looked up and sniffed the air, expanding her senses.

Ao Shun started to speak, but White Crane put her hand on his wrist to silence him.

It was an unconscious gesture to keep him from distracting her, but she felt an electric tingle pass through her body as she did.

She turned to smile awkwardly at the man as she blushed.

Her brain clicked.

There had been power floating in the air around her. There always was. It was what made heroes and villains work.

It had just disappeared.

The last time she had felt something similar was just before Marauder attacked her, when he sucked in as much energy as he could.

White Crane locked eyes with Redlance across six feet of space.

Itala was unable to sense the power. But she was already sliding her chair backwards, apparently just from the look on Kate's face. The lance clicked into a single piece and began to hum.

White Crane turned back to *Ao Shun* as the storm gathered in the aether above her.

"Trouble," she said flatly.

The flying suit resided in a special-made backpack. It was close enough to respond to her wishes, without her having to be in physical contact with the plate.

It did.

The organic, steel spider origamied itself outwards and engulfed her like a grenade going off in reverse.

Around the room, all hell broke loose.

Part of her power, the part Kai Di had always known about, was the instinctive ability to slow down time. It didn't really slow down, but she was able to process things many, many times faster when she locked in. She could think, respond, and catalog at a speed that made football's slow motion replay look fast.

A door shattered behind her.

On the roof, someone had just landed lightly, grabbed hold of the metal in a corner, and begun to rip it open like a box of animal crackers. A world-ending-screeching-sheet-of-metal box of animal crackers.

White Crane had her timing down perfect after so much practice. She threw herself backwards into the air, spilling her chair onto the concrete while the flying suit finished embracing her and lifted her into the air.

A woman stood in the shattered doorway where White Crane had first entered the warehouse. Her costume seemed to have been cut down from an expensive one-piece swimsuit, held together by string, wishes, and boob-tape. She had green-hued skin and long, flowing purple hair and was surrounded by a nimbus of energy White Crane could taste from here.

Starchild.

Modern God.

Powerful one, too. Probably more powerful than White Crane. Certainly more dangerous than Redlance.

The ceiling surrendered to the night sky.

A man hovered in the air over the space.

He had short black hair with a curl over his forehead, and a face so beautiful that Michelangelo would have carved it in stone centuries ago. His rippling muscles were visible through a royal blue bodysuit with white trim, white boots, and a nine-point white star on his chest.

He was the first person, hero or villain, that White Crane had ever seen that wore a cape. They didn't do that anymore.

But he was from a previous age.

Provost.

Possibly the greatest of the Modern Gods. Looked thirty, but had to have been at least sixty, as he had been active in the business for more than four decades. Rumored to be an alien sent to Earth as a child. Rumored to be immortal.

Rumored to be a real god.

The greatest hero of the heroic age.

Very, very dangerous.

Northern Dragon King's arch nemesis.

White Crane heard a howl beneath and behind her. She arched away and to her right, looking down in time to see *Ao Shun* complete his transformation into a giant, golden-scaled dragon.

With a flurry of wings, the monster leapt into the air and charged the hero in blue.

Provost flew backwards and up into the night sky, clearing space between himself and the dragon, lest the beast catch him in giant claws that might test the legendary bullet-proof invincibility.

White Crane considered the battle about to occur above her and stayed low. *Ao Shun* should be able keep Provost busy long enough for she and Redlance to sort out an escape.

Inside the warehouse, everyone was scattering to the four winds. All the hired help went for the walls to get out of any field of fire. Henchmen and goons ran towards a panel truck tucked back in a corner. A few men were returning from that direction armed, so apparently there was an arsenal in back. Or something. The rest ran for the fire exits.

Starchild had come into the larger room. Apparently, she could fly as well, riding a stream of purple fire like a contrail. She ignored White Crane to focus her attention on the two men below, mostly on the man in green.

His gas mask was back in place, and the table was flipped over on a side like a bulwark for him to stand behind.

White Crane watched him raise a hand and point a finger at Starchild. A bolt of lime-green flames flashed out.

He missed, but only because Starchild had been expecting the move and ducked at the last moment.

White Crane watched the blast strike the already-damaged roof, well away from her, and punch a small hole in it.

Starchild responded with her own mystic bolt, a flash of purple energy that struck the overturned table and shattered it to pieces.

So much for the security deposit.

White Crane couldn't, as far as she knew, throw any sort of energy bolt, not that she had ever considered trying.

And now was not the time to be distracted finding out.

She glanced up. *Ao Shun* and Provost had disappeared from sight, but she saw a flash of light she suspected was dragonflame below the horizon of the roofline.

She needed to grab Redlance and get gone, or at least get some distance where they could defend themselves better.

A few of *Ao Shun's* goons began to open fire as they got closer to the action. As with every trope and meme from the movies and interwebs, these men couldn't hit the broad side of a planet.

That didn't stop them from trying. Bullets suddenly began to ring on the roof in dangerous ways. Some of them went on through, but a few began to hit the big metal whale's ribs and ricochet back down into the space below.

White Crane went for the deck as fast as she could, happy she had spent as much time training on the indoor obstacle course as she had.

Two men were trying to shoot Starchild, at least she hoped they were aiming at the other woman, as she blasted between them at full speed.

Rather than try to find altitude, White Crane flipped her feet forward, rotating end for end as she stalled to the ground like a gymnast landing. At least, how Itala had taught her to do it, and the petite Frenchwoman was also a gymnast.

White Crane spun around, looking for Redlance in the fury and the melee.

There.

And look who came to the party!

A pack of *Ao Shun*'s goons were already down, either unconscious or knocked silly by the man standing just inside the warehouse door.

He had a yellow-gold spandex costume, skin-tight, with a similar colored gi as a tunic over it. There were black stripes running horizontally, wrapped around his body from his spine to his sides. Tiger stripes.

Golden Tiger.

The pictures and the graphic novels didn't do him justice. He was lean and tall, but moved with a grace like a man trained in ballet and sky-diving.

His masque looked more like an oversized bandana wrapped around his skull, with eyeholes cut out, except the eyes were all white, so she assumed he had lenses to protect his vision.

Golden Tiger appeared to be a white guy. He had a good California tan and blond hair long enough to show under the hood. And his gi and his top were both open enough to show off his trademark Glowing Tiger brand on his chest. The one that had been burned into his chest in the monastery in Tibet, when he was recognized as a supreme master of the martial arts.

White Crane looked closer as she began to head in his direction. Sure enough, his gauntlets were also glowing, ever so slightly. It was the mark of a Modern God.

Golden Tiger had finished off all the goons within easy reach as she watched. He was obviously a master of southern Kung Fu, using many of the animal forms she had studied, with a pronounced emphasis on Tiger form, one of the most deadly.

The man was ignoring her, or had missed her in the chaotic scrum. It didn't help that Starchild was busy blasting anything that both moved and wasn't wearing black. At least she was using big bolts that seemed to impact on goons and furniture like a giant medicine ball, knocking things over and squishing them slightly, but not killing folks.

Not yet, anyway.

Golden Tiger was working his way towards Devilback. Devilback had pulled his mask back down and was concentrating on something.

It took her a moment to realize what was distracting the big man. Devilback was trying to draw energy into himself from the air around him, and not finding any. She guessed that the heroes had taken it all. She wondered briefly if that had been part of their plan, to handicap any villains who were unprepared.

Lesson: always stay as charged as possible. Too many Modern Gods in a room and there will be no power to absorb. It was almost like lacking oxygen.

Devilback appeared to be low on battery power. She watched him glare at his left hand and hold it out, pointed at Golden Tiger. It did glow, however briefly, but nothing happened.

"Too bad, 'devil,'" Golden Tiger taunted the man in red as they closed.

Apparently, not an unknown issue. Even better to know.

White Crane spotted Redlance in the mess. Her partner was keeping her head on a swivel, trying to spot gun-crazy goons, flying heroes, and ground-level problems all at the same time.

They made eye contact across the space and both began to close on Golden Tiger.

For White Crane, it had all come down to this.

She watched as the two big men, Golden Tiger and Devilback, closed to melee range and began to exchange blows. Devilback was a shade taller, and much broader across the chest, but slower, clumsier.

Devilback swung a mighty right hand at the martial artist. White Crane watched the man lean into the blow, like he was supposed to, blocking the fist with his own left hand at the last moment to just miss his head, rotating on his hips as he did.

Because she had trained in many of the same forms, White Crane could observe what was coming next scientifically. The left hand blocking set up a counter-rhythm. Even the feet moved to it. Golden Tiger's right hand lashed straight out like a piston coming up from the hip and turning into a fist at the last instant.

It sounded like a giant taiko drum when the blow struck Devilback's chest, a dull, hollow thump that drove the man backwards several steps. It looked like it hurt. It sounded like it hurt.

Golden Tiger obviously wanted to follow up and finish Devilback, but Redlance suddenly came at him from his left. White Crane still had space to cross before she could help, so she concentrated on how and where to hit the man if she needed to do a charging, flying tackle.

Hopefully, it wouldn't come to that, but he was a Modern God and Itala was still only human. In peak form. Well trained. Taking Kai Di's serum to make herself better. But only human.

If he hurt Itala, she would pull him apart slowly like a fly.

Redlance thrust the red end of her shaft at the man like she was holding a spear. White Crane cringed mentally. That was almost the worst possible way to use a bo-stick against a good martial artist. It left the hands and feet out of position. It put you off balance. It opened you up to a deadly counter-strike.

Golden Tiger flowed into a block. White Crane wasn't sure how much of the tip of the Redlance itself was dangerous, but Golden Tiger blocked by sweeping his right foot into the air and catching the shaft midway. It passed harmlessly by his right.

At the same time, the tiger hopped powerfully into the air from his left foot, flipping his weight to his right, cocking his left fist in the air, and preparing to hammer Redlance in the side of the skull as she was over-extended.

White Crane blanched and leaned forward to charge into the man's back before he could get a second blow in, the kind that might do serious damage once he knocked Redlance down.

And then White Crane learned a whole new way to use a bo-stick. All the Chinese forms treated it like a very long, very light sword, or possibly a whip. You held it at one end and poked or swept or tripped.

Redlance pivoted in place and shifted her hands by pulling on the black end of the staff. Suddenly, her hands were at the thirds of the lance, instead of one end. She blocked Golden Tiger's punch with a stick move Kate remembered from her youth, from an ancient kid's cartoon about Robin Hood.

Friar Tuck Fu, also known as English Quarterstaff.

Apparently, Golden Tiger wasn't any more familiar with English forms than Kate was. The black end of the Redlance continued across and caught the man hard on the side of the thigh. Not quite a kneecapping blow, but it was going to leave a lovely, painful bruise tomorrow. And someone would walk with a good limp for a week.

White Crane smiled and began to close with the scumbag. Now was her opportunity to pay that man back for everything he had done to her, however unknowingly.

Out of nowhere, a flying tackle engulfed her and lifted her into the air.

Crap. Lost track of Starchild.

The green, alien woman was bigger than White Crane, almost Provost's size. Big enough to lift her up like a child and carry her away from the battle she needed to join.

"Going somewhere, my dear?" the woman purred. Starchild had a deep voice for a woman, an alto low and sultry, but with a very strange accent Kai Di could not place, even though she herself spoke a dozen languages.

White Crane struggled, but Starchild had her wrapped up tight enough that there was no leverage, no matter how hard she tried.

"Can't have you hurting Golden Tiger, villain," Starchild continued. "I'll take care of you first and then go help him."

White Crane was trapped, and she knew it. Her first big battle, and she was desperately outclassed. The only other person on her side who could fly was gone away outside somewhere, probably desperately battling the greatest of their kind.

She couldn't use hands or feet trapped like this. She didn't throw energy bolts. She couldn't try Wei De's trick of summoning help from the nether reaches of the universe.

She was about to fail completely.

Fail herself. Fail her family. Fail Itala. *Fail Miranda.*

The Empress stepped to the fore in her mind and growled. It was like being struck by lightning on a clear day.

"I don't think so," she snarled at the green hero.

Starchild was strong. She had muscles like a gymnast, or a swimmer. White Crane could feel the energy of the universe, the raw power itself, flowing through the green woman, powering strength and flight and everything else.

Below, the bug-eyed man in green was out cold, apparently the loser in his first-round tussle with Starchild.

The Empress would not be her next victim.

Starchild wanted to get her into the air. That much was obvious. Get her away from Golden Tiger and Devilback. Even the odds a little.

But White Crane was heavier than she looked. Kate hadn't told anybody how much she really weighed. It was more than just adding muscle. Her very bones seemed to have turned to granite, for a Chinese woman with a lean athletic body to weigh close to two hundred pounds.

Her chest was *not* that big.

But her anger was.

The Empress took control in that split second.

Instead of struggling against Starchild's strength, her grip, The Empress put every erg of energy, of dedication, of desire, of *Rage* into the flying suit.

Sing for me, oh muse. Sing a song of the rage of Achilles.

The Empress drove them straight down as hard as she could.

Starchild squawked in surprise. But she didn't want to win this battle more than The Empress did.

Nobody did. Nobody would.

The Empress would not be denied.

Ever.

White Crane rolled herself like a gator as her force became irresistible. Starchild continued to struggle to lift them, even as the horizon suddenly snuck past her.

White Crane grabbed the bigger woman by the front of the barely-there costume and held tight. Because she had a helmet and Starchild didn't, White Crane head-butted the woman for good measure.

Nothing like a good training stinger on the nose to blind you and make your eyes water.

White Crane relaxed as she approached the ground. The first lesson of Kung Fu is how to fall and not hurt yourself. Instead, she twisted on her hips as hard as she could, rotating in place inside the other woman's arms while not letting go.

White Crane twisted harder, and then tucked herself tightly underneath the woman as her bottom touched the floor, trusting the metal to protect her from a friction burn.

Starchild was flying full speed, concentrated on keeping control of her prisoner. And she was blinded. She did not see that she was flying down instead of up. She looked like a diver about to enter the water.

Starchild face-planted the concrete floor hard enough to craze it several feet across and leave a small crater.

White Crane twisted more, and then let go. She put all her focus into stopping, as Starchild bounced back into the air, apparently unconscious, and slammed headlong into the side of the panel truck that had held all the catering equipment.

The vehicle tipped over with a sound like someone throwing a symphony down a stair case.

White Crane let instinct float herself upright. The Empress seemed to have a handle on things.

She shook her head once. Everything was still intact and didn't seem to rattle too much.

Thirty seconds had elapsed since Starchild had kicked the door in.

The Northern Dragon King was gone.

Provost was as well.

Whether they were still engaged, or chasing, or something else, neither had come back to the warehouse.

Bug-eyed villain was down.

Devilback was down.

Redlance was slowly being driven back by the martial artist who was the very bane of their existence, barely holding her own from a whirlwind of strikes and kicks.

The Empress was angry. Raging. No, she was *Vengeance* itself. Tisiphone revived from legend and made flesh.

Now she was going to destroy that man.

RABBIT

Before she could move, Golden Tiger turned her direction. Or rather, the fight continued to rotate and they found themselves facing each other across the vast distance of the warehouse.

She could see the moment of recognition on his face. That moment he first knew fear.

Starchild was one of the most powerful Modern Gods. And she was down.

White Crane stood triumphant. And was coming for him next.

He erupted into a flurry of blows that pushed Redlance back and completely defensive, lest she get her head bashed in.

And then the man was gone, sprinting towards the door and hopping over several of *Ao Shun*'s unconscious and soon-to-be-captured men and women.

White Crane covered the space to Redlance at the speed of thought.

Itala was down on one knee, but did not seem to be badly injured.

"You okay?" Kate asked.

It wasn't White Crane speaking. This was her friend, her partner, her right hand.

"I'm fine," Itala answered.

Again, not the being known as Redlance, but a petite-if-very-strong Frenchwoman with an attitude problem the size of a cinder block.

"He's good," Redlance was back. "Better than you, maybe."

"We'll see about that," The Empress snarled. "We'll just see about that."

From outside the shattered door to the warehouse, an engine started up.

Both women listened as they began to move.

"That's not *Cheval*," White Crane observed as they crossed the empty space.

"No," Redlance agreed. "Bastard's on an Italian scooter. Had one just like it when I was there."

"He's not getting away," The Empress announced as she began to fly at the door.

She would just pull her wings in and dive through like a swimmer entering water. Hopefully there wasn't anybody standing there with a net.

"Not if I can help it," Redlance agreed, pounding silently in her wake.

After the cool of the warehouse, the hot, dry night air was a slap in the face as White Crane exploded through the open door and swooped straight up.

Nobody jumped her, or netted her. Or embarrassed her again.

There.

Sure enough, that bastard was on a pale yellow scooter that sounded like a lawn mower, powering down the street as fast as the damned thing could whiz.

Not exactly the most macho of conveyances.

White Crane took a moment to roll over onto her back, like a swimmer floating in calm water. Provost and *Ao Shun* were out here somewhere. It wouldn't do to accidentally fly into their battle and let her victim escape.

Nothing but stars and night above her. Nothing in the parking lot but weeds, and elbows and butts as wait staff and henchmen ran like hell to get away from the battle.

So far, so good.

Where the hell had the two big guys gone off to?

"Where is he?" Redlance yelled from below.

White Crane rolled back over, feeling like a raptor about to catch a rabbit.

"Follow me," she hollered back, swooping down to a lower altitude to give chase.

The roads were lit reasonably well, but this was still a warehouse district, all light industrial boxes in identical paint jobs. If she got too high, she might lose perspective and let him escape down an alley.

Not a chance in hell.

Golden Tiger had gotten to the end of the block and turned left.

White Crane pushed herself in pursuit. She could fly faster than he could drive, as long as there weren't too many wires, trees, and buildings in the way.

Better still, behind her, she heard *Cheval* roar to life like a pack of angry wolves.

Golden Tiger heard it as well. White Crane saw his head rotate back once for confirmation, and saw White Crane coming after him, and then he leaned forward over the handle bars like he was on a racing pony smelling the finish line.

She wondered what the man would do now. He didn't take long to show her.

Golden Tiger popped the scooter into a driveway and began to race like hell towards the back, White Crane staying hard on his heels.

The Frenchwoman's roar continued to close.

White Crane realized that she would lose Redlance in all this maneuvering, if she stayed close to the ground, so she angled her flight up into the night air so she could be seen from below.

The scooter was in an alley between buildings, so she climbed into the air and pivoted back. She heard the warhorse's howl as Redlance closed, but didn't see her.

Nothing to do but hope at this point.

White Crane arched over and pushed. Golden Tiger was only a hundred yards ahead of her, and slowly losing this race. It would be nice to have Redlance at her side, as she should be, but White Crane was willing to face the man alone.

Apparently, Redlance had seen her, or had the right instincts. *Cheval's* booming thunder suddenly trebled as the bike skidded around the corner of the building at the short end of the alley, even as Golden Tiger raced around the far end.

White Crane decided to cut the corner instead. She popped up over the ledge of the building and prepared to drop down atop the man when they both got to the other corner. If she timed it right, she could grab him right off the back of his scooter and carry him into the air.

Then they would both find out how well he could fly.

White Crane snarled as she emerged into the night sky, and pulled up so short she would have stalled an aircraft and fallen back on her tail.

Provost was standing there.

Well, flying.

Hovering ten feet above the roof, smiling serenely at her from twenty feet away.

God, that man was gorgeous.

None of the Hollywood hunks she could name would hold a candle to the raw magnetism, the power this man exuded. What she had felt around *Ao Shun* simply paled by comparison.

Kai Di wondered, deep in the corner, if that was part of what made the man one of the greatest of the Modern Gods, that ability to make women wet just being in the same room with him.

She would need to research the sorts of pheromones he must be exuding into night air. It could be a useful trick.

They stared at each other for a second.

White Crane could hear Golden Tiger's ban sidhe being chased by baying wolves, but time seemed to have stopped.

"We haven't been introduced," the gorgeous hero said politely, confidently. "I'm Provost. You must be new in town."

God, even his voice was pure sex, distilled down and poured directly into her brain like a bolt of lightning.

"White Crane," she replied, a little breathless, feeling like a groupie trapped in an elevator with a rock star, trying not to *squeeeee* all over the man.

"If you're chasing Golden Tiger, we have a problem," he continued. "That makes you a villain."

The Empress was impressed with the man, but not overwhelmed. She pushed White Crane to one side to speak.

"No, silly man," The Empress Bird pronounced. "I am Vengeance."

Provost nodded to himself at her words.

"Then you will have to go through me," he answered with a smile.

White Crane was suddenly nervous. This man had been one of the greatest heroes of the entire Age of Modern Gods. Supposedly an alien rocketed to Earth as a child to hide him, so he could grow up to be a hero, a protector.

Undefeated. Unconquered.

As King Arthur myths went, not bad.

Still, this man was going to let Golden Tiger get away from her.

She would not surrender her revenge.

There was some power floating in the air. Not much. Presumably this man, Provost, had absorbed as much of it as he needed, or hadn't recharged his batteries after chasing off, evading, or defeating *Ao Shun*.

Certainly, the Northern Dragon King was nowhere to be seen.

White Crane pulled all of the energy available into herself.

She flew at him.

She thought about the anger that had engulfed her when she heard Miranda had been killed. The sorrow at her friend's funeral. The helplessness when Marauder netted her. The fear and anger that he was going to rape her.

She pushed all of that down into her soul and compressed it, a diamond of wrath from the coals that life had gifted her recently.

Provost did not move, apparently confident that there was nothing this petite villainess, this *woman*, could do to him.

She grabbed that ball of energy and let it flow into her fist as she charged him. The energy seemed to make her feathers glow. She wondered, fleetingly, if she was leaving her own contrail right now.

They closed. Provost smiled like a mastiff confronting a Chihuahua.

White Crane punched the man in the jaw.

The Chihuahua barked.

There weren't any witnesses, so White Crane didn't know if the explosion of sound from the impact was as loud outside her head as it was within.

The crack of thunder deafened her.

The flash of lightning blinded her.

The world seemed to end in one cataclysmic psychic earthquake.

White Crane found herself floating in the air, tumbling softly like she was in zero-gravity.

Provost was floating nearby, also tumbling, possibly out cold.

They had drifted beyond the warehouse roof, and were over the back alley now.

The night returned.

White Crane shook her head to clear the cobwebs and got her bearings by the distant thunder of *Cheval*'s engine.

She turned and began to fly to Redlance's aid.

Provost grabbed her by the ankle and stopped her short.

"Not so fast, young lady," he said.

PROVOST

White Crane felt the man's iron grip on the bones of her right ankle, even through the flying suit. Right now, the suit felt like tissue paper, barely protecting her modesty or her soul.

Provost tugged her lightly, walking his grip hand over hand up her leg to her bottom, her backpack, her shoulder.

She found herself face to face with the man, this greatest of the heroes, close enough to dance. There was a musky edge to the night that bored into her soul through her nostrils.

She wasn't sure if she wanted to kiss the man, or knee him in the balls. Maybe both.

He smiled down at her, his arms wrapped around her sides and up under her wings to trap her.

For the fleetingest moment, she was sad that her hair was under the helmet, where this amazingly sexy god couldn't get to it, couldn't run his fingers through it.

"Not a bad punch, little girl," he murmured.

White Crane could see the beginnings of a shiner on his right eye. Considering that he was supposed to be bullet-proof, she must have really hammered him.

Good.

Because Golden Tiger is getting away.

Something about the man's smile changed. She couldn't put her finger on it, but it took on a new flavor as she watched. She could see thoughts chasing each other in his eyes.

For a comical moment, she had a vision of a children's cartoon, with a good conscience and a bad conscience, each seated on a different shoulder, offering countervailing suggestions about what to do with this woman they had caught.

The man's smell was driving her sideways, but Kai Di had finally unlocked it. Where others could fire bolts of energy, or summon demons, this man, this Modern God, this *hero*, constantly surrounded himself with a cloud of pheromones, human desire, that would overwhelm the average person.

No wonder he had been so popular for so long. Every man who got near him wanted to be his friend. Every woman in range wanted to be his lover, White Crane, Kai Di, and Kate included.

Provost leaned forward, smiling at her. Except the smile was a leer.

She felt one of his hands let go of the tangle of feathers so it could run down the muscles of her back to her bottom, caressing it, kneading it like fresh bread.

He leaned close and began to kiss her on the neck.

Three of the girls were in heaven at the possibilities.

The Empress Bird, however, was just pissed.

He was too close, and at the wrong angle to kick him in the balls, or to do much of anything except get groped by this alien defender, this man-child, this rapist.

She settled for head-butting him in the face as hard as she could when he leaned back to admire her. It sounded like a bell ringing vespers in her head. She wondered what he heard.

Provost snarled at her. His grip had loosened, but not enough to let her get away.

She could see a dark fire ignite in the backs of his eyes. It was ugly and cruel.

This was probably more what this man was like, when he was at home alone, watching soap operas in his underwear.

He glared at her for a moment.

"It could have been easy," he whispered hotly.

The Empress fixed him with her predator's smile.

"It still would have been rape, you worthless shit," she said. "Have you ever asked a woman first, or just taken them because they couldn't resist you?"

Not that she was resisting well. Most of her was already so far gone that she could barely think.

If that hadn't been Golden Tiger getting away down there, if it hadn't been for Miranda, and Itala, she might not have resisted this man's charms, or his powers.

Maybe she was more powerful, more dangerous, than she realized.

Time seemed to stop.

Provost cocked a fist back and held it there behind his ear.

She couldn't tell if he was posing for a comic-book artist, or making sure she would see the wallop coming.

White Crane steeled herself for a telling blow.

Bullies don't like being told *No*.

Before the man could move, the night erupted in an earth-rending crash.

A hurricane of energy slammed into the two flying lovers, embracing them in a titanic whirlwind, tearing them apart.

White Crane found herself flying sideways through the air, carefully held in gigantic claws.

Itala had never touched her so softly. Miranda had kissed her harder.

The claws were yellow-gold with glowing red flakes worked into the keratin itself.

White Crane looked up in surprise.

She was being carried by a giant, golden dragon.

Ao Shun craned his long, swan-like neck around to smile down at her.

"You should leave the big, blue schoolboy to me, my dear White Crane," he smiled at her in those clipped, British tones. "I'll handle him. Your playmate is getting away from your assistant. Can you fly?"

White Crane shook her head. Most of the cobwebs fell away.

Just how powerful were Provost's pheromones, anyway?

"I'm fine, *Ao Shun*," she said, hoping the words would make the deed.

"Provost is a very dangerous opponent," the Dragon King intoned. "You just stick with Golden Tiger for now."

The dragon pivoted so sharply on his left wingtip that he stopped moving forward. In the middle of the turn, he let go of White Crane and floated her softly out into space.

She started to fall, thought about it, and hovered with a thought.

Below, she could see the dragon swooping down on a man floating in space. Round Two in tonight's epic grudge match.

At least he had saved her from getting beaten up.

Or worse.

She would owe the Crime Lord of Angel City for that help.

But she was a villain, now.

Guanxi.

Movement below caught her eye.

Ao Shun had carried her to the very back of the warehouse complex, where the fences were twelve feet tall and topped with spirals of razor wire.

There was a little Italian scooter near the farthest corner. *Cheval* was parked close by.

Redlance and Golden Tiger were madly dancing to a deadly tune nobody else could hear.

White Crane took a moment to look inside herself. The candle was burning fitfully.

She reached out and found only the faintest bits and pieces of cotton candy energy floating around.

It wasn't much, but it would have to do as she sucked it in as hard as she could.

She turned over in the air like a pearl diver and began to swoop.

Below, the two dancers had separated.

She could tell that they were both exhausted by the way limbs and heads drooped.

Something got Golden Tiger's attention. He looked up and saw her plunging out of the night sky.

Below, Redlance took a deep breath and stood fully upright, beginning to swing the stick like a drum major as she came for him.

Something came over Golden Tiger as White Crane watched and drew closer. He shook his head once, as if to clear non-existent hair out of his eyes.

Instead of dropping back into a fighting stance, he stood erect and held out his right arm, a fist pointed at Redlance.

His fist began to glow.

Shit. Ki-bolt. Itala.

Miranda.

White Crane tried to yell, tried to fly faster. Something. Anything. Everything.

She was too far away to stop him.

Redlance saw it coming and tried to move, but she was human, facing a Modern God. The woman started to fall to her right to duck, but Golden Tiger was faster.

His bolt struck Redlance square in her chest, lifting her in the air with a soft whomp and slamming her backwards into the chain-link fence.

The fence held, barely, nearly torn from the ground by the force of impact.

Redlance was down, unmoving.

Golden Tiger started to move forward to finish her off.

White Crane screamed pure rage as she got to him, an owl atop the rabbit.

He tried to duck, but wasn't fast enough either.

She clipped his shoulder with a wing-tip, stood on her other wing-tip, and came to ground hard, with Redlance on the ground behind her, and Golden Tiger knocked down fifteen feet away.

He did some sort of gymnastic move as she watched, and was suddenly on his feet facing her.

The Empress spoke.

"In the comic books," she began darkly. "The villain would say something like, *If you've hurt her, I'll kill you.* But I was already going to kill you, Golden Tiger. Make your peace with whatever Gods will listen."

GOLDEN TIGER

White Crane didn't have time to glance down to see how badly hurt Redlance was. Golden Tiger was raising his fist and pointing it at her.

As with Provost, time seemed to stand still as she pushed herself to a higher level of consciousness than even she thought possible.

White Crane could see the way his eyes squinted and his face contorted as he aimed at her, that damnable right fist tracking her like the barrel of a battleship's cannon.

She had an advantage, though. Itala was human. Normally, that distinction was meaningless. But among the Modern Gods, the ability to wield power meant that they could do things that were impossible for the rest of mankind.

It meant that Golden Tiger could cast an energy bolt at her from twenty feet away.

But it also meant she could duck.

His fist began to glow slowly. Kai Di, deep inside, recognized it as a capacitor charging in a machine. It had that feel.

But it also meant that there was a distinction between thought and action as he tried to shoot her.

She required no thought. Only the muscle memory pounded into her by Itala, in the rain and snow, on all those nasty weekdays up at the campgrounds and the Cascades.

She and the flying suit were one. Her thought was action.

She became the great, red-headed, White Crane of legend, symbol of the Empress of China. Protector and master of lesser birds.

And she did it at the speed of light.

His bolt flared, encasing his hand for the briefest instant in a corona of amber fire. It wasn't as bright as the bolt that had hurt Redlance. Maybe he was almost done.

White Crane leapt into the air hard and tumbled in a tight circle, a somersault that ended with her left foot planted in the middle of his chest as the bolt passed harmlessly beneath her.

Golden Tiger landed awkwardly on his ass.

White Crane had almost no energy to put into the kick. It wasn't hard enough to break anything, just enough to drive him backwards again.

She had used almost everything just getting Provost's attention.

Tomorrow, she would figure out how to take that big, blue, bastard down, but right now, she had a man to kill.

White Crane took a deep breath. It felt like she had already run all the way to the airport, back in Emerald, and was on her way twenty miles home, most of it uphill.

Where had this exhaustion come from?

Not even the day she killed Marauder had it been this bad.

At least Golden Tiger felt it as well.

Instead of kipping up to his feet in a display of awesome acrobatic prowess, he rolled onto his side and kind of threw himself to his feet before she could lurch over and hit him again.

Everything was moving slow except her perception of time itself.

That was so jazzed up right now she could see the man's pupils dilate as he considered what to do next.

There was the twelve-foot-high-razor-topped fence behind him, but White Crane could fly. There was a way back up the alley to the front of the property, but he had to get by her to get there.

This felt like a last stand. Hopefully, he would die well.

Golden Tiger set his feet and raised his claws.

She recognized the stance and the hands from the southern forms. At the very end, he had fallen back on a lifetime of training and was willing to let the tiger be his weapon.

White Crane felt the same way. The battles, first with Starchild and then with Provost, had drained her. There would be no fantastic surge of superhuman strength to crush him, no explosion of razor-tipped feathers to slash this man to kibble. Just years of Master Daniel, and months of Itala, pushing her.

Crane form used a different stance than tiger, shifting side to side where the great cat wanted to rush ahead and pounce. She became the protector bird and waited for him to move.

She didn't know how good a fighter he was. Obviously good enough to make a career out of it. And Itala, the person who would know, had thought that he might be better.

But he wasn't nearly as angry.

There was nobody nearly as angry tonight as Kai Di Peng.

Best to let him commit and then counter-strike. It was what the crane form was all about. Block him with a wing or a leg. Sweep in with the back of a wrist for a devastating crossing strike.

The faster she got this over, the sooner she could tend to Redlance, get her medical help. Maybe save her life.

Golden Tiger growled deep in his chest. His hands curled into ripping claws, set to rend and tear.

If she had more time, or a weaker opponent, Master Daniel had once taught her a wonderful variant on the snake form for fighting tigers. But it would end up with her chest-to-chest with a bigger man at a time when exhaustion threatened to overwhelm her.

Kai Di Peng has not come this far to die at your hands, you rat bastard.

She growled back at him.

There was nothing mocking about the sound. It was primordial, the dance of death itself, the sound a field of freshly-cut hay makes when you burn it in the fall to clear the land for spring planting.

His growl turned into a roar as he leapt.

For a Modern God, he jumped like a white guy. Apparently he was out of juice as well.

White Crane's immediate reaction had been to leap with him, meet him in the air, where she was mistress of all she surveyed. Instead, she nearly flew over his head.

She caught a glimpse of surprise in his eyes as she flailed at him with a boot, her hands well above his strike.

She recovered and started to turn.

Golden Tiger had landed first. His hand shot out and caught her foot.

What is it with you people and ankles?

She tried to kick weakly, but his grip was iron.

She tried to fly away, even carrying him with her, but there was no power left to do more than just barely hover.

He jerked hard on her leg, nearly dislocating her hip, and leapt up.

She was facing away at an awkward angle, nearly with her butt to the man.

She couldn't block, couldn't evade, couldn't strike.

She was barely able to get the feathers of her left wing in the way of his fist as he punched the side of her head.

Even then, her head rang. She could only imagine what a clean blow would have done.

White Crane let go as the Empress demanded control.

She spun in place, two feet off the ground, as he pulled her in for a punishing second blow. She got an elbow in the way, or that punch would have taken her in the kidneys so hard she would have been peeing blood for a week.

She pivoted on the elbow, lashing out with the back of her right wrist to his face. It was soft, no more than a lover's slap. Nothing that would stop him.

But it opened him up by pushing his hands out of the way.

The left hand, trailing into the opening made by the right, connected with a sound like a triple smashed to right field, bone meeting bone in a sharp crack.

Golden Tiger went down like a sack of potatoes. He did not, however, let go, and White Crane ended up on top of him, straddling his body, riding him like a cowgirl.

I don't think so, pretty boy.

She leaned forward and punched as hard as she could. No technique, no subtlety, no form. Just knuckles to cheek bone before he could get a hand up to stop her.

At the least the flying suit understood the situation. Instead of breaking her hand, her gauntlet stiffened around her fingers, turned back into the kind of armor it could do when she demanded it.

Like now.

She connected with a sound like brass knuckles.

Golden Tiger's head bounced off the asphalt with hollow thump.

She hit him twice more, just in case, but he had already gone utterly limp beneath her.

White Crane staggered to her feet.

The blow to her head, followed by a jab to her ribs, had rattled her. Thinking was a fuzzy, painful concept.

Redlance.

Itala.

There.

She stumbled over to where her friend lay at the foot of the nearly-destroyed fence.

Everything looked intact, even if Itala was crumpled up in a ball.

Kate fell to her knees and stuck a hand in, looking for a pulse on Itala's neck.

There. Thready, but there. Weak. But not dead. Breath shallow but in and out.

She peeled Itala's eyes open.

Okay, mild concussion, but mostly just got the wind knocked out of her.

No blood on the front. None on the back. Whatever he did to her was a bolt of energy, and not a bullet.

Itala's eyes fluttered open, focused about a million miles away.

Slowly, they came back to the present and focused on Kate's face.

"Ow," Itala muttered.

Kate laughed.

"I thought I had lost you, like I did Miranda."

"Harder to kill than that," Itala retorted softly.

"I know."

Kate let the relief flow through her. She wasn't sure she could have survived losing another best friend, not to Golden Tiger.

"Oh, shit," Redlance yelled and started to move.

What?

White Crane looked up and realized that Golden Tiger was awake, was on his feet, was looming over her.

She tried to move, but he pummeled her with a heavy fist to the ear, driving her sideways and face first flat on the pavement.

White Crane saw stars, little flashing supernovae popping into her field of vision and receding.

Out of the corner of her eye, she saw Redlance lurch almost to her feet between them.

"Stay down, bitch," Golden Tiger snarled as he punched Redlance. Once to the stomach. A second fist followed. Crossing down-strike to the side of her head.

Redlance collapsed like a landslide.

Golden Tiger turned to scowl at her. He stomped closer. Perhaps staggered. Nobody was anywhere close to even twenty-five percent at this point, let alone one hundred.

White Crane was having a hard enough time just getting her eyes to focus on the same target as he approached her.

"What is your problem, woman?" he howled down at her.

White Crane blinked. She had a little energy left, a candle guttering and about to fail.

She looked over at Itala, motionless on the pavement next to her. She felt a round lump near her right hand.

"You are," she replied simply.

"What?"

"Miranda Devereux was my friend, Golden Tiger," Kate hissed. "Scarlet Titan. You killed her."

"Who?" the man stopped and blinked, confusion carved into the tired lines on his face. "Do you have any idea how many stupid punks and wanna-be villains I've killed over the years?"

"Only one matters to me," The Empress replied.

"Well, you can join her in hell," Golden Tiger staggered another step forward. "When you get there, tell her I said hi."

She watched his fist come up and begin to piston forward.

Her death was right behind it.

No.

White Crane burned every drop of power she had left, lit it like a Roman candle firecracker and let it explode into the air.

Her mind cleared.

Time slowed down again.

She grabbed the thing her fingers had found.

Itala's stick. The Redlance.

Before that bastard could dodge, she rolled onto her side and jammed the red tip into his chest and held it there as the taser discharged everything it had into the man's heart.

She had never been willing to test the weapon. The man who built it originally had sworn it would knock a moose on its ass. Golden Tiger wasn't as big as a moose. Or as mean.

White Crane pushed him over backwards, but the man was out cold.

And he would stay that way for a while.

White Crane crawled over to Itala and rolled her over.

Redlance was bleeding from the nose, and a cut on her cheek, but breathing. Her heart was beating normal.

They would both need a week of sleep tomorrow.

The Empress was in charge now. She pushed to her feet and walked, a bit drunkenly, over to Golden Tiger.

Something about the man tugged at her, demanded her attention, tried to touch her soul.

Kai Di kneeled next to the man, ready to hit him again with the lance if he moved.

Something tugged at her mind.

She reached out a hand and put it on his chest. The golden tiger logo, that dimly glowing brand on his chest that signified his power, his membership as a Modern God, it was an outline on the man's undertunic.

His gi was the open-front style. Kai Di the scientist pulled the two sides of the tunic open and found a small electronic board hanging from a necklace under the cloth, shaped like a tiger pouncing.

It sparked feebly under her hand.

She tugged sharply and snapped the chain that held it in place.

It was a device, a machine, a thing, like the *Getaway* had been, or *Cheval*. An apparatus that could focus the energy of a Modern God and create an effect. In this case, the glowing tattoo of an eastern mystic warrior. A fraud.

White Crane made a pocket appear in her flying suit, and slid the necklace in for future research. She had access to four such tools now: the flying suit, *Cheval*, the *Getaway*, and now this.

She wondered…

Kai Di ran an open hand loosely over the man's body, feeling for such a tug.

The bandana on his head demanded power.

She pulled hard on it, and discovered a blond wig underneath, and a brown, close-cropped, flattop beneath that.

So the blond hero was a lie, as well.

The cloth of the bandana contained wires. The solid white lenses, what she had taken for something akin to sunglasses, were a *thing* as well.

She held them to her own eyes and pushed just enough power into them to suddenly turn the dim night into day. She rolled up the cloth and added it to the pocket with the tattoo.

It was the two gauntlets that pulled the hardest. Those bloody hands that had slain Miranda. That had nearly killed Itala. That would have done her in.

She pulled them loose and inspected.

There were wires here as well, but much more complicated and finer. Expensive workmanship. *Property of US Army* was printed in indelible black ink just inside of both cuffs.

It made sense that the government would want to research how a soldier could fight without a weapon. She wondered if he had stolen it, or been gifted as a guinea pig so he could be a hero for them.

Modern Gods as soldiers were just as dangerous as Modern Gods as heroes. Or villains.

The gauntlets lay flat against her thigh as she opened a different pocket to add them in.

Nothing else about the man wanted her attention.

White Crane stood up and considered.

She had come here to kill a man. To exact revenge for the death of Miranda Devereux.

She had already heard *Ao Shun's* saying that revenge is about forgiveness, redemption, or the futility of revenge.

She had no forgiveness for this man. Blood demanded blood.

And he would not be redeemed. Nor would she.

Revenge was not futile. She hadn't bothered digging two graves, like all the old western movies told her to do. Like her father had suggested.

She had won.

White Crane considered Provost, long said to be the greatest of the heroes. A man who had been saving the world and fighting villains since long before she was even born. And yet he looked thirty.

The Peng clan itself was named for an ancient scholar who was said to have unlocked the secrets of immortality. Perhaps that was in the realm of possibilities for a Modern God.

But being a hero in this town appeared to be just the spin that the evening news put on things. In the end, Provost was no different than Marauder had been, except in the amount of charm he brought to the rape.

And Golden Tiger was a killer, a vigilante with a good PR department.

She could sleep at night after putting this man down like a mad dog. Marauder had given her no sleepless nights.

White Crane smiled.

There was a much greater way to get her revenge. Even better than killing him.

She considered again and got to work.

It took less than a minute to strip this rat bastard *hero* of his tunic, his gi, his pants, his red polka-dot boxers. Everything.

Even the cute little ballet slippers with the steel soles went.

She stuffed it all into a saddle-bag pouch on *Cheval*, and threw the blond wig in on top of it. She rooted around until she found the tool kit Carlos had included, and pulled out a screwdriver.

Golden Tiger's scooter was a simple, off-the-lot model. Both tires blew happily when she stabbed them with the spike end of the screwdriver.

She walked over and checked on the man, but he was out.

Not dead, but those pupils weren't coming back to earth any time soon. *Good.*

White Crane sent a flickering thought to the flying suit, and suddenly it was gone. She was just a woman in a skin-tight white body suit.

She moved on to Redlance.

Itala was stirring. Fuzzy and concussed, but at least awake.

Kate helped the woman to her feet, and walked her over to *Cheval*.

"No good," Itala muttered. "Can't drive."

"You hang on to me, my friend," Kate said soothingly. "I'll get us home."

She climbed atop the big beast, pulled on her helmet, and thumbed the starter. The lance separated into two halves and went into the rifle holster.

The mighty warhorse seemed to understand things. It started with a soft purr and rumbled warmly at the two women.

Itala moved like an old woman in her helmet, but she climbed up behind Kate and wrapped her arms around Kate's chest, squishing her breasts for a moment before she gripped lower.

"Sorry," Itala murmured.

Kate smiled. That was still the best offer she'd gotten all day.

The sound of *Cheval* seemed to cut through the gunk coating Golden Tiger's brain. He stirred and sat up, stark naked in the warm, evening air.

"Why don't you just kill me, you bitch?" he screamed over the rumble of the mighty warhorse.

The Empress looked over at the scooter with two flat tires. She smiled evilly at the dorky, naked, white guy, deep in an industrial, Hispanic neighborhood without a phone, a wallet, or pants.

"I already have," she called back as she rolled the grip.

Cheval growled once, and they were gone.

EPILOGUE: EMERALD

Wei De's study had not changed, as far as Kai Di could tell. It was simply not allowed to change.

Dinner with Yi Wen had been fabulous. Mu Ren had taken the time to show off.

It being summer, Ge Ke and Han Rong, little brothers Gregory and Harry, were home from their respective schools, studying just as hard, but also free to enjoy Sunday dinner with family. And perhaps to ogle Itala and be surprised at the transformation their sister had undergone.

Last summer had been utterly boring, by comparison.

Now the three of them were alone in Father's study: Wei De, Kai Di, and Itala.

He had brought out the very expensive brandy tonight. The caramel taste sat atop the smell of jasmine and the sweet oils to imprint the room on her brain.

It was good to be home.

They sat in companionable silence, swirling and sipping.

Wei De held a piece of bright green cloth in his hand, a shiny, metallic taffeta. It was a triangle cut roughly from a much larger piece. Father studied it intently in the silence.

White Crane had kept the part of Golden Tiger's cowl that was wired for sensors and night vision, but there was enough left over for a trophy. It was not the man's head literally, but a very close figurative approximation.

Jean-Michel would eventually get the matching piece, when she could come up with a reasonable explanation.

If there was such a thing.

Father ran his fingers back and forth over the cloth as if he could divine some deeper connection to the fabric with his own powers. It wouldn't take necromancy, at least as far as she knew. The man who had previously owned it wasn't dead.

Golden Tiger, a man apparently named Danny Fazekas, had managed to find a cop before the local gang-bangers had found him. Most of what happened next was an open record: public indecency, resisting arrest, assaulting an officer. If he hadn't been white, they probably would have shot him.

As it was, all records stopped suddenly and the man had vanished from human history, as far as the interwebs were concerned.

Fortunately, Carlos had a friend who had a cousin who had connections.

Fazekas had apparently been politely gathered up in the dead of night by officials from the US Defense Department, who were not happy about the equipment he had apparently stolen from them. Having subsequently lost it made them positively beside themselves.

Golden Tiger was currently being held in a top-secret military prison facility for super-villains, in the Rocky Mountains.

Good riddance.

Wei De smiled, as if he could read her thoughts.

Who knew? Maybe he could. She had never asked what his powers really encompassed, beyond the traces he had shown her.

But she knew it had a very strong genetic component. And that she was apparently much more in Provost's league than she was that of Marauder or Golden Tiger, when it came to raw power.

Father was probably just as powerful, if he wanted to be.

Wei De sat the piece of cloth on his desk and rested his hand on the small box that had been his other present this evening.

It had started out as a simple wooden box, purchased in a craft store, but Carlos had carefully stained and painted it, showing a whole new side of himself that Kate had never suspected existed. It was perhaps six inches on a side, and three inches tall, with a highly stylized image of a tiger painted on, in a technique that suggested a mastery of both water-color and sumi-e.

Truly, the layers Carlos was hiding were astounding.

Father did not open the box again at this time. The first time had been worth the entire evening.

After finishing the box, Carlos had gotten out the metal-working tools and hand-crafted a wind-up music box as a present for her father.

And what proper Chinese gentleman didn't need a music box that played the instrumental chorus of Low Rider?

Kai Di smiled at her father's flash of discomfort.

He relaxed and smiled back, letting it grow until it embraced both her and Itala in its warmth.

He leaned forward a little and grew serious.

"Are you complete?" he asked.

It was an odd choice of words from a man with a complete mastery of seventeen languages.

Kai Di considered herself.

"A year ago," she replied. "I would have said so. Miranda has been avenged. Not only has Golden Tiger been utterly defeated, he must live the rest of his days with such a knowledge."

Wei De nodded.

"A samurai would have taken the honorable path," he observed quietly. "Beware the ronin."

Kai Di and Itala both nodded back. The old Japanese legend was known on all sides of the Pacific.

"But?" Father continued, one eyebrow arching perfectly.

Kate could see the first gray hairs appearing in her father. She knew Yi Wen carefully and precisely dyed her own hair, but Wei De was only beginning to show the mark of time.

She made a mental note to fix that, too.

"But something else happened on the path to vengeance," she clarified.

She took a sip of the very lovely brandy to steel her nerves.

"A man known as Marauder tried to kidnap me," she said simply. "He would have raped me. The only question is whether he would have killed me first or afterwards."

Itala growled under her breath, but otherwise remained silent. This was Kate's story.

"In Angel City, something similar happened," she continued after a deep breath. "Provost would have done the same."

"Provost?" Father exclaimed in surprise.

"He can generate a cloud of pheromones, Father," Kai Di explained. "Once you get close, it will overwhelm you. Very few women would be able to resist themselves and their lusts."

Wei De was silent, but let his eyes prod her.

"He would have taken me," she said. "There would have been no asking, no choice. When I resisted him, he was intent on using force. *Ao Shun* rescued me at that moment."

"So this man is not a hero?" Wei De asked.

"No woman has probably ever told him no, Father," Kai Di replied. "He cannot even fathom the possibility of not getting anything, everything, he wishes."

"And so we owe favors to the Northern Dragon King?" Father said.

"I owe him, not you," she said hotly.

"*Guanxi*, daughter," he replied, just as sharp. "I have raised you better than that. It is a duty of the clan, not just a daughter."

He paused.

"Are you complete?"

She understood, finally, what he was asking.

"No, Father," she murmured, deep inside herself.

Itala reached out and put a hand on her arm. Nothing more than that, but enough human touch to help her breathe.

Friends.

"When this started, my target was a man known universally as a hero," she enunciated slowly. "So I set out to become a villain. It made for a round symmetry, the Tao made flesh, if you will."

She took a moment to think.

"Now, I have destroyed one hero who turned out to be a wolf in sheep's clothes. But I have found another."

"Is he truly not what he says he is?" Itala spoke up for the first time.

The Frenchwoman had been raised on the man's exploits, a global hero for freedom and justice in the bad, old days of the Cold War. The one American hero even Europe understood and embraced.

Learning the truth about the man had been hard on Itala.

But she was still Redlance underneath.

"I have read the stories about Golden Tiger's origins," Kai Di explained. "The monastery, the training, the years necessary to master the *ki-bolt*. All of it is lies."

"So Provost is not an alien? Is he truly vulnerable to the green stones supposedly left from the remains of his homeworld?" Father knew the stories as well, but gave them less credence than his other daughter.

Kai Di shrugged.

"The only green stone that I can think of that might be dangerous to him would be Trinitite."

She watched both of her companions mouth the word, confused.

"Alamogordo glass," she continued. "Burnham's theory is that there have always been people around with the potential to use the raw power available, to be Gods, but until very recently, there simply wasn't enough of that power available for them to express that will. Trinitite is a radioactive glass made from sand and quartz, plus all manner of trace minerals, from one of the original nuclear weapons test sites, when they used to detonate the bombs above ground. There is something similar in the nations of the former Soviet Union. You would probably find the same sort of thing at Bikini Atoll, if you went diving, but those would probably be green pearls, since the material would have cooled in the air and then fallen into the water."

"Green pearls?" Father asked suddenly.

His face took on a very concerned look, almost apprehensive.

She watched him stand and walk around to the side of his massive, oak desk, closest to her and Itala. He put a hand on the wood panel and muttered something under his breath.

Kai Di felt the small surge of power transiting from her father's hand to the wood of the desk. A panel popped up to reveal a space like the inside of a safe.

"How does that fit inside with your file drawers?" Itala asked with wonder.

Wei De fixed them both with a knowing smile.

"It's not really there, daughter," he said. "But in a different place. Much like how The White Crane can store things inside the flying suit. It is merely anchored to the desk."

He reached in and pulled out a large jewelry box that appeared to have been cut from a single piece of polished volcanic glass originally the size of a grapefruit.

Wei De weighed the box in his right palm for several seconds before he came to a decision and opened it.

Inside was a pearl. At first glance, it appeared to be jade, but there was a depth and glow to the stone that jade never achieved. It was almost as though someone had polished a green diamond nearly an inch across.

Even from where she sat, White Crane could feel the power pulsing off the pearl.

"This is much older than Bikini," Father began. "It has been in the family for at least seven hundred years, passed secretly to the most powerful child of each generation. Family legend has it that it originated in a Siberian volcano, possibly Kamchatka."

He handed the box carefully to Itala first. She held it without touching the pearl, and then passed it on.

"Seven hundred years?" Itala asked.

Kai Di could taste the power as the box rested in her palm. It was not the clean, pure sort of stuff that floated in the air like cotton candy, ready to be harvested. Power pulled from this pearl would be tainted by something dark and malevolent.

But it would be a price any wizard worth his salt would have gladly paid, in the era before the rise of Modern Gods.

"The clan has always had sorcerers, daughter Itala," Wei De observed with great seriousness. "Great seers as well. It is why we left China in 1852 to come to a place where we could survive. Where we could thrive."

He fixed Kai Di with a hard stare, the grand patriarch of the Peng clan, the general marshalling his army.

"Would this power be enough to slay a god like Provost?" he asked. It was a voice that brooked no nonsense.

The White Crane considered the power in her hand.

"We shall see, Father," The Empress answered. "We shall see."

ABOUT THE AUTHOR

Blaze Ward writes science fiction in the *Alexandria Station* universe as well as *The Collective*. He also write fantasy stories with several characters and series, from an alternate Rome to epic high fantasy in the desert. You can find out more at his website www.blazeward.com, as well as Facebook, Goodreads, and other places.

Blaze's works are available as ebooks, paper, and audio, and can be found at a variety of online vendors (Kobo, Amazon, and others). His newsletter comes out quarterly, and you can also follow his blog on his website. He really enjoys interacting with fans, and looks forward to any and all questions—even ones about his books!

Never miss a release!

If you'd like to be notified of new releases, sign up for my newsletter.

I only send out newsletters once a quarter, will never spam you, or use your email for nefarious purposes. You can also unsubscribe at any time.

http://www.blazeward.com/newsletter/

ABOUT KNOTTED ROAD PRESS

Knotted Road Press fiction specializes in dynamic writing set in mysterious, exotic locations.

Knotted Road Press non-fiction publishes autobiographies, business books, cookbooks, and how-to books with unique voices.

Knotted Road Press creates DRM-free ebooks as well as high-quality print books for readers around the world.

With authors in a variety of genres including literary, poetry, mystery, fantasy, and science fiction, Knotted Road Press has something for everyone.

Knotted Road Press
www.KnottedRoadPress.com

www.ingramcontent.com/pod-product-compliance
Lightning Source LLC
Chambersburg PA
CBHW071747190726
48292CB00003B/893